CW00502036

Lemon Drop Cottage

K.T. DADY

Lemon Drop Cottage
K.T. Dady

Copyright © 2022 K.T. Dady

All rights reserved.

This is a work of fiction. Names, characters, places, and incidents are the product of the author's imagination or, if real, are used fictitiously.

Change can be a beautiful thing.

1

Scott

Hey, Lady Light.

I've been feeling a bit up and down lately. I think I'm still adjusting to being back home. I still need to sort my house out and get moved in. Sometimes I wish I were still travelling, but mostly, I'm glad to be home. I've been keeping myself to myself since I've been back. Just work and bed pretty much sums me up nowadays.

I'm glad your move went well and that you managed to finally settle into your new home, even if the quietness did freak you out a bit. I'm pleased you made some new friends as well. Moving to a new place can be daunting. Where I live is pretty quiet, but I find that soothing.

Etsy sales have been a bit slow recently on my prints. Hopefully, you're having better luck than me with your work. I know we said we would keep to the basics with nothing too personal, but sometimes I'd like to know a bit more about your work life. Obviously, it's something artistic, seeing how we met through the Artline forum. I'm not trying to be pushy though. I guess, sometimes, it would be nice if we knew more about each other. I know we agreed in the beginning to keep things simple. I'm just saying that sometimes I get the urge to shake things up a bit. We've been talking for a long time now, and maybe

when you feel ready one day, we could try a video chat or a phone call.

Anyway, how is your aunt? Was the retirement home everything you expected, and do you have any gossip on your new neighbours yet?

Speak soon.
CK x

Scott Harper stared at his laptop, wondering if he should edit the part about her job. It was the second time he'd asked for more details of her work life, knowing full well she was wary about giving up too much information that could expose her identity. He didn't blame her. She didn't really know the man she had been having email chats with for the past six months. In some ways he was glad that she was responsible. He'd only worry about her if she was telling strangers everything about her life.

What did he know already? Well, she was forty, single, creative, lived in England, and had just moved to start a new life in a new place and was attempting to expand her business.

There would be no more stories from her old home, so he never was going to find out if Mr Jacoby and Mrs Williams finally stopped bickering over their shared drive and realised how insanely in love they were with each other. He still didn't know who won the annual cold-water race in January or if Maisie and Florence were still sleeping with the same married man, who was a complete and utter git in LL's opinion.

He did get the feeling that she had been hurt via the cheating route herself once, as her foul language when talking about the married man in question had been rather impressive and a tad personal in areas, in his opinion. He also guessed that she must live on the coast. Her cold-water race mentioning the bitter chill of the sea was a clear slip on her part, but he didn't remark upon the subject.

He adjusted his position on his aunt's puffy pink sofa so that his legs were crossed on its bottom cushion. If it were possible to die at the hands of a sofa, it would be that particular piece of furniture doing the honours. It was as old as him, and considering he was forty-five, that was pretty old for a couch. He could feel himself slowly sinking into the abyss of the extremely soft materials that made the seat. It was no good. There was little escape once sat there. He gave in to the motion and waited until he could sink no lower before reaching over to the olive-green, leather-topped coffee table, which was handcrafted back in 1990 and never to be thrown, according to his aunt, and pulled his laptop onto his lap.

He pressed *Send* and settled back into the melting marshmallow whilst once again imagining what LL looked like.

Today, I'm going to give her pink hair to match this sofa. She's vibrant and doesn't care that people point at her bright hair and whisper about her behind her back. She has big red hoop earrings, very plasticky, and wears lipstick just as animated as the rest of her. She lives along the East Coast of England and is currently walking along the beach enjoying the current heatwave we're having this June. She's listening to "Girls Just Wanna Have Fun" on her headphones and doing an arms-only dance.

He moved his laptop to his side, knowing she probably wouldn't reply that day. He also knew that his aunt would be home any minute, and he really needed to talk to her about his living arrangements.

Roseberry Cottage in Pepper Bay had been his home since he was eight years old, when his dad had left him on the doorstep of his aunt's house and buggered off, but Scott had another home along Pepper Lane. Lemon Drop Cottage. That was the one he was born in, and the one that was left to him by his late father twenty years ago. Aunt Ruby had taken care of everything, just like she always did. The small yellow cottage with the thatched roof had always been rented out, and Scott had always lived with her whenever he was home. Now, he felt the time was right for him to live alone, and Lemon Drop Cottage was the option he had chosen. He just had to tell Ruby.

Whilst he patiently waited for her to come home from her job at the local tea shop, he started to think about LL again. He loved talking with her, even though they shared little and often used each other just to vent. She was funnier than him, and her anecdotes way more amusing. He was looking forward to all the things she had to say about her new life and the new people around her.

Scott never watched telly, so Lady Light's tales were his soap operas and dramas. In between reading and painting, her emails kept him occupied, intrigued, and amused, especially now he was part-retired. She was the smile in his day. He'd just never told anyone that, including her.

Having his online friend gave him a safe space where he could just be himself. He appreciated the fact that she was in some ways like an imaginary friend that only he could see.

An incoming call came through the laptop, gaining attention. He sighed at the screen and tapped the keyboard.

'Hey, want to know something that's really funny?' asked the blonde man staring out from the monitor.

8

'Not really, Giles. Why are you calling me? I'm retired from my job with you. You should be leaving me alone.'

Giles frowned and faked being hurt by the comment. 'We're still friends, Harper. I wanted to see how you were getting on down there in Sleepyville.'

'Well, I was enjoying the peace and quiet. Get to your point, Giles.'

'A job's come up in Rio…'

'No.'

'You don't know all the details yet.'

'It doesn't matter, Giles. I retired after my last job, and well you know it.'

Giles shook his head and glanced down at something in front of him. 'That's not what it says in your file.'

'What does it say in my file?'

'Semi-retired.'

Scott clenched his fists. 'I didn't write that.'

'It's here in black and white, my friend.'

'Well, you can un-black and white it. I'm done.'

Giles huffed loudly for dramatic effect. 'Come on, Harps. One for the road?'

'No.'

'So, what? What are you going to do instead? What do people do on the Isle of Wight?'

'We lives happy, peaceful lives.'

Giles scoffed, clearly unimpressed. 'So, you're just going to sit around all day painting your pictures, working part-time in a book and art shop, and talk to the stranger online? That's it? That's your life now?'

Scott frowned into the screen. 'Wait, how do you know I've been talking to someone online?'

Giles waved one hand in the air as he tossed his head to his left side. 'Oh please. I'm a tech wizard. I can see what you're up to by tapping into your smoke detector if I want to.'

Scott glanced up at the one on the ceiling in the hallway. 'You had better not bloody well put a camera in my aunt's house.'

'Relax. I only bug your shoes.'

Scott stared into his eyes. 'Really, Giles!'

'Hey, I had to check out your mystery emailer. Security, Scotty boy. What were you thinking getting involved with someone online?'

'I knew she was safe.'

'Oh yeah, how? Did you run a check on her? No, you didn't. How do I know that? Because if you wanted a check done on her, you would have called me. You're on dangerous grounds, Harps. You should know better than that.'

'I met her on an art forum. I hardly think anyone in our line of work will be hanging around there.'

Giles shook his head in disbelief. 'Rookie mistake. And you're no rookie. So, what are you playing at? If anyone back at the ranch found out about this, you'd be in big trouble, buddy boy.'

'I hardly think they'd care. I am allowed a life, you know. Besides, I'm retired now.'

'Semi-retired.'

'Giles, amend that file. Wait. Did you hack into base and change my outline? Don't answer that. I know you did.'

'Hey, I'm wounded. This is clearly a clerical error. It has nothing to do with me. I don't do errors. I'm a pro.'

'Yeah, and I'm retired, so go play pro with someone else.'

Giles pouted and whined. 'But you're my favourite Ethan Hunt.'

'I'm nothing like Ethan Hunt.'

'True. Ethan Hunt wouldn't make a rookie mistake.'

'It's not a mistake. I know what I'm doing.'

Giles blew out a sarcastic laugh. 'You do not. She could be a catfish for all you know.'

'She's not though, is she, Giles? You've checked her out, haven't you? Tell me she's real.'

Giles rubbed his hands together with glee as he neared the screen, grinning widely. 'Ha! Now you want to know.'

Scott was hiding his amusement from his former work colleague whilst desperately waiting to hear what he had found out.

Giles sat back, looking smug and milking his moment for all that it was worth.

Scott arched his eyebrows. 'Are you going to speak?'

'I read all your messages. It seems you two don't want to know much about each other.'

'You read my messages? That's an invasion of my privacy.'

'Pfft! Your business is my business.' He revealed his palms in a bid to calm the situation. 'Anyway, she is who she says she is.'

Now it was Scott's turn to look smug.

Giles scoffed. 'Don't give me that look. For all you knew, she could have been a twelve-year-old kid with braces.'

'There's nothing wrong with braces. I had to wear them. And anyway, I knew she wasn't a kid. I'm not as stupid as I look.'

'Oh, you're not one bit stupid. It's everyone else around you who is. Are you still pulling off the Clark Kent persona around town? I can't believe people actually fall for that.'

'Shy and quiet keeps them away.'

'Not when you look like you. Your online bit will think she's won the jackpot when she lays eyes on you.'

11

'Well, thank you for the compliment, but I won't be seeing my *online bit* anytime soon.'

'Hmm.'

Scott pushed his glasses up his nose as he studied the look on Giles' face. He wasn't giving away much, but it was obvious he knew more than he was letting on.

'Giles, I'm going now. I love you, but don't call me again.'

'Oh, come on, mate. Rio.'

'No.'

'Please.'

'No.'

'Pretty please.'

Scott attempted to sigh quietly. 'How long have I got?'

Giles grinned widely. 'I'd have to know by the end of August.'

'Fine. Let me think it over. I'll let you know by then. Meanwhile, leave me to enjoy my peace.'

'Okay, but can you stop talking to the stranger?'

'No can do, I'm afraid. I like her.'

'But you know it's tricky for people like us to maintain relationships.'

'That's why I keep her at arm's length, and that suits her too. So, we're all good over here. Perhaps you should find someone to talk to.'

'I can just read your messages. That's entertaining enough.'

'Keep your nose out, Giles.'

'Fine. I'm going now. Some of us need to workout to look good. We can't all be as lucky as you.'

'I exercise too. I'm going out for a bike ride in a minute.'

Giles scoffed and waved one hand. 'Yeah. Bye.'

'Erm, wait a minute. Before you go, I want to know what it is you're not telling me.'

'You know I can't disclose info until you agree to the gig.'

'Not Rio. I'm talking about what else you found out about Lady Light.'

'Well, first of all, she should choose a better name than that.'

'She sells candles in her Etsy shop. That much I worked out by myself. I'm just waiting for her to confirm things.'

Giles looked unimpressed and was happy to show that.

'Tell me, Giles. Is there something important I should know?'

He pulled in his lips and shook his head unconvincingly. 'Nope. She's all good.'

'Have you seen her?'

'Not in person. Yet.'

'Leave her alone.'

'I promise you, I have not bugged her home. Yet.'

Scott laughed. 'Leave her alone, Giles.'

'She seems safe. I give her a green light, but I don't think she's your type. Not really.'

'How would you know what my type is?'

'Please, I've known you for years. Besides, I see the women who snuggle up to you.'

'Snuggle?'

Giles shrugged. 'I'm just saying, she's slightly different.'

'You cannot compare her to the women I have to do business with.'

'Yeah, she's definitely nothing like them.'

'Good. Because they're not my type. When I'm with them, I'm just doing my job.'

'You sound like a male escort.'

'Maybe that can be my new line of work. At least then I'm not risking my life.'

'007 doesn't complain.'

'James Bond is a fictional character. I'm real. And I enjoy breathing.'

'You know, you used to be more fun.'

'I used to be younger. Now, I'd very much like to live out the rest of my days in the tranquil setting of Pepper Bay. People here don't tend to shoot at me.'

Giles scoffed. 'When was the last time someone shot at you, and don't say Yemen, or Prague, or Mexico, and don't count that little old lady in Florida. That was your own fault. People in Florida don't take kindly to Englishmen trespassing on their land. Mind you, I still say she was a field agent. She had that shifty look in her eyes.'

Scott frowned and touched his eyebrow. 'I don't have a shifty look.'

'That's because you're British, Harps. Our agents are trained in the art of the deadpan stare.'

'My aunt says I have gentle eyes.'

'What's gentle about bright blue eyes?'

'Blue eyes can be gentle, thank you.'

'Warmth lies within dark eyes.'

'You would say that. Yours are dark.' He zoomed in on the monitor. 'Now that I think about it, you have eyes like a shark.'

'Sharks are misunderstood.'

'Goodbye, Giles. Leave me alone for the summer, please.'

'I'll think about it.'

The call ended and Scott closed his laptop. He bent over the sofa and picked up one of his red trainers to examine the sole for any signs of interference.

Bloody liar.
He gazed once more over at the smoke detector.

2

Dolly

It was a beautiful sunny day in June, and Dolly was enjoying the warmth on her face as she sat upon a small stile along Pepper Lane, eating an apple whilst breathing in the light fragrance of wild flowers and freshly cut grass coming from a nearby cottage. She had not long moved from Hastings to Pepper Bay, and she was noticing how quiet it was sitting uphill by the chocolate box cottages that lined the road.

It was in that tranquil moment that she finally decided on the new name for her shop down by the seafront.

For many years, the pastel-yellow shop in Pepper Lane was known as Dolly's Haberdashery, and owned by Dolly Parker.

Since Dolly Lynch bought the shop from her retired aunt, and the flat above it, she'd had the dilemma of renaming the place. Haberdashery was no longer selling, and Dolly had her own ideas about what she would like to sell instead.

Ever since she was a little girl, Dolly had been into arts and crafts. Starting with Fuzzy-Felt as a toddler and building her way up to the art of candle making as an adult. She loved her homemade scented candles and wax melts. Plus, she was a huge fan of crystals and dragon ornaments, dreamcatchers and essential oils. Her aunt had left a lot of home-accessory stock on the shelves. Items such as photo frames, vases, and tea towels. So, that's what Dolly decided to sell in her shop. Viewing the place as a home gift shop, she knew that it needed a new name.

Every evening, whilst eating dinner, she would throw out ideas to her fifteen-year-old son, Dexter, to see what he thought. So far, he had scrunched his button nose at all of them and not come out with any good suggestions himself.

She liked The Doll's House, but Dexter said it sounded misleading. Dolly Mixtures was another idea, but Dexter trashed that idea too, stating there was a chance she'd get into trouble with the sweet manufacturer over copyrights or something similar. He then went off to do a thorough google search on the subject, because neither of them understood any of it.

'Doll's Gift House.'

The flowers and weeds along the grassy verge on her side of the road gave little feedback, even though she stared hard over her shoulder as though expecting a response.

She watched a teeny-tiny ladybird sitting on a leaf. 'What do you think, little lady? I can get a new sign painted so that it fits in with all the other shop signs down there. There's a local artist who has painted them all. He works in a shop over the road. The Book Gallery. You've probably flown over there before, no doubt. I've seen him around from time to time, but I've not actually met him yet. I'll pop over and ask. Should be all right.'

She finished off her apple whilst watching some seagulls fly overhead, smiling at their familiar cry.

Surprised they haven't swooped down for my apple core. Well, greedy guts, you're not getting it. There might be a hedgehog or something else that will appreciate a nibble.

Turning quickly back to the road, she tossed her apple core across to the bushes and small ditch on the other side.

'Ow! What the bloody...'

Dolly froze with her mouth gaping at the man who had just swerved into the ditch after being hit in the face by a flying apple core. His bicycle's front wheel was twisted towards the greenery, and so was his head.

She jumped up from the stile and slapped one hand to her mouth. 'Oh my God! Are you all right?'

The dishevelled man could be heard swearing quietly as he clambered out of the bushes, pulling foliage from his dark hair and wiping earth from his hands.

Dolly remained on her side of the road, feeling it a safer place to be, considering how annoyed he looked.

He grabbed the handles of his bike and tugged till it was out of the ditch. Turning sharply, he scowled in her direction. 'What the hell did you do that for?'

'I didn't mean it.' Her soft Irish accent seemed to momentarily silence him. At least, she reckoned that was what caused him to stare. No one else in the bay was Irish, so she figured she might stick out a touch.

He bent over and rummaged in the ditch and then straightened up with a pair of dark glasses, which he wiped and returned to his face.

Oh, you're him. The one they call Clark Kent. I can see it now you're close and you've put your glasses on. Blimey, you're gorgeous. Look at you. I wish I had light-brown skin like you. If I stay in this sun any longer, I'll have bright pink, that's for sure.

She attempted to tidy her mousey hair in the two seconds he took looking down at his bike. The flick back of her thin strands from front to over her shoulder was all she had time for before his bright blue eyes were scowling her way again.

Scott rubbed his cheek where the apple had connected. 'Try and look next time. Why are you throwing food, anyway? Use a bin.'

'It's an apple core, and I was throwing it into the bush for the wildlife.' She glanced down at the munched apple now on the road where it had deflected to. 'So, you'd better move it out of the road, as it's dangerous for animals there.'

He went to speak but closed his mouth.

Dolly was pretty sure at that point that if he could beam lasers out of his eyes, he would. At her. 'Or, I can do that.'

He was looking over his bike and wiggling the handlebars from side to side. His face was filled with thunder, and his glasses looked slightly wonky on his face, but she wasn't about to mention that fact, in case they were broken.

It was just an accident. There's no need for the daggers. Anyone would think he's just had to pull out of the Tour de France.

'I think it's okay,' he mumbled, seemingly talking to himself as though she no longer existed.

She took a steady breath and waited for him to glance over. 'I am really sorry. I didn't even hear you, let alone see you. I didn't throw an apple at your head on purpose.'

The memory hit her and she laughed at the same time his face had softened a touch. He snapped straight back into angry mode.

'It wasn't funny. It hurt and caused me to fall. I could have broken my arm or something.'

She placed one hand over her mouth, but her giggle was still seeping through her fingers. 'I know. I'm sorry.'

He flapped a hand her way. 'Clearly!'

As she was so busy concentrating on him, she didn't notice the small herd of cows walking downhill towards her until one passed by, bent its head, and gobbled up the apple core.

Her mouth gaped as she turned to see the rest of its crew taking up the full width of Pepper Lane. A mooing sound made her jump, and a hefty body forced her to leap up on the stile, for health and safety reasons.

Scott stepped into the ditch on his side with his bike whilst keeping his eyes firmly on her. The slight twitch of a grin in the corner of his mouth didn't go unnoticed, and she silently cursed him in her mind. She also cursed the hefty animal that almost knocked her off the stile.

'Where did this lot come from?'

It was obvious Scott was fighting to hold back his laughter. 'Pepper Pot Farm.'

'Then why are they in the road?'

'Lee likes to take them for a walk around the block every now and again.'

A young man in his twenties came into view at the back of the herd. Dolly watched him casually walk past as though walking cows was a natural everyday occurrence in his life.

'Evening,' said Lee, tipping his white baseball cap at Scott.

Scott checked his watch. 'Wow, is it that time already? How are you doing, Lee?'

'Fine, thanks, Scott.' He turned to Dolly and smiled before heading off.

She smiled back and then looked over at Scott. 'Where is he taking them?'

'Walk Walk Road.'

'Walk Walk where?'

Scott gestured towards a turnoff on her side a bit further downhill. 'It's that road there.'

Dolly frowned with confusion. 'That dirt track is a road?'

'It leads to Dreamcatcher Farm and The Post Office Shop.'

Her big chestnut eyes widened. 'There's a post office down there? No one told me. I've been going all the way over to Sandly on the tram every time I want to send off my parcels.'

'Well, now you know.'

'Aye, of that I do,' she mumbled.

He turned back to his bike, showing he was finished with the pleasantries.

Dolly huffed to herself and stepped down from the old wooden stile. Her foot buckled, she twisted sideways, and fell straight into a bunch of stinging nettles that hugged her bare legs like a long-lost relative. Her mid-length, pink, flowery dress lifted to her waist, revealing her caramel-coloured, tummy-control knickers.

Scott rushed to her side and pulled her up before she had a chance to groan or think about her unsightly underwear.

'Are you hurt?' His hand was in her hair, pushing it away from her flustered face. 'Did you bang your head?'

Oh, now you want to be nice. Get off. Stop touching me with your sexy man hands, and I swear to God, if you so much as mention my drawers, I'll find that cow, have it regurgitate that apple, and I'll lob it straight at your head, this time on purpose.

She pushed him away and straightened her dress. 'I'm fine.'

His eyes were on her legs, and she followed his gaze to see the lumps that were already waiting to irritate her.

'You're going to need some cream on that.'

State the obvious, why don't you.

'Shouldn't we look for a dock leaf? Isn't that what you're supposed to do?' She started to examine the grassy verge for signs of big leaves, not having any idea what she was looking for. She just knew they were big leaves that grew next to stinging nettles.

Well, clearly not on the Isle of Wight, they don't. I can't see anything big, but that leaf is the biggest here, so...

She ripped the greenery out of the ground and proceeded to rub the leaf on her itchy bumps whilst Scott watched with bemusement.

'Why don't you just go home, wash your legs, and put some anti-itch cream on them? Wouldn't that make more sense than staining your skin green with a leaf some fox has probably peed on at some point today.'

Dolly dropped the leaf. He was right about one thing. Her leg was now tinted green. She drooped her shoulders and sighed to herself. 'I don't have any cream, and I'm in no mood to jump on the tram to Sandly to go to the chemist.'

He rolled his eyes. 'I have some back at mine, if you want to come there.'

'Where is yours?'

He nodded behind him to a cute yellow thatched cottage sitting not far back from the road.

She failed to hide the dreamy look in her eyes as she glanced over at his home. 'Oh, that's my favourite one out of all the cottages along Pepper Lane.'

He had no response to that except, 'Follow me.'

She took a step and winced. 'Ow!'

'What's wrong?'

'I think I've bruised my ankle.'

He waved his hand towards her left foot. 'Try again.'

Another painful step forward was enough to confirm the diagnosis.

She saw him roll his eyes again and heard his muffled huff. Watching him walk back over to retrieve his bike, she did wonder if he was simply going to ride off and leave her. But he came back and told her to climb on.

'Erm, what?'

'Get on the bike. I'll push you to my house.'

'Oh, I'm not very good on a bike. I'm quite clumsy, you see.'

'Hmm. Well, you won't be riding. You'll just be sitting, and I'll be steering and pushing you along.'

Dolly could already feel her cheeks flushing, and she knew it wasn't down to the warm sunshine. She reluctantly sat on the bike, knowing that would be the sensible option. Plus, she could hear Dexter in her head telling her off for delaying help. Had he been there, he would have already conferred with the 999 operator and morphed into a paramedic. She lifted her legs away from the pedals and off they went.

The short driveway up to the yellow cottage was gravelly and led to a narrow pathway made of stepping stones with pretty flowers lining the sides.

'Oh, it's so pretty.'

'It's called Lemon Drop Cottage.'

She cupped her hands across her chest, lost a bit of balance, and leaned into him. Clearing her throat, she straightened. 'Sorry.'

My God, man, you smell as good as you look.

He helped her off the bike and opened the door. 'I've not moved in properly yet, but I've got the kitchen stocked.' He swooped her up into his arms and casually carried her to the quaint kitchen as though carrying her was something he often did. 'The medicine cupboard is full, so you'll soon be sorted.'

Dolly was still gobsmacked as she was placed on the small oak table in the middle of the room. She looked around at the matching oak cupboards, and her eyes lit up when she spotted a green range cooker.

Oh, I've always wanted one of those, and he has a butler sink. I'd like one of those too. This is a really sweet kitchen.

23

Very country. Could do with modernising a touch and definitely a few candles. Ooh, and a suncatcher would look nice hanging in front of that little square window. You've got to love a cute square window, so you have. This place has a nice vibe. Good energy here. Yeah, I like it.

A warm cloth was placed on her leg, followed by Scott sitting in a chair in front of her and placing her poorly ankle up onto his thigh. His soft touch was causing way more than a flutter in her stomach.

'See if you can wiggle it around.' His eyes were only on her ankle. A deep look of concentration filled his face.

Dexter would definitely appreciate this man's attentiveness.

She did as she was instructed to find that her joint didn't feel too bad. 'I don't think it's sprained. I just landed funny, that's all.'

He looked up. 'Yes, that's how it usually works.' He leaned closer to her, reaching his arm out to her side.

She swallowed hard and hoped he didn't notice.

Where's he going with that arm?

Scott pulled a white hand towel off the table behind her and started to dry her damp leg.

Feeling quite perplexed and slightly irritated by the appearance of butterflies in her stomach, she watched him wash and dry her legs as though he were her carer.

'Here.' He handed her the cloth and towel. She scrunched them into a ball and placed them behind her as he opened a tube of anti-itch cream and proceeded to gently wipe some on her wounds.

'Thank you for doing this.' As he didn't respond or even look up from his task, she added, 'You have a nice home.'

'Thanks.'

'I'm Dolly, by the way.'

'I know.'

'And you're Scott Harper, aren't you?'

'Hmm. I am.'

'I understand you're an artist.'

'That's right.'

And clearly you don't like small talk.

'I was wondering if you would be able to paint a new sign on my shop. It's Dolly's Haberdashery. The yellow...'

'I know your shop.'

Finally, he looked up. Now she wished he'd kept his eyes on her legs. The bright blue almost bore into the depth of her soul. She was sure he could see things she had hidden away.

'When do you want me to start?'

'Oh, erm, whenever you have time.'

'Does tomorrow evening suit you? I close The Book Gallery at four, so I can come over then.'

Wow, I wasn't expecting him to agree, seeing how I threw an apple at his head. Christ, don't start laughing again.

'What are you grinning about?'

'Nothing.'

'Are you thinking about that apple hitting me again?'

Without thinking, she reached forward and touched the top of his cheekbone. 'Are you bruised?'

They stilled at the same time, both focusing on her hand. She removed her fingers, made a fist, and slowly pulled her arm back.

'I'm okay, but thank you for asking.' His voice was soft and low, and she was sure he was feeling just as awkward as she was.

'I'd better get back. Dexter will be wondering where I've got to. Plus, I need to start dinner.'

He nodded and gently removed her foot from his lap.

'Dexter's my son,' she felt the sudden need to add.

'I know.'

'You seem to know a lot.'

She caught his smile just as he turned to the sink to wash his hands.

'Pepper Bay is a small place. Everyone knows everyone's business around here.'

'Aye, I'm starting to realise that.'

'I'll put you back on my bike and wheel you home. Your ankle will feel better in a couple of days. Just try not to walk much.'

She slid off the table, attempting to put weight on her foot, as she really didn't want to be seen being pushed along on his bike. 'Nope!'

He turned and sighed. 'What are you doing?'

'I was testing it out.'

'Just leave it alone. You're lucky it isn't swollen. Don't make it worse. It needs time to heal.'

'Aye, you're right. I'll put a crystal on it when I get home.'

He arched an eyebrow as he lifted her into his arms. 'Yes, that'll work.' His flat tone made her wonder if he was being sarcastic or not.

'I wish you would give me a warning when you're about to swoop me up.'

For the first time since meeting him properly, his eyes lowered submissively, and Clark Kent was in the room. She had heard the locals call him by that name, saying that he acted shy and awkward like the character, but she wasn't getting full-on introvert vibes from him. She wasn't quite sure what she was getting from him. He had the bright blue eyes and the big glasses, and there was something gentle about his face, but there didn't seem any other reason for his nickname. But what did she know. They'd only just met.

And now she was in his arms for the second time, and it kind of felt nice, but she still felt the need to let him know that he shouldn't just pick her up whenever he felt the need. Or at the very least, ask first.

'Of course. You're right. I'm so sorry.' The hint of nerves in his voice made Dolly feel awful. She had no intention of chastising his actions. She just wanted to know what to expect, that was all.

As he had stopped walking towards the front door, she explained that she was fine and that he could carry on.

The journey back to her shop seemed to drag, especially as neither of them spoke, which went against her usual bubbly, chatty personality. She had tipped into his body a couple of times, but he never complained, and all she could do was secretly inhale his rosemary-infused aftershave every time she neared his neck. The scent stayed with her all night.

3

Scott

The bottom end of Pepper Lane had a few small quaint shops on both sides and a large family-friendly pub on the corner at the top end. The shops were an array of pastel colours, and the pavements were lined with flowerboxes filled with colourful flowers, as were the windowsills of the flats above each shop. A narrow conduit ran alongside the left side of the road, if heading downhill, all the way from the top of the shops down to the small stony beachfront at the bottom.

The quaint pastel-green shop, The Book Gallery, that was the first shop on the lane, had been quiet for the last half an hour, so Scott flipped open his laptop on the counter to see if his online friend had sent an email.

Hello, CK.

I'm not an artist like you. I'm just into arts and crafts. Maybe soon I'll share the link to my online shop with you. We have been talking for quite some time now. There's only so long we can talk about the weather, right? It's just, I've had so much going on over the last few months. I didn't want to add to it. I'm not sure what we should try next, but we should try something soon.

My aunt's really enjoying the retirement village. She's the youngest one there and likes to remind everyone about that fact. I don't know what she's playing at over there, but she's already got herself into trouble, over

quite a hostile game of bingo, I might add. Who fights over bingo? I was called in to speak with her. I had to give her a talk about how to play nicely with others. She called me a cheeky mare and sent me on my way, then rang me five minutes later to ask me to come back with a bottle of cherryade and a packet of Skips. I'm not sure you're supposed to dip your false teeth in such a drink, but my aunt reckons it hits your teeth anyway, so what's the difference?

Not sure about the gossip round my way yet, but my aunt said there's an old man at the home who keeps wiggling his walking stick at her. One of the care workers told me he has a bit of a crush on my aunt, so I guess that's his way of showing off. Poor fella. Didn't end well for him. He fell over the other day whilst waving his stick in the air. My aunt laughed. 'That'll teach him,' she said. She's all heart.

I did meet another neighbour recently. Not sure about him yet. He seems to have two sides to his character and I think I saw both of them. I prefer friendly, chatty folk. I never know what to do with standoffish people. Mind you, I didn't make a good first impression on the man, so it's my own fault, I guess.

What about you? Have you met anyone nice where you live? What's your neighbourhood gossip?

I'm glad to hear you're finally getting your home sorted. I've been trying my hand at a bit of tiling in the bathroom. So far, so good. Well, no tiles have fallen off the wall. Okay, so maybe one did, but one hardly counts.

It only had to go and fall in the middle of the night. Scared the bejesus out of me.

My son got a place in the local school, but he won't start till September. Most kids would be happy about the delay, but not him. I think he worries he might lose brain cells if he misses any lessons. He has already emailed his head teacher to ask for assignments to be sent home. He's been home-schooling himself, because I know about as much as sticky toffee.

How is your family? Is your brother still with his girlfriend?

Speak soon.
Lady Light x

Scott smiled warmly into the screen. There was something about this woman that made everything in his life feel calm.

Someone passing by stopped to browse the collection of books in the right-side window, catching his eye. They moved on, and he went back to smiling at his laptop.

I hope Giles has stopped reading my emails now that he's checked her out. I should have got him to tell me what she looks like. I can see her today in dirty overalls, tied-up hair, and glasses. She obviously doesn't mind getting stuck in. Tiling. I'll have to give it a go myself, which reminds me. I need to buy some paint for the ceilings. They definitely need a spruce up.

Scott's aunt opened the door. Her bright red hair was the first thing he noticed as he peered over the top of his laptop.

'Quiet in here, love.'

'Lunchtime. Everyone's off for a bite to eat over the road at the pub, no doubt, or in Edith's Tearoom. Why are you here? Haven't you got a rush on?'

'That temporary baker Joey hired for while she's on honeymoon has about six arms. He's got it all covered. Plus, Molly's working. Anyway, you need your lunch too.' She held up a cloth shopping bag.

Scott stretched his neck, attempting to peer inside. 'Ooh, what you got?'

'I got you a Ploughman's from The Ugly Duckling.' She gestured outside to the old pub across the road. 'Our Fred slipped one out the back for you.'

Scott breathed out a laugh. 'Ruby! You have to pay for it.'

'Yeah, of course. I'm not about to rip off the Sparrows, am I? They're my friends. Freddy said he'll pop the money in the till after the rush. He's busy cooking. He's training a new chef to help out in the kitchen. About time, I say. He works so hard over there.'

Scott was busy unravelling the foil from the plate his aunt had handed over. 'He loves it.'

She nodded her agreement and started to mooch around the romance section.

'I think you've read them all,' he called over before popping a chunk of cheese in his mouth.

Ruby glanced over her shoulder. 'I can sense your sarcasm. There's nothing wrong with reading love stories.'

'I could fix you up an online dating profile if you're that interested in love.'

'Cheeky sod. I'll have you know I'm happy being a divorcee.'

Liar. You would love to still be married to Wes. I know you still love him. I wish you were together. The divorce should never have happened. Oh well.

'Speaking of which, did you know that Wes stuck an envelope through the letterbox with twenty quid inside?'

Ruby stopped browsing and frowned with amusement. 'No. Who was that for?'

'Me.' He arched a dark eyebrow as she laughed. 'It's not funny. I'm forty-five not ten. What's with the pocket money?'

'Aw, your uncle helped me raise you, didn't he. He still likes to chip in every so often.'

'He's a fisherman. I know he doesn't have much money. I'd rather he didn't give me any.'

Ruby approached the counter, picked up a slice of crusty bread, and lightly pressed the buttered side on the tip of his nose.

Scott quickly wiped it off and laughed. 'Get off me, woman.'

She nodded at the window. 'You need to go over and have dinner with him one night.'

He followed her eyes. 'Who, Freddy?'

'No. Wes. He misses you, you know.'

'I will. I've already spoken to him, but you know what he's like. He hardly speaks. I'm only going when Fred's there with Molly. At least I'll get some conversation that way.'

'Your uncle is a man of few words. Always has been. You're not much different.'

Scott almost choked on air. 'I'm nothing like him.'

Ruby placed her hands over his, stopping him from eating. 'Scott Harper, you spend so much time away from home, and when you are here, you spend your time mostly on your own.'

'I like myself.'

She laughed and patted his knuckles. 'Perhaps you should think about online dating.'

Lady Light came to mind.

'I'm happy on my own, thank you. You know, some people actually are, Ruby.'

'Well, at least hang out more with your friends here.'

'I do.'

'You don't.'

'I hang out with Freddy.'

'He's your cousin. It doesn't count.'

'Don't let him hear you calling me his cousin. You know he likes to call me his brother.'

She nodded and glanced over her shoulder as though checking he wasn't there. 'That's true. Well, he did grow up around you, and he looks up to you so much, Scotty. I'm just glad he didn't grow up and join the army as well.'

Scott raised his brow. He knew what was coming next.

Ruby leaned over and pointed at her hair. 'See those grey hairs. You did that when you signed up. I was only in my forties then. I didn't deserve to have grey hairs.'

He homed in on her saturated red hair, unable to spot any signs of grey peeking out from the dye. 'Will I forever be blamed for your natural aging?'

'Yes.'

'If it's any consolation, you don't look a day older than sixty-six.'

'Cheeky bugger. That's my age. You're supposed to lower it.'

He chewed his food with a big smile on his face as his aunt went back over to a bookstand.

I give her five seconds before she starts talking about love again.

'You know,' she said quietly, 'there's a new girl over the road. Dolly. She seems nice.'

He rolled his eyes. 'I've met her. In fact, I'm going over there after work to repaint her shop sign.'

Ruby spun around with a gleam in her eyes and practically skipped towards him. 'Ooh, that's good of you.'

'It's not a favour. It's a job. She liked all the other signs I've done around here so asked me.'

'She's a single parent, came over from Hastings, but she's originally from Ireland, so she's Irish.'

'It's a good thing you told me. I would have never noticed from her accent.'

Ruby ignored his sarcasm. Clearly, there were more important matters at hand. 'She's forty, a widow, and good with her hands.'

The corners of his mouth twitched. 'Good with her hands, eh? Maybe I'll paint that above her door.'

'She's very friendly, and runs her own business, and she owns that flat above the shop, so she's not short of a few quid.'

'You should offer to help write her dating bio. I think you missed your calling there, Rubes.'

Ruby crossed her arms in a huff. 'Can you just be serious for a moment.'

He clasped one hand in the other, sat up straight, and gave her his best serious face.

Ruby scoffed. 'Oh, now you're just being daft.'

He smiled and leaned back in his office chair. 'I'm not dating her.'

'But you never date anyone.'

'You make it sound like a bad thing.'

'Aren't you lonely, love?'

Not anymore.

'I'm moving in to Lemon Drop Cottage in a couple of days, and I plan to enjoy the peace and quiet.'

'Ooh, that reminds me. Josephine called earlier to say all the furniture deliveries have arrived, so she's gone home.'

'Did she sage my house?'

'How did you know about that?'

'Because it's Josephine Walker, Pepper Bay's witch. I knew she would. I bet she's left a crystal lurking around somewhere too.'

'She used her own broom to sweep out any negative energy, you know. She doesn't do that for anyone. You should feel honoured.'

He slapped one hand over his heart. 'I truly am.'

'Scott.'

'I'll thank her. She was only supposed to be housesitting whilst waiting on the deliveries. I do hope she hasn't slaughtered any lambs on my doorstep.'

Ruby chuckled, then frowned. 'She wouldn't use actual blood, would she? God, you can't tell with her. No. I'm sure she wouldn't. Probably salt. Yes. Joey said her gran often left salt on the doorstep.'

'Good to know. Perhaps she missed a few ghosts and I'll be able to talk to the dead once I move in. At least you won't have to worry about me being lonely then.'

Ruby waggled her finger at him. 'Hey, you're a long time dead, you know. You get out there, Scotty, and start living.'

He stared glumly out at the sunlit street as his aunt left the shop.

If only you knew just how much living I've done. That'll take the red out of your hair.

He made his way over to the door and stepped outside, shaded from the sun by the pale-green-and-white stripy canopy that Anna had added to the shop front for the summer season. His eyes looked left down the street to see a mum dusting remnants of food off her toddler's dinosaur tee-shirt. A young girl taking selfies with the beach as her background caught his eye next. He moved away from her to follow the lively family of six about to enter Pepper Pot Farm Shop, and then he rolled his eyes next door to Dolly's shop. The old sign above it was dirty and faded. The whole premises needed a lick of paint.

Shouldn't be too hard to fix that sign. Weather's good all week. Yeah, I'm looking forward to that job.

Scott spent the rest of the day doodling design ideas in between serving customers and talking art. He was looking forward to closing the shop and getting started over at Dolly's so much, the day seemed to drag.

Tourists were still mooching along the lane, taking pictures of the view and paddling in the sea. The shops had started to close, which steered a lot of visitors off towards the pub at the top end, opposite The Book Gallery, and Scott thought it was a good time to take his ladder over the road to Dolly's to have a closer look at the sign before bringing over the rest of his things.

He climbed up and wiped one hand over the old faded swirls of orange and grey lettering.

Dolly's Haberdashery. What a shame you have to go. You've been here for as long as I can remember.

Nostalgia washed over him as he smiled warmly up at the sign, then the ladder vibrated against the wall as the door below his legs banged to a close. He quickly glanced down, hearing muffled chatter, and before he could say a word the ladder was knocked away from the wall, and he came crashing down to land upon his side on the pavement.

4

Dolly

'Oh my God!' cried Dolly. 'Are you okay?' She squatted down to Scott's curled body on the ground, with one hand dithering close to his head.

'No, I'm bloody not.' His scowling face caused her to stand.

'Should I call an ambulance?' Her voice was feeble and pathetic, and she knew it.

He tossed the ladder off his legs and sat up whilst groaning, clutching his hip. Dolly wanted so badly to check his head for any signs of growing lumps, or worse, but she was too afraid to offer assistance, because his face was filled with thunder. He was taking big, deep, calming breaths, and she wasn't sure if that was to ease any pain or stop himself from killing her.

'Erm...' She cleared her throat. 'I didn't notice you out here. I wasn't looking.'

'Habit of yours, it would appear.'

After their last encounter, she felt she had little defence.

'I'm so sorry, Scott. Please let me help you.'

He flinched away from her touch, picked up his glasses from the floor, and took his time standing. One of his legs was dipped slightly at the knee, and she wondered if he could put pressure on it. Her own ankle was still hurting, causing her to limp, so she had a rough idea how he was feeling.

'Will you come inside so I can check you over?' She waited patiently for a response. Anything would have been good, even a death glare. But his blank face gave away no clues, and she didn't know what to say next to ease the huge amount of tension between them. 'Please,' she opted for.

Dexter came out of the shop and slapped his one hand to his mouth. 'Mum, you didn't?'

Scott scoffed. 'Oh, she did.'

Dexter approached him, looking down at his bent leg. 'Come inside and sit down. You could have concussion or something.'

She was about to tell her son that the injured man probably just wanted to go home, when Scott agreed and limped past her.

Dexter led him towards the backroom whilst Dolly locked the shop up for the day. She glanced outside to see the small gathering disperse and was so glad no one took any photos of Scott on the ground. At least, she was pretty sure she didn't see anyone whip out their phone. She could only imagine how much angrier he would have been if that had taken place.

Sheepishly making her way to the small table and two chairs situated in her work studio, she could feel her heartbeat pick up the pace, and so placed one hand over her chest, hoping it would slow down the thump she was sure was showing through her bright blue tee-shirt.

Dexter had taken charge. He sat Scott on one of the old, white-washed, wooden seats and flicked the switch on the kettle, because tea always helped. He started asking medical questions as though he were on Grey's Anatomy, and Dolly edged towards the doorway, feeling like a spare part.

'You should take your jeans off so we can examine your leg for any signs of swelling or bleeding.' Dexter was one hundred percent serious, and Dolly wondered what Scott's next move would be.

His hand reached for the buttons on his jeans and pulled them open, causing an instant dryness in her mouth. When he pulled them off and stood there in just his white tee-shirt and dark Calvin Klein boxers, she pondered over the idea of averting her eyes.

No, it's okay. I'd see more if he was on the beach. It's grand. He's grand. He has very nice legs about him. Okay, that's enough of that. I don't need to stare. He didn't stare at Dexter's arm, I noticed. That doesn't happen very often. My boy doesn't seem to care about anyone staring, and he definitely isn't bothered about anything at the moment except for looking after Scott. Aww, bless my boy. He's such a good kid. Fifteen going on fifty, but still. He'd make a fine doctor. He likes a bit of blood and broken bones. Oh, don't think about it, Doll. I feel a bit queasy, actually. This doesn't happen in the books I read. If he was the protagonist in my books, we'd be at it on the table right about now. Obviously, not with my son watching. Oh, good lord, I need to stop reading erotic romance, and I definitely need to stop staring at Scott Harper's legs.

She sat on the spare chair, opposite the casualty, willing the kettle to hurry and boil so she could have some ginger tea to help settle her stomach.

'Are you okay, Dolly?'

'Hmm?' Surprised he was talking to her, let alone concerned, she looked up in a daze.

Doctor Dexter interjected. 'You've gone a bit green around the gills, Mum.'

She glanced at the kettle as it clicked. 'Erm, I'll just make some tea.'

Dexter gave her his fatherly, stern glare. 'No, you won't. You look ready to pass out. I'll make it.'

Scott's eyes followed the boy. 'Do you need some help?'

He turned and smiled. 'What, because of my arm?' He gestured down towards his left elbow where his arm ended. 'It's okay. I can manage. You'd be surprised with what you can do with only one hand.'

'I'm sorry,' said Scott, lowering his eyes. 'I wasn't trying to insinuate anything.'

Dexter went back to making the tea. 'It's okay. People often ask me if I need help, and guess what? Just like every other human out there, sometimes I do.'

Scott breathed out a laugh as he sat back down. He turned to Dolly to ask how she was feeling.

Still queasy and very much stressed.

'Don't you worry about me. You're the one who fell off a ladder.'

'Fell?'

She slumped her shoulders, hoping she could slump all the way down into the ground. 'Knocked off.' She cleared her throat, as her words had sounded broken, which was pretty much how she was feeling.

Scott was leaning over, checking out his legs. There didn't seem to be anything obvious there, but Dolly was sure bruising would appear at one point. He glanced her way, jolting her out of the trance she had with his right knee.

'How's your ankle?'

She slowly looked down at her three-hundred-year-old brown flipflops that she simply refused to toss out, even after a long-drawn-out discussion with Dexter about buying new footwear at some point in her life, as all of her shoes seemed to be hanging on by a thread. At the same time, he had held up a pair of her shoes, claiming Emmeline Pankhurst wore the same pair. Dolly told him that she didn't care if she shopped in the same shoe shop as Jane Austen, she wasn't throwing away any of her footwear, not even the ones Dexter called Anne Boleyn.

She rubbed one hand down towards her ankle. 'It still hurts a bit.'

Scott was looking in the same direction. 'It didn't swell up in the end, so that's good.'

Dexter waved a teabag at them. 'I'm having chamomile, and I'm guessing Mum's having ginger. We have all sorts here. What heals you?'

Scott smiled, revealing a gorgeous smile that made Dolly's need for ginger increase. 'I'm a green tea drinker.'

'Ooh, lovely.' Dexter turned back to the kettle. 'How long do you like to leave the teabag in for?' He glanced over his shoulder. 'Mum does thirty seconds with her herbal teas. I'm more a minute and ten.'

'No one's ever asked me that before.'

Dexter shrugged one shoulder to his ear. 'Hey, there are different strengths, and each to their own, right?'

Scott glanced at Dolly. 'I like your kid.'

'Thank you,' said Dexter.

'I prefer two minutes,' Scott told him.

Dexter brought the tea over. 'Ooh, risky.' He smiled as he placed a saucer on the table by the bright yellow mug.

Scott leaned forward and removed the teaspoon from the cup and placed it on the saucer. 'Thank you.' He took a sip to test its strength.

Dexter frowned and waggled his hand close to Scott's face. 'Ooh, that's still really hot.'

'It's okay. I can only drink hot drinks when they're really hot.'

Dolly daren't pick hers up in case she accidentally spilled it on his bare legs or somewhere more delicate. She was quite sure something else would go terribly wrong, and then he'd hate her even more. At least he was getting on with Dexter.

Without any warning whatsoever, she started to cry. Dexter quickly rushed over and hugged her tightly, leaning over her shoulders.

'Oh no, Mum. Come on. Don't cry. He's alive. Look.'

Dolly snuffled her nose into his *Science Rocks* logo and quickly took the tissue he waggled her way that he had pulled from the pocket of his shorts.

Scott was up out of his chair and squatting at her side, with one hand resting lightly on her knee.

'Aww, group hug,' said Dexter, but nobody moved. 'Just me then.'

'What's wrong, Dolly?' The softness in Scott's voice caused a second wave of silent tears to fall.

Oh, flipping heck. Get a grip now, Dolly. Come on. What you crying for anyway?

'Mum hasn't cried in years.' Dexter gently stroked her mousey hair away from her forehead. 'You'll be okay, won't you, Mum?' He turned his blue eyes towards Scott. 'It's all been a bit chaotic the last few months, what with moving and opening this place.'

Dolly felt Scott's hand gently squeeze her knee. 'I'm okay,' she assured him, not sounding too convincing. 'You need to straighten your legs. Go on. Sit back down.'

Scott hesitated but then went back to his chair. 'I'm all right, you know. Please don't cry.'

She wiped away her embarrassing snot bubbles and dried her cheeks. 'I'm sorry. I don't know what came over me.'

'You got a fright, that's all.' Scott slowly pushed her tea towards her.

'Maybe I should make you chamomile, Mum.'

She nodded and watched Dexter go back to the kettle.

'Hey,' said Scott, gaining her attention. 'I think we all need a break. How about this Sunday, you two come and help me settle in to Lemon Drop Cottage by sharing a picnic lunch with me in the garden?'

Dexter spun his head around so fast, his nose met the conversation before his eyes had time to assess what was going on. 'You own Lemon Drop? Oh, that's my favourite. We'll definitely be there, won't we, Mum?' He waited a second, then added, 'That dazed look means yes.'

Scott gave Dolly a wink, which did little to wash away the haze in her head.

I'm not quite sure what's happening to me right now. I could have killed a man. He's now sitting in my work studio in his underwear. I just cried like an eejit, and Clark Kent just winked at me. I think I need sleep.

5

Scott

'It's Mum's famous chocolate mini rolls trifle,' announced Dexter as soon as Scott opened the front door of Lemon Drop Cottage.

Dolly wasn't looking overly chuffed about the large glass bowl in her hands that was covered in crinkled clingfilm.

'It's pretty decent,' added Dexter.

Scott welcomed them inside. 'There was no need to bring anything, but thank you. It looks very nice.'

Dolly headed straight for the kitchen. 'I wouldn't get too excited. It's just shop-bought chocolate mini rolls sliced on the bottom covered in a packet of chocolate Angel Delight, and topped with Dream Topping and a crumbled Cadbury Flake.'

'And Mum always sings the Flake song as soon as one's in her hand.'

'I do not.' She scrunched her nose. 'Do I?'

He nodded.

Dolly frowned down into her dessert. 'I've never noticed. I like that song. You don't hear it much nowadays. Stays with you. Now, that's good advertising.'

'Yes, Mum. You should be on commission.'

'You're right there, son.'

Dexter grinned over at Scott. 'Next time we come, we'll bring a shop-bought Arctic Roll and a tin of squirty cream, because we like to go all out.'

'Oi, cheeky. I'll have you know that everyone loves Arctic Roll.'

Scott laughed. 'Well, I wouldn't say no.'

'Mum slices a circle onto a plate, squirts a swirl of cream on top, then adds a thin slice of banana and says, ta-dah! She's very creative.'

'I'll give you very creative in a minute, Dexter Lynch.'

Dexter giggled. 'Shame there isn't an Arctic Roll song. Someone needs to work on that.'

Scott removed the hefty bowl from Dolly and made some room for it inside the fridge. 'We're just out the back garden.'

Dolly tried to stretch her head around his body to look at the doorway as though someone was there.

He followed her eyes. 'It's just my aunt, cousin, and his girlfriend. I believe you have already met them all when you first arrived.'

She smiled widely and casually strolled to the garden.

Whoever the gardener was, they had been doing a fine job. Neat borders, trimmed grass, washed-down paving, and the prettiest of flowers were in full bloom. Mini gnomes clearly owned the area. They even had a door at the base of the biggest tree at the end of the garden.

Dexter clapped his hand over his heart. 'Oh, I love gnomes.'

Dolly smiled at Scott's family sitting at a patio table beneath a large brown cantilever parasol. 'What my son meant to say was, hello, everyone.'

Dexter turned on his heels. 'Oh, yes, sorry. Hello, everyone. I was just caught in gnome-zone for a moment.'

Scott placed a glass jug of Pimm's on the table. 'Feel free to walk around and check them all out. There are plenty to be found.'

'Come on, Mum. You know you want to.'

Dolly twisted her lips to one side as she gingerly took a step towards the winding pathway swirling through the lawn.

Scott moved to her side. 'I'll introduce you.' He glanced back over his shoulder to see Freddy and Molly engaged in each other's hair, and his aunt giving him the thumbs-up sign. Ignoring her completely, he walked behind Dolly and Dexter as they explored.

'Wow, this one looks old.' Dexter squatted to get a better look at the little gnome watering the earth with a dull-silver watering can. The gnome's eyes were as faded as his shorts, and there was a tiny chip on the tip of his hat.

'That's Mr Summer. He's the first gnome to claim this garden. My mum bought him a long time ago.'

'Where's your mum now?' asked Dexter, still examining old Mr Summer.

Scott swallowed down the dry June air whilst leaning back onto one heel to take the weight off his bruised hip that hadn't healed yet from the fall off the ladder. 'She passed away when I was a kid.'

Dexter's blue eyes held softness and compassion as they rolled up at him. 'I lost my dad when I was a kid.'

Dolly smiled warmly. 'You're still a kid, Dex.'

He flapped his hand. 'Oh, you know what I mean.' He stood and turned back to Scott. 'I was five. Almost six.'

I'm not going to ask him how he lost his dad. I get the feeling Dolly won't want to talk about it. And if she did, it wouldn't be out here in front of my family whilst gnome hunting.

He pointed into a peach rose bush. 'Now, that's Beryl. Named after a character from an old comic.'

'Beryl the Peril,' said Dexter, admiring the young gnome with the bright red hair and a definite look of mischief in her eyes.

47

Scott grinned. 'I didn't think you would have heard of her, Dexter.'

Dolly huffed out a laugh and nudged his elbow. 'Please, Dexter here knows every character from every comic ever made.'

'Slight exaggeration, Mum.' He smiled at Scott, an abundance of delight oozing from his face. 'Almost every comic, is correct.'

Scott was still staring at his elbow, wondering why her touch had bothered him.

Dolly hadn't seemed to notice the brief encounter. She was busy staring up at the tall tree where all the gnomes went home to every night, Scott said his mum used to say.

'This is a lovely tree you have here, Scott.' Her hand reached out to touch the bark. Her palm pressed flatly on it and stayed put as though going for the Guinness Book of Records longest high-five.

'And it has a swing,' cheered Dexter. He gave the old rope a tug, checking for sturdiness.

'It's safe,' said Scott. 'Try it out.'

Dexter didn't need to be asked twice. He plonked his bum down and pushed with his feet. 'Oh, I haven't been on a swing for ages.'

Dolly started to fuss around him, stepping closer and holding her arms out as if to balance him without actually touching him.

Dexter laughed. 'Mum, I'm fine. I can hold on with one and a half arms.'

'I know. I know. Just don't go too high. It's only made of old wood, you know.'

For reasons unknown to him, Scott gravitated to her side, practically gluing himself to her mousey hair. 'I assure you, it's very safe.'

She turned sharply, bumped into his chest, and wobbled. A gentle breeze whipped her loose locks onto his cheek. He slowly returned her hair whilst watching her chestnut eyes shyly roll down to his feet.

Remove your hand, Harper. Why is it still there?

He swallowed hard and turned back to the swing. 'Erm, would you like a go, Dolly?'

She laughed out loud, then seemed to chastise herself. 'I'm forty years old. I'm thinking that I'm a little too old for that now, wouldn't you say?'

Dexter brought himself to an abrupt stop and jumped off. 'Don't be daft, Mum. There are no age restrictions to having fun. Right, Scott?'

'That's right, Dexter. So, come on, Dolly. Hop on. You never know, you might actually enjoy it.'

Before she could find her voice, she was manhandled onto the thick plank of wood by her grinning son.

'You can push Mum, Scott. I'm going to look for more gnomes.'

Dolly looked ready to jump off, hop on the nearest bus, and flee the island altogether.

So, Scott thought he'd tease her. 'You're not afraid, are you Dolly?'

'I might be. What's it to you?'

Oh crap, maybe she actually is afraid, and there's me grinning like an idiot.

'Are you scared of heights? I wasn't going to push you high.'

The hint of a twinkle hit her eyes. 'No, I am not afraid. I'm just saying, I might have been. Wasn't exactly asked, was I?'

'No, you wasn't.'

'Go on then, one little push. Take me back to my childhood.'

Scott smiled to himself and stepped behind her, taking the sides of the seat in his hands. He pulled her towards him until her back was almost resting on his chest, and then he let go.

Dolly laughed out loud, and it warmed him. He shook his head and widened his smile. Then he noticed his family down by the house, watching. He lost his stupid grin and went back to the front of the swing.

'Do you want me to push you now, Scott?'

Oh God, no. I'll probably end up in the rose bush, with a heap of thorns sticking out my backside if I let you near me.

'How about we have some lunch now instead?'

He bit his lip as she tided her pink floral dress and mumbled, 'Coward.'

Ah, I think she read my mind.

Ruby stood to give Dolly a tight hug as soon as she reached the table. 'Finally, I get to say a proper hello.'

'Leave her alone, Mum,' said Freddy. He swiped his thick apricot curls from his eyes and beamed widely at Dolly. 'Sit down before she knocks you down.'

Molly reached her hand over the table, tapping at Dolly with a bright yellow nail. 'I was so pleased to hear you were coming today. Now I won't be the only one left out of the loop when it comes to family in-jokes.'

Freddy breathed out a huff of a laugh. 'She's a fine one to talk. Her family is full of jokes I don't understand.'

Dolly gazed down the garden at her son. 'I think all families are like that, Moll.'

Scott frowned in amusement at the gnome whisperer, wondering what in the hell Dexter had to talk about to a gnome. Scarlet Pumpernickel did, however, look as though she were listening whilst catching butterflies with her net.

Ruby bundled herself back into the black sun lounger and reached out for a sip of her fruity drink. Pulling a piece of pith from her lips, she gestured towards Dexter. 'How did your boy lose his arm?'

Both Scott and Freddy huffed out at the same time. 'Mum!'

She quickly turned to Dolly. 'I don't mean any harm, love. It's not a bad thing to ask, is it?'

Scott sat by Dolly's side, leaning closer to his aunt. 'Dexter's probably sick to death of people asking him.'

'Well, I'm not asking him, am I? I'm asking his mum.'

'It's okay,' said Dolly. 'People ask sometimes. He was in an accident when he was two. A bus driver had a heart attack at the wheel and crashed into the bus stop. Dexter was in his pram on the other side of that bus stop. It was nobody's fault. The driver didn't know he would keel over that day.'

A moment of silence filled the air, which caused Dexter to glance up from his conversation with Scarlet Pumpernickel.

'Well,' said Ruby quietly. 'I'm not sure what I was expecting you to say, but it wasn't that.'

Dolly shrugged. 'That's Dexter's story.'

Silence filled the air once more until Molly's light voice cut through. 'The thing I get asked the most is, are you single?'

Freddy frowned at her. 'Who's asking you if you're single?'

Molly beamed a smile his way and snuggled his hand into hers. 'I love you, Freddy Morland, that's all you have to know.'

He arched one eyebrow at her and lightly moved her dark hair behind her ear. 'Hmm.'

She leaned over and kissed his cheek, and his thick lips returned the gesture.

Ruby was staring into space. 'I think the question I get asked the most is if my hair colour is real. Of course it isn't real. Who is born with blood hair?'

Dolly looked at Dexter. 'He was quite red when he was born. As you can see, it's just plain old rusty now.'

Ruby smiled over at him. 'I like his colour. Suits him.'

Scott could see Dolly from his peripheral vision before he shifted more her way. Her cogs were turning. He sensed that much. She wanted to know more about him. Her silent words were as strong as her sweet perfume that seemed to have wrapped around his face, refusing to leave his nostrils. Not that he minded. He had grown accustomed to her scent already. He liked it. He liked her and was happy to share some titbits about himself.

He met her eyes. 'I get asked if I was born here.'

She frowned in confusion. 'What, in Pepper Bay?'

'No. England.'

Ruby tapped his arm. 'Scott's mum was Indian, you see. That's why he has that lovely skin tone. Unlike mine, which looks about as pale and lifeless as an oven chip.' She nodded at Freddy. 'Fred's got my skin. Shame, because his dad, Wes, has got tough old skin that has some sort of permanent suntan.'

'What's known as weather-worn from being a fisherman,' said Freddy, grinning at Scott. 'I get asked if I workout,' he added proudly.

Scott shook his head. 'Only because you're always flashing off your abs any chance you get.'

Molly giggled as she stroked Freddy's stomach. 'I don't mind.'

Scott turned his attention back to Dolly. There was so much more he wanted to know about her, but as there was only one question flying around at the moment, he asked her the same thing.

She gave a half-shrug. 'Not sure. About Dexter, I guess. As for me personally, for some strange reason people like to point out that I'm Irish.' She laughed. 'Ooh, you're Irish, they'd say. Obviously, they don't say that in Ireland.'

'Why did you move to England?' asked Ruby, who, unlike Scott, got to the point when she wanted to know something. She had no shame.

He listened carefully to any morsels he could collect, slightly intrigued by the fact that he was slightly intrigued by the woman.

'My husband got a job with my brother in Hastings, so we moved there. That's pretty much where Dexter grew up, which is probably why he doesn't have an Irish accent like me and his dad. I'm not sure who Dexter sounds like. He always reminds me of some history or science professor you might find at Oxford or somewhere similar.'

Ruby nodded, and Scott knew she had more questions. She was in interrogation mode. He had to save Dolly from the spotlight, but he didn't want to. For once, he allowed his aunt to interfere.

'So, Dolly. When did your husband die?'

Blunt as ever, Rubes.

'About ten years ago now.'

Dolly doesn't seem fazed. I guess that's another question she's used to hearing. What's Ruby got up her sleeve next?

'How did he die?'

She just comes right out and says it, doesn't she? Amazing.

'Carbon monoxide poisoning. He was away with my brother on one of their fishing trips. They went to sleep one night and didn't wake up.'

Bloody hell!

Scott reached out and held her hand. 'I'm sorry you lost them both.'

'Yeah,' said Freddy, as Molly quickly wiped her eye. 'That's really sad. Was anyone held accountable?'

Scott felt uncomfortable as Dolly removed her hand from his.

'Eventually. It took years. I was handed compensation through the courts, and that was the end of that.'

'Well, I think that's enough of question time,' said Ruby, scraping her chair back. 'How about I serve us up some lunch now.'

Dolly stood. 'I'll help.'

Ruby flapped one hand. 'It's okay, love. I've only got to carry it all through. Our Freddy's already made everything.'

'I can help with that.'

Ruby smiled. 'Okay.' She looked at Freddy and Molly. 'You two can set the table.'

Freddy frowned over at Scott. 'What about Scotty?'

Ruby affectionately patted Scott on the shoulder as she passed him. 'It's his housewarming lunch. He can just rest.'

Freddy rolled his eyes, then turned to Dolly. 'Any old excuse. She never lets him do anything.'

'It's true.' Scott leaned back in his chair, placing his hands behind his head whilst closing his eyes and grinning widely. 'I am spoiled.'

He jolted forward as he felt the back of his hair get swiped. Dolly was glaring down at him.

'Well, not on my watch. Get up, and get helping.' She winked over at Freddy. 'In my family, it's all hands on deck.'

Scott slid his hand through his dark hair and peered over his shoulder at her. 'I work hard when I'm away. That's why I get to relax when I come home.'

'Is that right?'

He kind of guessed that his futile attempt at remaining seated wasn't going to work on her. Big chestnut eyes were boring into his soul. He wasn't quite sure if the slight fluttering feeling in his solar plexus was coming from her or if it was simply indigestion. Either way, it made him stand.

'I can help,' he muttered.

The small hint of a smile that raised one side of her mouth was extremely cute and ever so kissable, and now was definitely the time to go and get the salad cream out of the fridge, because he was about three seconds out from his cousin noticing him standing there looking dazed and dreamy.

6

Dolly

I can see why they call him Clark Kent. That way he lowers his eyes beneath his glasses. Nervous. Submissive. He has the good looks, the bright blue eyes, and the slightest droop to the shoulders. He's definitely got that pose down to a tee. But I've seen him when he thinks no one is watching. I've noticed the changes when he drops his guard, or when he's too annoyed to think about his expressions. There is so much more to that man than he lets on. So, I guess the real question is, why? Does he really have two personalities? If not, why is he pretending to be someone else? He's way more Superman than Clark. Wouldn't you want to be Superman? Why does Superman hide his true identity? Christ, I'm starting to think like Dexter. But why does Superman hide himself? Because he has something to hide. So... what does Scott Harper have to hide?

Dolly had finished the washing up in Lemon Drop Cottage, much to Scott's disapproving eyes. But she wasn't about to let Ruby do any more. It was late evening. Lunch had extended to a BBQ dinner, thanks to Freddy, and Ruby was ready to put her feet up for the night.

Dolly heard the front door close after Scott said his goodbyes to his family. They had been so welcoming of her and her son. From the moment she stepped foot in Pepper Bay, everyone had been so nice. Scott was the last one she got to meet properly. Although, throwing an apple at someone's head could hardly be classed as a proper meet-and-greet.

Scott headed straight upstairs, she assumed to use the loo. So she popped her head around the living room door to see what Dexter was up to, as she always worried whenever he was quiet. Not that she had anything to worry about with him. If anyone had the best kid on the planet, it was her. She knew that. Dexter wasn't the type to break the rules, get into intentional trouble, or even have accidents. Nope. She was the accident-prone one in the family.

A low light was on in the corner where Dexter sat curled up on the sofa reading one of Scott's books about Viking gods.

The room was small, cosy, and in her opinion, a little on the dark side. She glanced around, imagining how she would decorate if it were her home. Her eyes came back to her content son.

I wish I was like Dexter. He's so smart, and nothing ever bothers him. He really should have been born into a better family. One with clever parents who can keep up with him. What has he got? Me. Poor kid.

'Hey, Dex. Do you want a cup of tea?' She kept her voice low as not to disturb his peace.

The warm light created golden flicks to his rusty hair as he lifted his head to smile softly at her.

Those blue eyes were his dad's, and they always smiled that way at her. The melting feeling in her heart was making her eyes glassy, and very soon she wouldn't be able to make him a cuppa, because she wouldn't be able to see the kettle.

'Thanks, Mum.'

Aww, Cianan, look at that beautiful child we made. Isn't he something? I swear to God, sometimes he looks at me and I see nothing but pure magic in his eyes. Bless him. What a gorgeous soul.

She silently sighed and headed back to the kitchen to see if Scott had more of a tea variety than green tea. The racing-green dome kettle hung low to her hip as she peered outside the little kitchen window.

Oh, how she loved the light nights. The warmth in the air. The tranquil feeling of summer. The sense that there was so much more time to the day.

The window was ajar, so she inhaled the smell of the low sun upon the grass outside. Dolly always thought that night-time being held back by the light had a slightly different undertone to full-on night.

She liked to sniff out as many fragrances she could find in life and attempt to recreate them into her homemade candles and wax melts. Tonight's smell would be labelled, Almost Night. The colours would be a mixture of sunset and summer sky. Not too dark. Not too light. Definitely a touch of shepherd's delight.

Another smell mingled. It was herby, with a hint of Scott Harper.

The need to swallow came about from nowhere, as did the awkwardness in her posture. She glanced down at her food baby, wondering if he would notice if she stuck the ironing board down her summer dress, and then she told herself off for worrying about her body shape. It wasn't something that normally bothered her.

'If you ever decide to put the kettle on, I have some teas to choose from,' said Scott softly.

She turned and smiled. 'Sorry. I was just enjoying the evening air.'

He sat on a chair and watched her fill the kettle. 'I like the smell of night-time around here. It reminds me of crying flowers.'

Dolly frowned into the sink.

Weeping Wisteria. Not sure that would sell. Although...
'You daydreaming over there, Dolly?'

She placed the kettle on the stove and turned to look for help. It was his kitchen. Only he would know where the tea and mugs were.

As though reading her mind, he got up and took over.

'It's so lovely here, Scott. Makes me wonder why you would ever leave such a place.'

He had his back to her, pottering around. His voice was low, blending into the relaxed atmosphere. 'Work reasons. That's all.'

'Will you be leaving again anytime soon?'

Not that it's of any interest to me. I'm just having some idle chit-chat. Not a thing wrong with that.

'No. I'm retired from that job now. Just have my part-time job in The Book Gallery to keep me on my toes. Although, it's full time at the moment while my boss is away on honeymoon.'

Dolly sat in the chair he had not long moved from. His posture had straightened again, and his voice was more controlled. Superman was on show for her tonight. Perhaps he was too chilled to care. She tried not to overthink it. 'You seem young to retire.'

'Forty-five going on eighty-five, that's me.' He breathed out a laugh as he turned to meet her eyes.

She felt the tiniest of flutters appear in her stomach.

And you can bugger off.

'Is that how old you feel, Scott?'

'Sometimes. I get a lot of aches and pains in my body. That's why I ride my bike a lot. I'm trying to keep myself well oiled.'

'Oh goodness, I haven't helped you much.'

He pursed his lips tightly and shook his head. 'Nope.'

Swiftly moving on…

'Was your last job very physical?'

He turned back to the kettle as it started to give off a faint whistle. 'At times.'

'What did you do?'

'I joined the army when I was younger, and when I got older, I went into a different field. Still military, but more on the communications side.'

'What, like a radio controller?'

He brought her tea over. 'I made you chamomile. Dexter told me it's your favourite.'

'Oh.' She glanced at the steam snaking out of the blue-glazed coffee mug.

'I'll just pop this in to him.'

The kitchen felt extra quiet as soon as he left. There was no breeze to rattle the window. The crickets were still in zen mode, and as Pepper Lane was absent of people, there wasn't the background noise that she sometimes heard from her flat when the locals cleared out of the pub.

'You've got a good kid there,' said Scott. He seemed to linger in the doorway before sitting at the table.

She smiled to herself. 'Yeah, I know.'

'Look, Dolly. I'm sorry we got off on the wrong foot. I was being a moody git. I don't make friends easily, and I'm not a people person at all, I...'

'And you worked in communications?'

He laughed along with her.

'There was a team of us, and I wasn't the talker.'

'What was your role?' She watched him mull over his answer.

'I guess we were all just trying to keep the peace.'

Oh, you just totally avoided the question. Maybe he can't talk about it, what with it being military stuff. Top secret, operation code whatever.

'So,' he asked, cupping his hands around his mug and shuffling closer to the table. 'Have you always had a shop?'

'No. I had a small business back in Hastings, but I worked from home. This was my aunt's idea. More outgoings, but I live in this beautiful place now, and I get to mix with more people. Unlike you, I like them.'

He smiled the cutest smile into his tea. 'Well, somebody has to.'

And back to you...

'So, the army was your life, was it?'

'I suppose. It is a bit of a lifestyle. Would you like a biscuit? I have chocolate fingers in the cupboard. Ruby always buys them for me. It's rude not to eat them. She calls them happy biscuits, because apparently they make people smile.'

Oh, you really don't want to talk about the army. Okay, Doll, let it go. Might be some trauma there.

'No, thanks. She's a nice lady, your aunt. Very blunt, bit like mine, but harmless enough.'

Scott laughed. 'Yes, Ruby is quite straightforward.'

'You call her Mum sometimes.'

'She raised me, that's why. I don't exactly know what happened to my dad, but I can only assume he fell apart after my mum died. He couldn't cope, so he dumped me on her doorstep one day with a note. I was eight. That was the last time I saw him.'

'Grief can do funny things to a person. We all know that. When my husband died, I was like a zombie for the first year. Probably the second too. Life felt surreal. I couldn't hear his voice anymore. His clothes no longer filled the laundry

61

basket. I no longer had someone to hold my hand. It didn't feel real for a very long time.' The breath lodged in her chest evaporated slowly. 'Sorry. I'm oversharing.'

'No, that's okay. You can say what you want. I don't mind.'

'Have you ever been married?'

Scott laughed. 'I meant about you, not me.'

'Oh, you don't like to talk about yourself, do you?' She watched him chew his lip, consider his answer, and sip his tea, stalling for time. 'Hey, Scott, I've got poisoned family members and a son with an amputated arm in my backstory. Yours cannot be that bad. Come on. Hit me.'

His eyes rolled up, filled with amusement and a hint of something she couldn't figure out. 'I was married when I was young, but it wasn't an ordinary marriage.'

'Okay, now I'm intrigued. Did you do it so that she could stay in the country?'

His gorgeous smile slightly swept her away to somewhere enchanted. 'No. She was a friend of mine. She was dying, and she wanted to get married. It was on her bucket list. She didn't have a boyfriend, so I volunteered.'

'Oh, wow. I wasn't expecting you to say that. That's a sad story, but very good of you to grant her a dying wish. How old was she?'

'Twenty-one.'

'Aw, Scott, that's horrible that she died so young. Her poor family must have been shattered to pieces. It takes its toll on a family when one of the kids die. I know.'

'Your brother. Were you the only two?'

'God no. He was the only boy. Our youngest. I have six older sisters.' She took a moment to appreciate how quiet her life was now. Growing up, there wasn't any peace. Not with the size of her lot. The thought of the chaotic family she grew up in caused her lips to curl. 'Ah, they were a mad bunch. It took me a long time to get used to such a small family. Now, I can't imagine living in a crowd again. Just the thought drives me insane.'

Scott laughed with her. 'Do you see much of each other?'

Dolly felt her heart warm with the love that came from her memories. 'No. My parents sold everything they owned many years ago and bought themselves a rather posh campervan. They go all over in the thing. I think they're currently in Portugal. I've not had a postcard in a while, and that's how they like to communicate. We keep telling them to buy a laptop or even a phone would be good, but they prefer to call from a phone box and send mail. I'm not sure they realise what year we're living in.'

'I like their style.'

'Hmm, you would. Well, it doesn't suit the rest of us who are up half the night at times worrying ourselves silly that they've gone and got themselves kidnapped or something.'

'I'm sure they're experienced travellers by now.'

'Aye, that they are. Still, you worry. Or maybe I just do. Do you know, sometimes, they leave their caravan parked up somewhere and just hop on a plane. They have no plans. No schedule. They're just out there in the world winging it.'

'What about your sisters? Do you have any local?'

Mary and Aoife were the first two who sprung to mind. They were always the first two. They were the hardest to talk about, so she decided to leave them to last.

'No. I have two back in Ireland. One in America, and one lives in a quaint cottage like yours up in the Cotswolds. I've been for a holiday. It's so lovely there. Very pretty. If I'm honest, I didn't want to go home, but our Kathleen doesn't like to play hostess for too long. She doesn't tell you when she's had enough, oh no, that would be far too normal. She starts putting on her pyjamas earlier and earlier and burns your dinner. That's her polite way of saying go home.'

Scott laughed as he got up and went over to a cupboard. He came back with the already opened packet of chocolate fingers.

Dolly took one as soon as he slid the tray out of the box. She smiled as she snapped it in half.

Scott was watching her. 'See, they do make you smile.'

'What's not to smile about with such a treat?'

He twiddled one in his fingers. 'So, what about your other two sisters?' He bit his biscuit and smiled her way.

Well, we've come this far in our oversharing night. Might as well tell him. It's no secret, after all.

Scott stopped smiling as he swallowed down what was in his mouth. 'You look uncomfortable, Dolly. Do you not want to talk about these sisters?'

He knows how to read someone. Army training, I bet. Or maybe I can't hide my emotions very well. Dexter always says I'm an open book.

'It's okay. We were teenagers when it happened. We took one of those cheap blow-up dinghy things out into the sea. We'd been drinking. We thought it would be funny. Wasn't exactly a calm night. The only thing we had about us was drunk logic. Stupid thing had a hole in it, didn't it. The long and short of it is, we sank, and me and Mary were the only ones who made it back to shore. Mary, being the oldest out of us three, ordered me to stay put while she went back in the water to find our Aoife. She never came back. I called the emergency services, but my sisters were not found till morning.'

Scott got up and sat in the chair next to her. His arm pulled her in for a hug, and she just let him. 'Look, I know you felt uncomfortable when I held your hand earlier today, but I really need to give you a hug right now. Jesus, Dolly. Your family have really been through the wars.'

The moment leaning on him had passed. She sat up to look at his bright, wondering eyes. 'I wasn't uncomfortable, Scott. It's just, I'm not used to having my hand held. And if I'm to be honest right now, I don't need a hug. Not really. I can cope with sad memories. They're a part of me now.'

He stretched his head back for a moment and sighed to the ceiling. 'Yeah, I guess. It's just something that you do, isn't it? Comfort someone.'

'Aye, but I'm okay.'

His head lowered, and he seemed to be studying her face through her eyes. 'Okay.'

'But thank you.'

'You're welcome.'

'We've shared a lot of sad stories today. Tell me something funny about your life, Scott Harper.'

The cute grin was back. He leaned away, thinking for a moment. 'Well, there was that time when I came home and told my aunt that I'd joined the army.'

7

Scott

Doll's Gift House was the new sign above the pastel-yellow shop in Pepper Lane. Scott stood back on the pavement, admiring his artwork. There was always something that could be improved, but he had reached a point where he had to let it go. It was a cute sign that matched all the other cute shop signs around it. The time had come for him to lower his paintbrush and walk away. He looked through the glass door and caught Dexter's eye.

Dexter smiled widely, called for his mum, and brought her outside.

The moment of truth. Why does this bit always make me nervous? There's not a lot that makes me nervous in life, but this is definitely something that gets me every time.

His eyes rolled down from the sign to watch for any tell-tale signs coming from Dolly's deadpan expression. The last thing he wanted was her hating it but being polite.

Dolly beamed his way, and he immediately felt relieved. 'Oh, Scott. It's adorable. I wish I could paint.'

'Me too,' said Dexter, tilting his head all angles before whipping out his phone to take a picture. 'Do you want to get in a picture, Scott, with your work?'

'No, that's okay, but I can take one of you and your mum with the new sign, if you like.'

'Yes, we like.' Dexter pulled his mum to his side, telling her not to do her goofy grin.

Scott laughed to himself as he walked out into the road to take the photo using Dexter's phone. 'Say cheese.'

Dexter frowned and gestured to the farm shop next door. 'That's their shop.' He turned to his mum. 'We'll say Dolly's.'

Dolly giggled and slung her arm around his shoulders, and Scott took quite a few shots.

Dexter retrieved his phone. 'Thank you, Scott. One of these will be framed and hanging behind the counter before the day is over.' He went back inside to get on with the job at hand.

Scott followed Dolly's eyes back up to the sign. She had a dreamy look and a wide smile. He could feel her emotions as though they were his own.

She lowered her head, quickly wiping away a tear. 'Oh, I'm having myself a moment here.' She breathed out a laugh, and all he wanted to do was take a step closer towards her.

Not sure how to play this one. Sod it. I'll just stand next to her.

He tried not to react when their arms touched. She didn't move away, so he stayed still.

'It's funny where life can take you, isn't it, Scott?' The softness in her voice settled his controlled awkwardness.

He glanced down at her, studying her features as though seeing her for the first time. 'Yes, it is.'

She sniffed, drew breath, and looked up at him. 'Would you care to have your dinner with us tonight?'

'Yes, thank you. I'd like that.'

He couldn't work out what kind of smile she gave him before she headed back inside her shop. There was still his own shop to see to, so he crossed the road to put away his equipment and lock up for the evening.

The laptop seemed to be mocking him, almost demanding his attention. He hadn't emailed Lady Light back since their last chat. There was an element of guilt running though him because he had been focusing on Dolly and not her.

He flipped it open and began to type.

Hey, Lady Light.

Hope you are okay. I'm glad your aunt is settling in nicely and making new friends, especially the old guy. That's funny. Not much has changed my end. My brother and his girlfriend are still making puppy dog eyes at each other.

I'm finally in my own home. Not sure if I miss my mum's old sofa. We became so attached, I feel as though I should have left it a note.

Cooking for one is lonely, don't you think? It somehow never fails to depress me. I'll get used to it, or I can keep going to my mum's for dinner. As much as she likes company, she also likes her alone time, and I don't want to intrude on that. Last night, I couldn't even be bothered to cook or order takeaway, so I had cornflakes. It was a big bowl and went down nicely, before you scold me for not eating properly.

So, what have I been up to that will thrill the socks off you when you read this? Well, I did some weeding in the front garden. Technically, I pulled out one large weed by the front door, but that is classed as gardening. I actually have a gardener. He comes once a week during the summer. He seems to enjoy it, so it's best left to him. God, I sound so lazy.

I did some artwork today, and I got paid, so, yay to those days. Who said we can't make a living as artists? Well, they were probably right, but hey.

Tell me something positive. I'm in need of a Lady Light hit today.

Speak soon.
CK x

He looked at the screen and sighed deeply.

I wish I could say more. If I could talk about my life, it wouldn't sound so boring. She's never boring, and now I miss her. That's it. No more distractions. I need to keep my head in the game. Wait, that won't be easy, I've agreed to have dinner with Dolly and Dexter later on. Why is this a problem? I'm not cheating on anyone. Nothing romantic has happened between us nor has anything resembling flirting happened with Lady Light.

He went to check that the back door to the shop was locked, then went upstairs to wash out his paintbrushes and clean his palette. Meticulous was the word when it came to him cleaning his art equipment. Everything had to wash up looking shiny and new.

He rolled back his arm and clicked his neck as he made his way back to the counter to collect his things. Just as he was about to close down his laptop, a message from Lady Light popped up.

It wasn't unusual for either of them to respond quickly to the other's emails. Some nights, they had stayed on all night emailing back and forth.

He smiled at her name, knowing that whatever she had to say, it would lighten his mood, clear his head, and settle his worries. She had that effect over him, and he liked it. He had felt a connection with her pretty much straight away on the art forum. There was something about her that he couldn't quite explain to himself. Why he gravitated towards her. He tried not to focus on that. Just hanging out online was good enough.

'What say you, Lady Light?'

He opened the email, leant on the counter, and smiled warmly into the screen.

Well, hello there, CK.

It sounds like someone needs cheering up. Let's see now. Well, I can't tickle you in the ribs from here, although, that would probably annoy you more than anything. I know it does when someone attempts that manoeuvre on me. It annoys them even more when they end up with a swift kick in the shin for their trouble.

My aunt's been behaving herself, so no news on that front, but watch this space. Trust me, it won't take her long. I suppose I could tell you about the grumpy man I met the other week. That was pretty funny. I think you'll appreciate this story.

Let me just start by saying I did not do this on purpose, but I did laugh. You should have seen his face. I didn't know he was there, you see. Anyway, I threw an apple core across the road, aiming for the bushes, and he just happened to ride by on his bicycle at that exact moment, and it hit him in the face. He swerved, dipped into a small ditch, and, needless to say, wasn't impressed with me.

We got off on the wrong foot, but since then, he's been okay with me. He might be more nice than grumpy.

Hopefully, my eejit self has cheered you up. Look at that. I'm giving away clues now.

We'll have a video chat next. Are you ready for that?

Speak soon.
Lady Light x

PS. My heart bleeds for you missing that old sofa.

Scott stared at the screen, with his mouth gaping, his eyes wide, and all traces of saliva in his mouth gone.

No. It can't be. No. Just no. No.

Four times he read the email, and each time didn't make a blind bit of difference. The words did not magically change.

Lady Light. Candles. Dolly makes candles. Lots of people make candles. They don't all throw apples at my head though, do they. Bloody hell. No. It can't be. It just...

He needed his phone. His other phone. The one he could call Giles on.

Giles was way ahead of him.

Scott closed his drooping mouth as the video call came in.

'Giles, you complete and utter git. You knew exactly who she was all this time and you didn't tell me.'

Giles showed his palms. 'Hey, it was only a matter of time before you sussed it out yourself. That was half the fun. Waiting. You know, you never used to be this slow. I'm starting to worry about you now.'

Scott slumped down into the office chair behind the counter and huffed loudly.

'Come on, Harps. Why aren't you smiling? Surely this is good news. Right on your doorstep. You can see her when you like. Oh, wait till you tell her you're Online Guy, that'll…'

'I'm not telling her.'

'Scott, you can't hide forever. One day, she'll figure it out. I don't see what the problem is, anyway. You were planning on meeting her at one point. I think she'll appreciate the fact that she already knows you.'

Scott wasn't feeling his friend's enthusiasm. 'I can't see this ending well, Giles.'

'Well, of course it won't if you don't tell her and she finds out later on down the line that you already knew. Come on, mate. I thought you'd find this hilarious.'

Scott shook his head whilst lifting his glasses to pinch the bridge of his nose. 'It doesn't feel right, Giles. I don't know what to do with this.'

'You're making problems where there aren't any, Scotty boy. The lady you've been seeing lately is the same lady you've been talking to online for months. That's a win in my book. Ooh, it's like that film with Meg Ryan. I always liked her.'

Scott slumped forward, removing his glasses so that his fingers could rub over his now weary eyes. He glanced up through his fingertips. 'Hang on a minute. How do you know I've been seeing Dolly lately?'

Giles grinned widely. 'Hey, I'm your big bro.'

'Stop, Giles. Just stop stalking me.'

'I can't. It's my job.'

'I don't work there anymore.'

'Wellll, officially, you kind of still do.'

Scott pointed sharply at the screen. 'Bloody well change my status, Giles.'

'It's not Facebook. I can't just tap a button to *It's Complicated.*'

Scott dropped his shoulders in a slump. 'Giles, do you hate me or something?'

'I love you, Harps. No one has your back like me. I miss you. Come back to work. At least then you won't have to worry about your *two* women.'

'Tempting, but no.'

'Sorry, I didn't hear that. The line went crackly.'

Scott rolled his eyes. 'I'm going now, Giles. Hope you had fun.'

'Not as much as you'll have tonight on your dinner date. Don't mind me. I'll just be here, all alone, eating cornflakes.'

Scott ended the chat.

What the hell am I going to do?

* * *

Spaghetti Bolognese was on the menu. Messy, slurpy, and not one of his preferred dinner choices. He ate slowly and quietly, pondering over her email and the survival odds of his white shirt.

He might be more nice than grumpy. What's she really saying? Does she like me more than him, me? Am I actually jealous of myself? What the hell is wrong with me? I need to get out of my own head before I lose my mind completely. Concentrate. Dinner. Say something.

'Thank you for dinner. It's very nice.'

Dexter sucked up his last strand of spaghetti and dabbed the corners of his mouth with a red napkin. 'It's my speciality.'

Dolly sipped her red wine. 'Aye, he'll make spag bol any chance he can.'

'It's different to others I've tasted in the past. What's your secret, Dex?'

'Soya mince.'

I wasn't eating meat? That explains the texture.

'Oh.'

Dexter finished his apple juice, then refilled Scott's wine glass before there was a chance to decline. 'What are you up to tomorrow, Scott? After work, that is.'

'Erm, not sure. Bit more decorating at the cottage, I guess.' He narrowed his eyes at the grinning boy. 'Why?'

'I'm learning how to ride a bicycle tomorrow up at Pepper Pot Farm. Daisy Walker said I can use her bike and practice along their drive, as it's long. You could come along for support and guidance. I'll need someone there who is on my side and big enough to handle my mum when she starts fussing. And she will fuss. Why do you think I'm fifteen and still can't ride a bike?' He rolled his eyes towards his mum.

Dolly lowered her glass from her lips instead of taking a gulp. 'Riding a bike with one hand is challenging, Dexter.'

Scott thought about his own riding ability. 'I can ride a bike with no hands.'

Dexter blurted out a huff of a laugh. 'See, Mum.'

The comment earned Scott a stern glare from Dolly. He adjusted his glasses and lowered his eyes. He could see her out the top of his lashes. The faint lines around her mouth meant she was trying not to smile.

I think she likes my submissive look.

'Well, you don't have to come, Scott. I'm sure you have more important things to be getting on with than watching Dexter's stunt rolls.'

'To be fair. I really can do excellent stunt rolls.'

Dolly scorned him in her motherly way. 'It's not funny, Dex. You'll do yourself a mischief one of these days.'

'I'd like to come. I can help. It'll be more fun than painting the ceiling.'

'And I can teach you how to stunt roll, Scott.'

Scott laughed as Dolly huffed. 'Well, thanks to your mum throwing an apple at my head, I kind of already know how to do one.' He checked out her expression. Her smile was itching to be released.

'I'm going to serve dessert,' she said, standing and avoiding his eyes.

'Mum has pulled out all the stops tonight. We're having Jaffa Cakes.'

Scott couldn't help but laugh.

Dexter nodded. 'It's not just them on their own. It's really nice what she does with them. She puts a couple at the bottom of a bowl, layers on some hot chocolate custard, squirts some cream on top, and then sprinkles some of those cake-decorating chocolate sprinkles.'

Dolly turned from the stove where she was stirring a crumbled Wispa bar into some vanilla custard. She waggled her wooden spoon. 'Stop giving away all my best recipes, son.'

Scott waited for Dexter to face him. 'I love Jaffa Cakes,' he whispered.

'Don't tell her, else she'll serve you them all week,' he whispered back.

'That would require me coming back all week.'

Dexter gave a half-shrug. 'That's fine with me.' He glanced over his shoulder. 'Mum, Scott can come again for dinner, can't he?'

'Sure,' she replied, without turning. 'Anytime, Scott. We don't mind.'

Hmm, maybe she does like me more than other me. If I hang out with her more often, she might just forget about him, me, altogether, and then I wouldn't have to explain anything. It's a plan. It could work. Stupid plan, but hey-ho!

8

Dolly

Daisy Walker was two days away from turning fourteen, which she happily announced to Dexter before inviting him to her birthday sleepover, which was taking place in a tent on a field on Pepper Pot Farm where she lived. Her parents and sister were camping out too, and it was all because she was going through a stargazing faze, and that was what she had chosen to do for her big day.

Dexter was excited to attend and met his mother with pleading eyes.

It was rare for Dolly to spend a night without Dexter in the house. He wasn't one for sleepovers, and she wasn't one for babysitters.

'Okay, seeing how Tessie and Nate will be there.'

He gave her a quick eye roll. 'I hardly think it matters if they weren't, Mum. We're only staying up all night to check out constellations.'

Daisy smiled sweetly as her blonde ponytail swished from side to side. 'It's true. Everyone else will probably fall asleep.' She turned to Dexter, and her smile widened. 'But we won't, will we, Dex?'

There was the W one and Orion's Belt to be spotted, and Dolly couldn't think of any more even though Dexter knew them all and had rattled them off many times in the past. There was every chance he was staying up all night. Her eyes rolled to Daisy's face.

Hmm, she seems smitten. She's got no chance of stealing a kiss from my boy that night. She'll learn.

77

'I'll need to buy you a sleeping bag, Dex.'

Daisy lifted her yellow bike from the grassy verge of the driveway. She dusted off the basket on the front and walked it over to Dexter. 'No need. We have one he can use. My dad has loads of camping equipment from when he used to sleepout in the fields as a kid.'

'Erm, wait. Don't you have cows in your fields?' Dolly glanced around the front section of the dairy farm.

Daisy pointed up at the big white farmhouse that seemed to be under construction. 'Not in all the fields, and not in the one we'll be in. Don't worry, Dolly, I won't let anything happen to him.'

Dolly watched the young girl beam her deep blue eyes at Dexter, but he was examining the bike with Scott as though they had just made the old contraption themselves.

'Come on then, let's get you on,' said Scott, causing immediate panic to set directly into Dolly's solar plexus.

'Already? Shouldn't he walk alongside it for a bit first?'

I know. I know. I sound as mad as a hatter, and no one here will understand my fears. I should just shut up.

'Doesn't he need a helmet? What about knee pads? Stabilisers?'

Before she knew what was happening, Scott had placed his arm around her shoulder whilst nodding towards the potential death trap. 'He'll be fine, Dolly. You'll see.'

She felt at a loss for words. The touch of a man's arm, his arm, which held his scent was causing a mild bout of giddiness, or it could just have been because Dexter was about to ride off like a bat out of hell. The song started to pound the back of her head. Dexter, all leathered up and raring to go.

What if he takes to the sky like E.T., or worse, starts jumping over cars like Evel Knievel? What if Scott Harper's aftershave is really a drug designed to make anyone who takes a sniff think irrational thoughts? Oh God, why has the man got his arm around me? Does he even know? He's acting extremely casual about the whole affair.

Scott answered that question by dropping his arm, taking a side step away, and revealing, if for all but a second, a touch of awkwardness. 'Right, let's get this show on the road. Jump on, Dex. Don't worry. I'm going to hold on to the bike while you ride along. I won't let go. I promise.'

Dolly noticed he aimed that last part at her.

Daisy stood at Dexter's side as he straddled the bike. 'It's all right, Dex. It's easy once you get into it. You really won't wobble for long.'

Dexter was looking just as optimistic as her, which wasn't a bad thing. Someone had to have faith. All Dolly had was a light head and a churning tummy.

I'm so glad Scott is here. I'm useless. Right. That's enough of that, Dolly. You be the parent your son needs. Get out there and get involved.

She moved to the front of the bike as his feet took charge of the pedals. 'Come on, son. You've got this.' She realised that flapping her hands in the air like a cheerleader was only attracting a smile from Scott. Dexter and Daisy looked more concerned.

'Mum, if you do a cartwheel next, I'll definitely fall off.'

She smiled to herself at the thought and at the fact that Scott still had that sexy tug in the corner of his mouth aimed her way.

Oh, if my lad rides that bike today by himself, I'm one hundred percent doing a cartwheel.

She took a breath as Scott started to roll her whole world off up the driveway. Daisy was jogging by his side, looking like a boxer in training, and Scott was holding on tightly whilst whispering words of wisdom.

I remember at this point Mary letting me go without telling me, and I just stopped and fell sideways. She laughed, I was bruised, and our Christopher was telling me to go again. Flipping heck, I was battered and bleeding that day. Mary wasn't the best teacher. She wasn't the kindest either. Aw, bless you, Mary. Are you watching now? Do you remember how harsh you were with me? Well, look at that. That's how it's done. Patience. A slow and steady approach. A... Jesus, he's let go.

She was off faster than Usain Bolt out of the blocks. 'Oh God, Dexter, are you all right?'

Dexter was being pulled up by Scott and dusted off by Daisy. Dolly grabbed his face. 'Are you hurt?'

He wriggled his squashed cheeks free from her clamp. 'I'm fine, Mum. Get off.' He turned to Scott. 'Ready when you are.'

Dolly tapped Scott's elbow. 'Why did you let go?'

'I asked him to, Mum. Stop fussing. I know what to expect now.'

She grabbed the handlebars. 'Maybe I should hold you this time.'

'And that's an easy nope,' he told her flatly. 'Stand back, Mother. I've got this.'

Daisy frowned at his residual limb. 'Dexter, have you thought about getting one of those fake arms? It might help with things like this.'

Dolly turned to her son. 'Prosthesis, and he has one. Won't wear it. Says it makes his arm sore.'

'Well, it does.'

Daisy gently stroked over his arm. 'You had some grass there.' She quickly moved her hand.

Aww, look at Daisy. She's very affectionate. I like her. Ooh, they're off again.

This time, Scott held on for longer, and Dexter had stopped leaning into him. There was a two-second moment of alone time, a major handlebars wobble, and Dexter slamming his feet down to save himself from another encounter with the grass.

Dolly took a calming breath. She decided to sit on the grass and watch her growing lad try to ride that bike over and over and over again. Proudness filled her, and every so often it burst out of her mouth in the form of some motivational words.

The weather was warm but bearable, and a lovely light breeze kept everyone cool. That and the cold bottles of water Daisy's mum, Tessie, brought over.

The small red-headed woman sat by Dolly's side, smiling over at Dexter. 'Well, he's determined, I'll give him that.'

The water was so refreshing and welcomed. Dolly cuffed her lips. 'He's a perfectionist. That's what he is. If he's going to learn something, he has to be good at it.' She fastened the cap back on her bottle and grinned at her son wobbling away in the near distance.

'Did Daisy invite him to her stargazing birthday night?'

Dolly nodded. 'Yes. And he said yes. That is so his cup of tea. He won't sleep that night, hope you know.'

Tessie smiled. 'That's okay. I don't think I will either. Can't say I've ever camped out before.'

'Yes, well, rather you than me.'

'Is there anything I need to know about Dexter? Any allergies? Food requirements?'

'Oh, no. He doesn't come with a list.' Dolly laughed to herself. 'That's what my mam used to say about my sister Aoife. She comes with a list, does that one.'

'Now that you mention it, I think my daughter Robyn comes with instructions.'

They both laughed and settled into a conversation about their own learning experiences in life. Tessie spoke about her first time on ice-skates, and how she ended up with a broken finger, and it brought Dolly straight back to the time she buckled on roller skates and crashed straight into her brother and sprained his wrist after landing awkwardly on him.

Tessie shifted the goal posts and started talking about Scott. 'Clark Kent over there is usually pretty quiet, but I've seen you two together a few times now. Has he finally gained some confidence?'

Laughter came from his direction. Whatever was going on in Camp Wheelie was obviously entertaining to the kids. And Scott was relaxed with them.

Dolly smiled softly at the vision. From an outsider's point of view, they looked like a happy family. A dad and his two kids having fun learning how to ride a bike on a lovely sunny day.

Cianan would have loved this. Mind you, if he were still alive, I reckon Dexter would have learnt this skill ages ago. Cianan would have made sure of that. I wonder what he would make of Scott? I'm sure he would just be happy that Dexter is smiling, and by the look of things, starting to get the hang of it.

'Go on, son,' she cheered, making Tessie jump. She gently tapped her knee. 'Sorry, Tess.'

Tessie grinned. Her green eyes sparkled Dolly's way. 'Are you avoiding talking about Scott?'

'What? No. I think he has more confidence than he lets on. I just don't think he likes to let people get to know him, that's all.'

82

'He's always been a loner. When he's around, anyway. Can't say what he's like outside of the bay.'

'Have you known him a long time?'

'All my life. I was born and grew up here, and the same for him. He's older than me. I'm in my thirties, but still, you just grow up around everyone here. We're a close community, as I'm sure you've figured out by now.'

'Aye, I got that message loud and clear the moment I arrived.'

Tessie smiled at her, then stood, glancing down at her knees that had just clicked. 'Right. I'd better get back inside. I have work to do. I'm starting a business course next week. I was supposed to do it in August, but what with the wedding and our Robyn's birthday that month, I brought it forward. I just feel so busy lately. Still, it's better than sitting around twiddling your thumbs. That's what my dad always says.'

Dolly agreed and thanked her for the water again and watched her walk off back to the farmhouse. She fumbled in her large cotton bag and pulled out her white flower-shaped sunglasses. Her jean shorts were starting to irritate her, making her bum feel sweaty and in need of looser clothing, but her green flowery tee-shirt was baggy and way more on the comfy side, so at least that was something good about her early morning what-to-wear decision. She awkwardly attempted to pull her knickers out of her bum without being noticed, but it was at that precise moment Dexter conquered the bike, squealed out her name, causing Scott to glance over.

Oh, blooming heck.

She jumped up, ignored the flush on her face, and started doing some warped version of star jumps. Her big boobs bounced even in her full cup bra, but that didn't bother her. It was an historic moment in the Lynch household. Dexter was riding a bike, and with one hand, just like a pro. She knew he'd get there in the end. Although, it had taken the best part of the afternoon, and now her stomach was rumbling for dinner.

Everything was suddenly wonderful. The fresh grassy smell in the air. The pale-blue sky still hanging on. The coolness in her mouth from the water. And her knickers had dislodged themselves somehow. Yep, life was grand.

Dexter rode by just in time to see his mum do a cartwheel. He laughed, wobbled, and was caught and steadied by Scott.

The bike was finally put away, and Daisy had permission to join them for dinner at The Ugly Duckling. She walked with Dexter in front of Dolly and Scott.

Dolly was straining her ears, desperately trying to earwig on their conversation.

Dexter said, 'Would you prefer it if I brought my artificial arm with me to your stargazing night?'

Daisy said, 'Only if you want to, Dexter. I don't care either way.'

Dexter said, 'It doesn't bother you that I only have one arm?'

Daisy said, 'You have one and a half arms, and no, Dex. I like you just the way you are.'

Dolly felt she could quite possibly melt into a slushy pool on Pepper Lane from the overload of sweetness she had just witnessed. She dreamily leaned her head on Scott's shoulder, then realised what she had done. She peeled herself off him, and he turned slightly to face her, then held out one hand.

She bit her lip to stop her smile from completely taking over her face like the Cheshire Cat, and then she slowly placed her hand in his. It felt like a perfect fit.

'Thank you for teaching Dexter how to ride a bike.'

'You're welcome.'

Come on, Dolly, just spit it out. You can do this. Draw courage from your brave son.

'Would you like to come to dinner at mine the night Dexter is on his sleepover?'

'I was thinking, perhaps I could take you out somewhere for dinner instead.'

'Fed up with my cooking already?'

Scott smiled warmly down at her. 'No. I want to take you out.'

'Like a date?'

'Yes. What do you say?'

I'm on the verge of doing another cartwheel.

'Okay.'

The rest of the walk down to the pub was done in companionable silence.

9

Scott

Dolly's midnight-blue skater dress was all Scott could gawp at when she stepped out of her shop, ready for their date. He offered his arm as she approached.

'You look beautiful, Dolly.'

Her eyes were on her dark heels as they walked up towards the small car park just past the shops.

'Thank you. I haven't had a chance to wear this dress until now. You look very nice too.'

He glanced at his navy shirt, then back at her. 'We match.'

She giggled and snuggled closer to his arm that she was clutching.

'I've borrowed Ruby's car to get us over to Sandly. It's the tiniest car you will ever see in your life, and I just about fit, but it'll do the job. Besides, we won't be in it for long.'

'Where are we going?'

'To the harbour.'

'Ooh, is it that new fish restaurant that's recently opened? I've heard good reviews about it.'

I think I can do better than that. I hope. Maybe I should've just booked local. She seems keen to try the place. No. Stick to the plan. Rule number one. Do not divert from the plan unless it's an emergency.

'No, sorry.' He opened the car door for her and watched her squeeze inside a lot easier than him.

She didn't look too disappointed and didn't ask for further details. He figured she liked surprises. Well, she was about to get one whether she did or not.

The drive to Sandly Harbour didn't take long. They were soon parked and walking towards the moored boats.

'You wouldn't know it was six o'clock. It's so light out. I love summer. You feel as if you have more of the day. If we didn't know the time, it could be lunch.' She smiled up at him, then dropped her bottom jaw as he gestured towards a white boat.

'That's ours for the night.' Scott waited for her to close her mouth. He reached out his hand and led her on board. 'Come on.'

Dolly stared down at the water as she crossed over onto the Princess Stevie. 'Oh wow! What a luxury. This is a bit posh, isn't it?'

Scott showed her around inside, feeling ever so slightly uncomfortable when she saw it had a bedroom.

'You could live here,' were her only words on the subject. She loved the kitchen and sat at a small polished white table.

Scott laughed. 'No, we're not eating here.' He took her hand and led her to the wheel and started the engine.

Dolly placed one hand over her chest, and he was sure he could hear her heart rapidly beating over the noise of the boat.

'Where are we going?' she asked, with one hand on the wheel as though worried he might steer them into another boat.

He lightly brushed over her fingers as he guided the vessel out of the harbour. 'We're going over the road to Lymington.'

She breathed out a laugh that relaxed his hidden nerves. 'Over the road.'

'I guess I should have asked you if you get seasick.'

Dolly shook her head as she peered forward. 'No. I'm okay at travelling by boat. But you should have seen the state of our Dexter coming over on the ferry. I honestly don't think he'll ever leave the island after that trip. He's stuck there now, bless him. I suppose he could fly. Why didn't we just get the ferry?'

He looked down to meet her eyes. They were filled with the excitement of adventure, which confirmed he had made the right call in hiring the boat. 'Now, where's the fun in that?'

She glanced over her shoulder. 'This is such a beautiful boat. Can you imagine owning something like this? I'd be on it every day. It would have to stay moored when Dexter came on board, but still. It's a nice dream. We could have eaten here. I could have brought a picnic.'

'Perhaps we can do that next time.'

'Next time? Are you lining up a second date before the first one is even over, Mr Harper? That's confidence for you.'

Scott laughed along with her. 'I was thinking more along the lines of us all having lunch here, moored of course so that Dexter doesn't turn green. But a second date wouldn't go amiss, now that you mention it.'

'I might second-date you just for this boat.'

He flashed her his best smile. 'Oh, I think I can get you to like me just for myself.'

She sat down, crossed her legs, and gave him one of her *is that right* looks.

'Get up here and steer this boat. Come on.' He gestured to the cream leather wheel.

Dolly didn't need a second nudge. She jumped at the chance. 'Okay. What do I do?'

He held her in front of him, placed her hands on the wheel, and kept his face low and to the side of her mousey hair that was tied up with some loose tendrils meeting her cheeks. 'Just keep it straight.'

Dolly stretched her head forward, peering through the glass. 'How do we know where we're going? There aren't any signs about.' She leaned back into his body, and once again her hair was close to his lips.

Scott inhaled her coconut shampoo and moved his face slightly towards hers.

I don't want to go anywhere right now. All I want is to take you downstairs to the bedroom and lose the world for a while.

His mouth dropped to her shoulder strap, and he nuzzled it to one side with his nose. The feel of her warm skin millimetres from his lips was almost too much to bear. He wanted so badly to touch her. To kiss her. To do so much more. But he also wanted their night together to play out the way he had planned. His hands reached around to her fingers, and she rested her head back against his.

'Scott?' Her voice was low and breathy.

His eyes were still taking in every inch of her neck and shoulder. 'Hmm?'

'There's a whole heap of boats up ahead.'

'What?' His eyes rolled up to see what she was on about, as just for a moment he had forgot they were even on a boat. He jolted back to life. 'That's Lymington Harbour.'

She slipped out from his gentle hold of her. 'You'd better take over. I don't want to crash this beauty.'

The space between him and the wheel suddenly felt cold and empty. He concentrated on his mooring task whilst she stood close to his side. Her bare arm touching his.

'I bet this thing costs a fortune. I'd cry if I damaged it.' She smiled up at him, and he caught her eye for a second.

'So would I.'

She laughed and it helped his need for her settle down a bit.

'Where do you even hire something like this from?' she asked. 'And don't say the harbour.'

'Well, that is normally where you find them.' He expertly steered the boat safely to its designated spot. 'This one belongs to a friend of mine.'

'Ooh, get you. Posh friends. And I suppose all you islanders just happen to know how to sail such a boat.'

Oh, you'd be surprised what I am trained in.

'You know my uncle who raised me is a fisherman, right? He has two boats. A trawler and a smaller boat that he uses for personal fishing and daytrips.'

'Ah, yes. Wes Morland. I've met him. He's quiet. A bit like everyone thinks you are.'

'I am quiet.'

She gave him a look as he led her off the boat. Dolly was too busy taking in the sights to answer. She pointed out other boats, the seaside town, shops, and restaurants. 'Aw, I've never been here before. It's a lovely place, isn't it, Scott?'

'I think we have a lovely country.'

'And by we, you mean you. I'm Irish, remember?'

He laughed and gave her hand a gentle squeeze. 'Yes, I know.'

'So, where we going now, Mr Englishman?'

'Not far. It's just up here.'

She followed his finger to a large white-washed hotel overlooking the harbour. 'You do like a place with a bedroom, don't you?'

Scott couldn't help but burst out laughing. 'Your mind is in the gutter, Ms Ireland.'

'Oh, is it now. Well, maybe I don't think that place is the gutter. Maybe I think it's a lovely place that happens to have the ability to be quite magical.'

'I like your thinking. Here, allow me.' He opened the door to the hotel and politely waited for her to step inside.

The lift took them to the top floor where they were guided to a big oak door by a staff member. Scott was watching Dolly's face as they entered the room. Her eyes lit up at the sight of the large veranda at the other side of a lounge. Fairy lights and candles were dulled in the light evening, as the sun was still shining, creating a mass of diamond-looking sprinkles over the sea.

Scott pulled out her chair, and she sat whilst staring down at the harbour below. 'Oh wow! Wouldn't it be nice to wake up to this view every morning?'

He felt a flutter hit his stomach as he stared down at her. 'Yes, it would be lovely.' He quickly looked away and sat next to her as she turned to face him.

As soon as they were seated, the staff member offered them a choice of wines and champagne. Dolly chose the bubbly and Scott asked for orange juice.

'You don't drink much, Scott.'

'I have a boat to sail.'

'Oh yes, I almost forgot.' She pointed over the glass walls of the veranda. 'Look, there's ours.'

'Yes, let's hope she's not lonely.'

Dolly flapped one hand. 'She's okay. She has all those other boats for company.'

The drinks were poured and a menu offered. With all the fancy dishes to choose from, Dolly asked for scampi, chips, and peas.

A girl after my own heart.

'I'll have the same.'

The waiter left them alone.

Dolly had the biggest grin, and Scott couldn't help but smile back. 'What are you grinning about, miss?'

'A couple of things.' She shifted more towards him and leaned her arms on the table. 'Firstly, I'm grinning at your sexy setup here.'

He held his stomach as he laughed. 'Sexy setup?'

'Yeah, you with your smart clothes and slick hair. Your bright eyes that flitter between submissive and dominant behind those particularly nice glasses. And then there's all this. The posh boat, this cute seaside town, and I don't even know what to call this room. Does it even have any more to it than a lounge area and private outdoor seating for two?'

Scott wasn't much of a blusher, but he felt the slight wave of heat hit his cheeks. 'I just wanted it to be memorable.'

Dolly looked him straight in the eyes. 'We could have sat on a bench eating sandwiches and it would have been memorable, Scott Harper. It's the company that counts.'

It took all of his willpower not to kiss her at that point.

She reached over and held his hand. 'Just so you know, I really do love this date.'

The corners of his mouth creased into a wide smile. 'It's not over yet. I might have some more surprises.'

'Well, if you're going to flash me your Union Jack boxers, then I'm off.'

He laughed and kissed the back of her hand. 'Oh, Dolly Lynch, you always make me laugh.'

Online and in person.

'I've had a couple of other memorable dates, you know,' she told him.

'Oh really? So, I have competition?'

'No. They were memorable for the wrong reason. You win hands down.'

92

'Now I'm intrigued. Come on. Do tell. What happened on these dates?'

'About three years ago, I decided to dip my toe in the water, so to speak. I'd never considered being with anyone ever again after Cianan, but a woman has needs.' She burst out laughing and tapped his hand. 'I'm just kidding. I guess, I just wanted to see if any of that was possible for me again. I never held much hope, and I didn't really care if it never happened for me again, but I gave it a go.'

'I'm surprised you didn't get swept off your feet.'

'Aw, you big softy. No such luck, I'm afraid. The first date I went on was with a fella who did nothing but talk about his ex. He even produced a photo of her that he still carried around in his wallet, and if that wasn't bad enough, he took a moment to give her a call. Needless to say, he wasn't ready for dating.'

'Oh my God. He actually did that?'

Dolly nodded. 'Hmm. Well, it gets better. The second man I dated was quite nice and it did lead on to a second and a third date, which then turned into a short-lived relationship. Three months. Turned out I wasn't the only woman in his life. There was his wife of fifteen years or something, another girlfriend of four years, another of eight months, and I was the new kid on the block. After that I gave up.'

'Oh wow, Dolly. How did you find out?'

'It was my seventeen-year-old niece. She's like the FBI. She went snooping, just because she's nosy. Well, her mam is. Anyway, she uncovered a lot more than she bargained for. So, that was the end of that. I still really hate that man, you know. Wasting people's time. Ruining lives. Pretending and lying. I really hate liars.'

Oh God, I should tell her I'm CK. Just say it, Scott. Say it right now.

The waiter brought their food, and Dolly was back to smiling again. She glanced up from her plate. 'So, you'd better not have a whole heap of women on the go, Scott Harper.'

He breathed out a laugh through his nose as he let go of her hand so that he could sprinkle pepper over his scampi. 'No. Just trying my luck with you at the moment.'

'Yeah, how's that working out for you?'

He laughed and lowered his face, and without warning, Dolly suddenly sneezed downwards, causing some of the peas to fly off his plate and stick to his glasses.

She slapped one hand over her mouth as her eyes filled with water. 'Oh my God. I'm so sorry.' She couldn't stop laughing. 'I'm so sorry.' The white napkin on the table was grabbed and scrunched tightly to her mouth as tears fell.

Scott slowly removed his glasses to look at them. A grin was tugging at his tight lips.

Dolly was holding her stomach. Her chair scraped back, and she bent over, crying with laughter. One hand was raised in the air, with a waggling finger pointing his way. 'I'm sorry. I… I…' She lifted her head, attempting to look his way, but as soon as they locked eyes, she burst out laughing again.

He started to clean his glasses with a napkin and some water. He had to laugh. She was in bits, and it took a while for her to compose herself. Their dinner was cold by the time it happened, but he didn't mind. Her laughter was infectious, and her smile adorable. And if took peas smeared on his glasses to make her night, then so be it. Plan A never ran smoothly anyway.

10

Dolly

The sun was finally setting as Dolly and Scott walked along, holding hands. She still had the odd fit of giggles when she looked at him, but he didn't seem to mind.

The area was quiet and felt a million miles away from home. She stopped to pick up something resembling a fossil. Not entirely sure what it was, she slipped it in her bag for Dexter, as he would know and appreciate the gift.

I haven't told Dexter about my date. He doesn't know where I am. Probably assumes I'm tucked up in bed, reading. Actually, I'm probably not on his mind at all. His eyes will shortly be in the sky or stuck to his telescope. I wonder if Daisy was thinking her night with him would be romantic? My night with Scott has been romantic. Well, except for the peas. Oh Lord, don't start laughing again. I can't cope.

Scott grinned down at her. 'You thinking about the peas again?'

'I'm sorry.'

'Hmm.'

She straightened and stepped closer to his chest, looking up at his glasses. 'I think they've given them a nice shine. What do you think?'

The fact that his eyes darkened didn't go unnoticed.

'I think I want to kiss you right now.' He lowered his mouth and held it a breath away from hers.

She swallowed hard, unsure what to do, but she didn't move away.

He closed the gap between them, and Dolly felt every part of her melt into his arms. She reached up and placed her fingers into his hair. She'd been wanting to do that for ages. And it was just as soft as she had imagined. One hand on her lower back tugged her closer to him, and his other hand held her jaw. It didn't take long for their tender kiss to become heated.

Dolly was all set to drop to the ground there and then. She couldn't get enough of his kiss, and she wanted more from him. His hands slid to her face, cupping her cheeks, drawing her closer, and she moaned out his name, hoping he'd get the message.

They came up for air, and he rested his forehead upon hers.

'Don't stop, Scott. Don't stop kissing me.'

Their eyes met, and he lowered his head and placed his lips back on her mouth. Giving her what she wanted.

'I want more,' she mumbled on his lips as soon as he took another breath.

'We can go back to the boat.'

The fact that his voice was breathy, low, and sounding as sexy as hell made her pull his mouth back onto hers.

'Oh, Scott, I don't think I can wait that long. I want you right now.'

He breathed out a laugh as he pulled back. 'You know, I was hoping for a kiss at the end of our first date, but I wasn't expecting more.'

'Fiddlesticks, Harper. We're grown-ups. We have sex when we want to without having to count dates. Now, do you want me or not?' She noticed his breath catch in his throat as his bright blue eyes sparkled her way.

'Oh, I definitely want you.'

'Then let's get back to that boat and let the motion of the ocean do the rest.'

He laughed as she tugged him away.

Scott pointed down a cobbled road. 'Do you want to stop off for a drink first?'

She tightened her grip on his arm and pulled him away. 'All I want is you, Scott.'

'You're not the shy type, are you, Dolly?'

'Life's too short to be shy.'

'Hey.' He brought her to a stop, and she could see the seriousness in his eyes. 'I want you to be sure. I don't want to rush this, and I don't want this to be a one-night stand. To me, this is the start of something. I don't know where it's going to take us, but I'm excited to find out. I want you to know that when I say I want you, I don't just mean your body. I mean I want you. I want to be able to see you every day and know that I can just kiss you. That I'm allowed to do that.'

Oh, this man. How beautiful is he. Look at his face. He really means his words. Such lovely words.

'You think this is the start of something, Scott?'

'I'd like to think so, Dolly. I want it to be where we begin, not where we end. I really like you. I want to mean something to you.'

'You do mean something to me, Scott. I wouldn't have kissed you if you didn't.'

'Then, we're agreed. This is our beginning?'

'Aye. Our beginning.'

'So, we can slow things down then?'

'You don't want to get jiggy with me?'

Scott laughed. 'I do. I really do, but I just want us to know each other that little bit more. I want us to grow together, not just go together.'

'Scott Harper, I don't think I've ever heard a man say such words before. You're actually turning down sex. Wild, sea shanty crying sex. Lustful, naked, with not a soul around sex. Rocking the boat till the sirens sing sex. That's what you're walking away from tonight?'

'Do you know what, Dolly Lynch? I'm about two seconds away from falling in love with you.'

'And you still don't want to rip off my knickers with your teeth and beat your chest like Tarzan?'

'Well, that's not my usual style but…'

'I'm not your usual girlfriend.'

'So, you are my girlfriend, are you?'

Dolly dropped back to rest on one heel. 'Some boyfriend you'd make if you won't give a girl what she needs.'

He stepped closer, pulled her into him, dipped his head, and lightly brushed his lips over hers. 'Oh, I plan to give you everything you need, and more. Just not tonight.'

'Are you playing hard to get?'

They smiled on each other's mouths.

'No,' he said quietly. 'I'm yours to keep. Just let me have tonight off.'

I feel as though I'm missing something here. He wants me, but he wants to wait. He was game a minute ago. So what's changed. Why does he have to be so desirable? Look at his eyes. He really likes me. He does want me. This isn't making any sense. Maybe he has some problems down below and that's why he wants me to get to know him better. Maybe he's embarrassed about it. I shouldn't push it. He said he likes me. He has done nothing but show me that he likes me. He's told me that he wants me, so, I'll wait. He'll do this in his own time.

'Okay, Scott. Let's go home. But I'm going to hold you to that kissing anytime rule. I want you to kiss me whenever you feel like it.'

He quickly wrapped her up in his arms and kissed her again, and again, and again.

The kisses on the boat seemed to be harder for him to back away from. They were almost on the table at one point. Her legs were wrapped around his, her dress hitched up, his hands sliding up her thighs, her fingers leaving nail marks in his back. He moaned out her name, wanting her, taking her, just not that far. She held on, willing him to go all the way, but something held him back, and it was confusing the hell out of her. It wasn't as though he wasn't able to perform. She could feel just how ready he was every time their bodies were pressed against each other. She was starting to feel frustrated.

'Please, Scott,' she whispered.

That was the moment he pulled away and took her home.

11

Work, a fifteen-mile bike ride, three cold showers, and half a skirting board painted, and Scott still couldn't get his date with Dolly out of his head.

He slumped down to the floor, leant his back against the sheet-covered sofa, and placed his head in his hands.

I can't believe I made a mess of last night. What must she be thinking? We had such a great time together. I don't think I've laughed so much. God, she's bloody brilliant, and I wanted her so badly. How the hell I managed to pull back is beyond me. I still can't get my head around it. What am I going to do? I can't sleep with her with this online business hanging over us. Why can't I just tell her the truth? Because, Scott, it will make things awkward and she'll stay away. Like I haven't already made things awkward.

He sighed into his knees. 'It shouldn't be this hard.'

'What shouldn't be this hard?' asked Freddy, walking through the opened front door. He took one look at Scott on the floor and sat down by his side. 'Hey, what's up?'

Scott kept his head buried until Freddy nudged his arm. If there was one thing that he knew about his little cousin, it was Freddy liked to be there for him. There wasn't anyone in the world who idolised him like Freddy. The last thing Scott wanted was to show him that he wasn't okay. He always put on a brave face for his family. He had poker-face down to a tee.

He glanced up through his fingers, lowered his hands, and reached out to the coffee table for his glasses. 'Oh, you know. All this decorating.'

Freddy was staring him straight in the face, studying him. 'You do realise I'm thirty-two now, Scott. You don't have to treat me like a kid anymore. I can see there's something wrong, and it's not the cottage.'

Wow, can he really see through me? I must be losing my touch. Or maybe he is one of the few who can actually tell when I'm lying. Do I tell him the truth or make something else up?

Scott watched him out of his peripheral vision whilst trying to figure out whether spilling the beans would be helpful. There was so much crap weighing him down, and he wasn't about to talk to Giles about it, and he hadn't yet found the courage to talk to Dolly.

Maybe Freddy would be a good ear.

He took a deep breath. 'There's this woman…'

'Thought so. Dolly, is it?'

'No. Well, yes. Sort of.'

Freddy frowned with confusion. 'Is there another woman?'

'Yes. Well, no. Sort of.'

'Scott, you're not making any sense, mate.'

Because nothing makes sense anymore, that's why. This is the exact reason it has always benefitted me to not get involved with people. You start mixing and everything goes wrong.

'Come on, Scott. What's happened? If you tell me, I might be able to help.'

'I've been talking to this woman online for a while now.'

'Yeah?'

'Well, I kind of like her.'

'Okay.'

'But I really like Dolly.'

'So, you have to just choose then.'

Scott shifted so that he was facing him. 'It's not that simple, Fred.'

Freddy's eyebrows lifted. 'It seems simple, Scott. Just pick the one you like the most and let the other one go.'

'But that's the problem. I've recently discovered that they are the same person.'

Freddy breathed out a laugh. 'What? You've been talking to Dolly online and you didn't know it was her?'

Scott had nothing to add. He merely lowered his head and put his glasses back on the table.

'Hang on a minute. You've been flirting with someone online and you haven't seen their face. Bloody hell, Scott. She could have been a catfish. You have to video chat. Check them out. She could have been anyone. A con artist after your bank account.' He huffed to himself. 'I feel the need to confiscate your laptop. Actually, I'm going to have to teach you about internet safety.'

'Fred, it's fine. I knew she wasn't a catfish. We met on the art forum I go on.'

'These weirdos are everywhere, mate. You can't trust people you don't know, have never seen, or met.'

Scott was starting to wish he didn't know who she was. Life was a lot simpler back then. Lady Light was his friend, and Dolly not so much.

'A friend of mine does these online checks for this sort of thing. I know him from the army. Tech guy, you know the type. He checked her out. That's how I found out she was legit, but then she emailed me the other day, and it was something she said that made me realise it was her.'

That's all I can tell you, anyway.

'Shouldn't this be a good thing, Scott?'

'You would think.'

'You don't?'

'I think it makes it complicated.'

'How do you know what way she'll take it? Just because it makes you feel awkward, it doesn't mean she'll feel the same way.'

'I don't feel awkward. I just think it makes the situation between us awkward.'

Freddy grinned widely and nudged his elbow. 'You totally feel awkward. That's what this is really about. You were fine with your online girl because you always knew you wouldn't meet her. You were fine with Dolly at first, and why? Because you kept your distance. Well, you tried. Scott, you never let yourself get close to anyone, and now that it's finally happening, you're scared.'

Scott huffed, then scoffed. 'I'm not scared.'

Freddy moved to sit up on the sofa, squashing in the dust sheet. 'Yeah, you're scared.'

I'm not scared. I'm not. Am I? Is he right? Is this my problem? But I like her. A lot. I'm not scared of anything. I was holding her. Kissing her. Wanting to do so much more with her. I wouldn't have done that if I were scared. So why aren't I telling her the truth. I am a bit worried about getting close to someone. If I weren't retired, this wouldn't be a problem. I would know not to let anyone into my life. Maybe I should just go back to my old job. Get out of here.

'What you thinking, Scott?'

Not much I can share with you.

'How best to play this.'

'Look, I know I'm not the best one to hand out relationship advice. It took me two years to let Molly in, but that was just me being wary, all because Dad accused Mum of cheating. The one thing I did take from it all was that I really loved Molly, and the thought of not being with her hurt way more than me keeping her at arm's length all throughout our time together.'

'It's different for you, Fred.'

'No, it's not. We're all human. We all have worries. My advice, move forward with her, not away. If you're struggling, for whatever reason, then take it slow. You like her, Scott. Don't waste an opportunity like that. Just slow it down. Get to know her a bit more, and while you're doing that you can work on all those walls you have built up around you.'

I definitely have walls.

'I'm not sure how she feels about me since I dumped her on her doorstep last night and ran off faster than Cinderella.'

'Well, there's only one way to find out.'

I knew that was coming next.

'Yes, I'll go and see her tomorrow. Perhaps it is time I told her the truth.'

Freddy patted him on the shoulder as he stood. 'Good thinking. Right, I came here to do some decorating, so I'll get on with the bathroom.'

Scott watched him sprint up the stairs, then turned to the laptop on the table in front of him. He was surprised to see a new email from Dolly sitting there, as he hadn't replied to the last one yet. She'd sent it last night, judging by the time, not long after he'd said goodnight, pecked her on the cheek, and scarpered.

I guess she's gone back to him. I don't blame her. I was giving off all sorts of mixed messages. I don't even want to read it. Online Me will get all the laughs, and I'll get a Dear John. Come on, Harper. Get a grip. Just read the blasted thing.

Hey, CK.

I just wanted to talk to someone. I've had a really weird night. My son is on a sleepover in a tent, stargazing all night, and it always feels lonely when he's not here.

If you're not up, it doesn't matter. I'm about to have a cuppa and watch a film. Not much else going on my end. I hope you're having a better night.

By the way, you can forget about the video call. I don't feel ready for that level of interaction yet.

Anyway, speak soon.

Lady Light x

Scott rested his fingertips on the screen. 'I'm so sorry, Dolly.'

I've set her back. She's gone in herself again. And we were just starting to get somewhere. She was lonely last night. I should have been with her. I could have been with her, holding her in bed all night. I need to tell her that I'm sorry.

Before he had any more time to think, he put on his glasses and started speed typing.

LL

Sorry you had such a crappy night. I wish I could have been there for you. You deserve better in your life. I want you to be happy. I hate that you felt lonely. Your

happiness makes everything right in my world, and I just want it to come back.

He clicked *Send* and stared blankly at the keyboard for a moment before rolling his eyes back up. 'I didn't sign it.'

Sign it? Bloody hell, why did I send it? What am I doing?

He quickly opened the email, looking for a way to unsend the message, even though he knew it was too late. His eyes scanned the words.

What the hell is that? Your happiness makes everything right in my world! Oh, crap, crap, crap. Why did I even send her a message? I'm supposed to be coming clean. I'm supposed to be seeing her tomorrow. I've avoided her all day, and now I've gone and done that. I really hate myself right now.

Giles came on the screen, without Scott even accepting his call.

'Really, Harps. You left her feeling lonely last night?'

Scott slammed the laptop shut and then slammed his head into his hands. He waited about five minutes before cautiously opening it back up again. Thankfully, Giles had buggered off. He was not in the mood for his sarcasm. His eyes widened at the response from Lady Light sitting there.

Hiya, CK.

I've got a plan. Meet me at the Mermaid Festival in Sandly on the Isle of Wight. It's not till mid-July, so you have a few weeks to mull it over. If you want to do this, don't tell me, just come. There is a row of beach huts along the promenade. Meet me in front of the pink one that has giant colourful spots on it. You can't miss it. It's the only one painted like that. I'll be there at midday.

Lady Light x

'Oh!' He shut down his laptop before Giles had a chance to pop back up.

Now what do I do? Actually, this is brilliant. I can use it to my advantage. I'll turn up and surprise her. It'll be romantic, and so much better than me just blurting out who I am. Yes, this will work. It won't be at all awkward this way. Meanwhile, I need to get Dolly to fall for me way more than she has for him, me. God, am I ever going to get used to that? I need to go back to how we were before sex became an issue. There is no way she would forgive me for sleeping with her whilst holding that secret. So, what have I got? Three weeks. A few weeks to make sure that when I'm the one she sees, her heart lifts, her smile returns, and she throws herself straight into my arms.

12

Dolly

Dolly sat under the shaded large patio at Wilson-Holmes Retirement Village. A large green stretched out towards a duck pond and tall trees. Pretty flowerbeds lined wide pathways, and hanging baskets draped from both sides of the accordion back door.

She leaned back in the wicker chair, admiring the peaceful view. An old couple was sitting on a bench by the pond. The white-haired man had his arm draped around the back of the top wooden plank, and the lady next to him was snuggled close to his side.

The thought of Cianan sitting with her like that in their old age was something she had mulled over during their time together. The talks they would have about retirement, travelling, and still holding hands in their nineties.

She glanced to her left to watch a man hunched over his walking frame, inching his way across the grass, accompanied by a young carer who was desperately trying to get him onto the pathway.

Dolly laughed to herself at his stubbornness and wondered what she would be like to handle at his age.

The laughter of two elderly women and two female carers came from a garden table over to her right. They were all drinking tea and smiling about something. The home was such a sanctuary, she could see why it appealed to her aunt. She could also see where all of the money from the sale of Dolly's Haberdashery had disappeared to. Just the huge fountain alone that sat proudly out on the front drive told her that.

A middle-aged male carer appeared with Dolly's aunt holding his arm. He helped her into a chair next to her niece.

'Ooh, thank you, my beaut.' She beamed her beady blue eyes up at him. 'Have you met my niece yet? Her name's Dolly as well. She's gorgeous, isn't she?'

'Yes, Doll. I have to keep confiscating cherryade from her every time she arrives.'

Dolly grinned at her disgruntled aunt. 'Hey, I bought the sugar-free version this time.'

'I'll have some of that then, young Artie. Go on, run along, and bring my niece some too.' She turned to Dolly as soon as he left. 'He's single, you know. His old dad, Arthur, used to be the postie in Pepper Bay. He's only just retired. In here now. Think he gets special rates because of his son. Not sure. It's all about who you know, our Dolly.'

Dolly reached forward and touched her aunt's frail hand. 'How are you, Auntie? You allowed to play dominoes with the others yet?'

'Oh, you heard about that, did you? Well, I cannot be blamed for winning someone's chocolate stash.'

'You're not allowed to play for people's food, Auntie.'

She scoffed and straightened her skirt. 'I knew I should have buggered off on a cruise before I came here. That would have been way more fun.'

'You came here for the peace and quiet.'

'I did, but sometimes it's a little too quiet.'

Dolly glanced over at the couple by the pond. 'I like it.'

'You're too young to like this place, my beaut. Now, tell me, what's going on in your world at the moment?'

109

Scott Mr Invisible Harper, that's what. I don't know what the hell he thinks he's playing at. Ghosting me, that's what Dexter called it. Plain ignorant is what my generation say.

'Well, Dexter is still hanging out with Daisy Walker most days. She's smitten, that's for sure. He went stargazing up at her farm. He loved it. Didn't get any sleep.'

'And what did you get up to that night? A whole night all to yourself. I'm expecting big things.'

'The biggest thing was a boat.'

'A boat?'

'I went on a date, and he took me over to Lymington on a private boat. You should have seen it, Auntie. It was a stunner.'

Those beady blue eyes were now wide and alert. 'Who are you walking out with, Dolly Underwood?'

Dolly smiled at hearing her maiden name. There weren't many who called her that anymore. She had been Mrs Lynch since she was nineteen. A young bride, completely in love, and ready to start a family. Little did she know back then how long it would take for her to fall pregnant with Dexter.

'Scott Harper took me out, Auntie.'

'That Superman fella?'

'Aye, that's the one.'

'And?'

'And what?'

Aunt Dolly rolled her eyes and tapped her hand on the arm of the chair. 'Was it just a boat trip, or did you see fireworks?'

'Lots of fireworks, but I haven't seen him since.'

'And how long has it been?'

'Two days.'

'Go and see him, I say. That's what I would do. Find out why he's hiding away.'

Dolly wasn't overly keen on that idea. Although her curiosity was getting the better of her, there was a part that didn't want to come across as desperate.

If Scott Harper doesn't want anything to do with me, sod him. I'm going to meet CK soon, and I'll see how that goes. If he's a no-show, then that's it. I'm quitting men altogether. No more of this dating nonsense for me.

'Do you have any news? What about Mr Waving-Stick. Is he still giving you the eye, Auntie?'

'Never mind him. We've got bigger problems here. We just found out last night the old girl who owns this place only went and snuffed it. Now there's this battle going on between her son and daughter about this home. He wants to sell up and move us all out, but she wants to keep things how they are. She's a good girl. Not like him. He's full of greed.'

Dolly felt her stomach churn at the thought of her aunt being transported to God knows where. 'They can't do that, Auntie. Surely there are laws. Everyone here paid good money for this place.'

She shrugged and lowered her head, revealing a rare glimpse of sadness. 'It all depends on whether the daughter can afford to buy out her brother's half. If she can't, he'll force her to sell.'

Dolly clenched her fists so tightly, she left nail marks in her palms. 'Ooh, I hate him already.'

'Join the club.'

'Well, don't you go worrying yourself over this, Auntie. You can always come home with me if push comes to shove. We'll figure it out.'

'You're a good girl, our Dolly, but I love it here. I've made so many friends, and some of my old mates are here too.'

I need to talk to Dexter. He'll have a plan. He's good at stuff like this. There has to be a way to save this place. Ooh, I want give that Wilson-Holmes a good telling off straight to his face. I just need to find out who he is.

* * *

Lemon Drop Cottage seemed to be calling her. Dolly had stepped off the tram and headed straight uphill towards Scott's home. She was itching to give him a piece of her mind, but at the same time, she had bigger fish to fry now, thanks to her aunt's news. She decided to sit on the stile where she'd had her first encounter with him. It wasn't that long ago, but it felt like ages. His home was just over the other side of the lane, and she couldn't stop staring at the thatched roof.

Missing Scott Harper wasn't in her plans, neither was sitting on a stile staring at his house. She was supposed to be going straight home. Why couldn't she just shake him off? It was starting to irritate her, and her bouncing foot was trying hard to release the tension that had been building inside her since their date ended.

A man in his late sixties came walking up Pepper Lane. His dark, weather-worn face beamed happily at her as he huffed and puffed all the way to her side.

Dolly pulled herself together and jumped up, pointing down at the stile. 'Here, you sit down. Catch your breath, Stan.'

Stan didn't need a second invite. He plonked himself upon the old wood and took a deep breath. 'Blimey, I keep forgetting how long this lane is till I walk it. Mind you, it's keeping me fit. The first time I walked this, I thought I was gonna have a heart attack.'

'Do you need a drink or anything?'

'No, love. I'm good. Just a little breather and I'll be on my way up to my Marsha Cottage.'

Dolly leaned on a small wooden post and looked uphill. 'I think it's so lovely that you named your cottage after your wife.'

Stan cleared his hoarse throat and smiled to himself. 'She would have loved this place.'

'It's hard, isn't it, when they're not with us anymore.'

'Funny old life. You never know what's around the corner.'

Dolly glanced over at Lemon Drop Cottage. A tight knot filled her stomach whilst tears formed in her eyes. She quickly rolled them back and cleared her throat.

Stan was fiddling with his shoe. 'So, what were you doing sitting here by yourself, Dolly?'

'Oh, not much. Just daydreaming, mainly.'

He rolled his dark eyes up to give her a look that told her that he wasn't one to be fooled.

'I don't know, Stan. I feel a bit deflated at the moment, if I'm to be honest. I've just got back from visiting my aunt in the retirement village, and she told me that the place might end up being sold off. Plus, I've got man troubles that I really shouldn't have at my age.'

Stan chuckled as he shook his head. 'How old are you, Dolly?'

'Forty.'

'Well, when it comes to love, trouble can come at any age.'

'I just thought I was done with all that.'

'Who's bothering you?'

She slid down to her backside, avoiding stinging nettles, weeds, and some mooching ants. Her bum was half on the road and half in the mixture of gravel and dirt that met the grassy verge. She crossed her legs and looked up at him. 'Scott Harper.'

'I know him. He works for my Anna in The Book Gallery.'

'That's the one. How's her honeymoon going, by the way?'

He chuckled whilst waving away a buzzing fly. 'The same way all honeymoons go, I'd expect.'

Dolly's mind went straight back to her own wedding. Pretty much the whole town had turned out for the day. The weather stayed dry, and Cianan looked so smart in his suit and tie, she could have devoured him right there and then at the altar. But that wouldn't have gone down too well with Father McElroy. 'Me and Cianan went to Wales for our honeymoon. One week in Pembrokeshire. It rained the entire time.'

'We spent a weekend in Leigh-on-Sea. That's all we could afford.'

Dolly nudged his knee and smiled up into his misty eyes. It was obvious he missed his wife so much. She knew the look. She knew the pain. 'It's not about the place is it? It's all about the company.'

They both sat in silence for a while, wrapped in their happy memories.

Dolly's eyes followed a white butterfly as it fluttered over Stan's head. She glanced his way to see him staring over at Scott's. She gazed at the thatched roof of Lemon Drop and stayed like that for a moment. 'Did you ever think about dating again, Stan?'

Stan coughed out a laugh. 'Gawd, no. I was even wary about moving from London to here. I'm not big on change. Besides, I don't think I could ever love anyone again.'

'I thought that once. Then I tried dating, then I decided I was right the first time.' They both laughed, and Dolly breathed in a big gulp of flower-scented air. 'You know what, Stan, I feel so blessed that I got the opportunity in my life to know what true love is like. So, if I don't get a second chance, at least I had that.'

He gestured at Lemon Drop Cottage. 'But you want another chance, don't you?'

'I don't know what happened, Stan. I just fell for him as soon as he touched my leg.'

Extra crinkles appeared on his head as he grinned down at her. 'Why was he touching your leg, or shouldn't I ask?'

She flapped one hand, waving away any wrong assumptions he might have. 'I fell off that stile, straight into the stinging nettles, and I twisted my ankle.'

'Ah, so that's the real reason you were sitting here looking dreamy.'

'I was not looking dreamy. Was I?'

He nodded.

Dolly shook her head at herself in disbelief. 'Jesus, I have got it bad.'

'Why aren't you over there?'

'We went on a date, and now he has ignored me for two days.'

'Oh, that doesn't sound like Scott. I help out down in the shop sometimes, and he always seems like a nice lad.'

I thought he was nice too, but what do I know about anyone? I once dated a serial cheater.

Dolly sighed deeply, dropping her shoulders. 'Not sure what to do now, if I'm honest.'

'Do you like him, Dolly? I mean really like him?'

Her mouth twisted to one side as her nose scrunched. 'Yeah,' she huffed out, wishing she didn't have any feelings for Scott whatsoever. At least that way, her life could go back to being uncomplicated.

'You wanna do something about it?' asked Stan, tapping her head.

Dolly couldn't hold back the smile that was twitching to be released. 'Like what?'

A whole heap of mischief washed across Stan's cheery face. 'Stick with me, kid. I've got an idea.'

13

Scott

Who the hell is banging down my door?

Scott swung it open, full agitation in his glare, and then lowered his jaw when he saw Dolly standing there.

She puffed out warm air as she grabbed the side of her waist with one hand and pointed the other over to the road.

'Dolly, what's wrong?' He peered over her shoulder, looking for signs of impending danger, only to see his flowerbeds and shrubbery being investigated by a loan pigeon.

'It's Stan,' she spluttered. 'He's sitting on the stile. He needs some water. He was breathless. I panicked.'

Scott sprinted to the fridge, grabbed a small bottle of still mineral water, and followed her down his pathway whilst asking numerous medical questions, all of which seemed to go over her head.

'I'm not a doctor, you know,' she snapped, silencing him.

Stan sat up straighter as they approached. He smiled warmly up at Scott and seemed to enjoy the cold refreshing liquid that was immediately handed over to him. 'Ooh, I needed that.'

Scott squatted in front of him, took his wrist, and started to time his pulse. 'Have you got any pain anywhere, Stan?'

'No. I had a bit of a stitch, that's all. So I sat down for five minutes. Next time I go on one of my walks in this heat, I'll take a bottle of water with me and a hat. I just thought it would be a bit cooler, being it's evening. Oh well, live and learn, as they say.' He raised his drink in a *cheers* motion.

Scott glanced up at Dolly. 'His rhythm is stable.'

Stan laughed. 'Good to know.' He winked at Dolly, and she smiled sweetly back.

They don't seem to be taking this very seriously. Anna will have my guts for garters if I don't make sure he's cared for. She's got cleaners, cooks, and carers up there seeing to him day in day out. I'd better walk him home.

'Are you okay to stand up, Stan?'

His achy legs creaked as he lifted himself from the stile, with Scott's help. 'Yeah, I'm good. Stop fussing. I'm off home now. Got a nice bit of salmon and rice waiting for me. Then, I'm spending the night with David Attenborough. Do you know how fast this planet is going under? Too bloody fast. We need to start doing stuff to help, so I might learn something later on about all that.'

Scott hadn't let go of his elbow, so Stan wriggled away.

'Stan, I'm going to walk you home.'

'No need, son. I'm fine now. I just needed five minutes off my feet and a sip of water. I've had that. I'm as good as new now.'

'I don't care. I'm still taking you home.'

'I'll come too,' said Dolly, avoiding eye contact.

I need to talk to her at some point. We haven't spoken since our date. What must she think of me. We'll get Stan back safely, and then I'll tell her how much I've missed her. No. I won't say that. I'll ask her to come for dinner tomorrow. Dexter too. Maybe. She's ignoring me now. She's got the hump with me. I can tell. I don't blame her. I've got the hump with me too.

The only one talking all the way up to Marsha Cottage was Stan, going on about global warming and polar bears.

The smallest house on Pepper Lane was newly built and sitting on the land that belonged to Starlight Cottage, a much bigger, grander property.

Stan proudly showed them his cosy home, offered them some water, asked if they needed to do a wee before they set off, and then hurried them out of his house.

Scott stood on the doorstep, shaking his head. 'Well, I think he seems fine. More than fine.'

Dolly shrugged as she headed off. 'I guess he just needed a breather, like he said.'

'Hmm.'

He jogged slightly to catch up to her side.

'You don't have to speak to me, Scott, just because we're walking the same way.'

Oh, I do. I really do need to talk to you. We need to clear the air before it suffocates us both.

'Dolly, I'm so sorry I didn't call you for two days. It wasn't intentional. There was work, and then sorting the cottage, and...'

'You don't have to explain yourself. We're grown-ups. You don't want to see me in a date way again. I get it. You shouldn't ghost people though. It's immature. Just be straight. It makes life so much easier, and I really cannot be bothered with stupid games at my age.'

'But I do want to see you again. In a date way.'

She stopped abruptly, threw her hands on her hips, and gave him some form of death glare. 'Well, you've got a funny way of showing it, lad.'

Did she just call me lad?

'Dolly, I got nervous. That's all. I promise.'

He watched her lower her arms, loosen her stance, and soften her face. She started back down the lane again. This time a bit slower, much to his relief.

119

Say some more. She's listening.

'I'm not very good at all this, Dolly.'

'You don't say.'

'I never meant to hurt you. That wasn't my intention. I know I messed up. I'm sorry.'

She glanced his way, and he smiled inside at the fact the corners of her mouth lifted. He so wanted to kiss her, but that wasn't on the cards.

'Okay. Apology accepted.'

He reached out and touched her arm, feeling a burst of fizz rush through him. She stopped walking again and gazed up into his eyes.

She might let me kiss her now.

'But,' she added sharply, 'just know, you are not my boyfriend. We are not dating, and from this moment on, we are back to being friends.'

I guess that's a no to the kiss.

'If that's what you want, Dolly.'

She folded her arms tightly, huffed loudly, and then stormed off.

What did I do now?

* * *

The next day, Scott turned up at Doll's Gift House with a spruced-up old bike of his. Dexter was pleased, but Dolly's face wasn't giving away much.

'I thought we could all go out for a ride one evening. I have another four bikes sitting around in Ruby's shed up at Roseberry, so I thought Dexter could have this one, and I have cleaned up another one for you, Dolly. It's back at mine. What do you say?'

'We say yes,' said Dexter, before she had a chance to speak. He looked over his new bike with so much joy, Scott figured Dolly wouldn't argue.

'How much do we owe you for the bike?' she asked, rattling the handlebars, giving the impression she was checking for sturdiness.

'It's a gift. I don't want money. The bikes are old ones that belonged to me and Freddy. They're just sitting around doing nothing. Dexter might as well have one.'

'Thanks, Scott.' Dexter beamed up at his mum, and Dolly caved instantly. 'Can we go now? We've just closed up for the day and dinner isn't for another couple of hours. The weather's nice, and...'

'Fine,' she cut in.

Perfect.

Scott realised he was smiling like the cat who'd got the cream. He tried to drop the corners of his mouth when she glared his way, but his lips were stuck. The smallest of smiles suddenly crept into her eyes, making his stomach flutter and his nerves settle. 'We can ride up to Wishing Point. Perhaps feed the ducks down by the river.'

Dexter was happy with that suggestion. 'I'll just go and pack my rucksack and I'll be right out.'

As much as Scott wanted to be alone with Dolly, he felt like running away as soon as Dexter went back inside the shop.

She stepped forward, holding one handle of the bike. 'Are you trying to woo me by giving my son gifts?'

'Woo you? No. You've got a big head about you there, Dolly. I'm just being friendly. I have no intention of wooing you. I thought we were mates again.'

Her eyes narrowed as she pulled one side of her bottom lip inwards. 'Aye, okay.'

121

His grin widened as she looked away, and then he quickly pursed his lips when she looked back. He glanced up at the cotton-wool ball clouds dotted in the baby-blue sky, then over at the shop's sign.

'I can't say I've been to Wishing Point yet,' she murmured, bringing his wandering eyes back to her.

He met the softness in her eyes and was pleased the blue bicycle was between them, because he was sure that if it wasn't, he would lean down and kiss all over that beautiful face looking up at him.

After dislodging the lump in his throat, he moved away from her eyes to glance uphill. 'It's a lovely place. Great for picnics and walks. It has a great sea view right at the top, and down the bottom by the river is quite tranquil. You often see walking groups along the trails and families with young children playing games on the flatter green areas. And don't forget to make a wish on a dandelion seed head if you see one. That's tradition there.'

'How many wishes have you made up there?'

'Only one.'

'You make the same wish each time?'

'No. I've only ever done it once.'

'Why? You not big on wishes, Scott Harper?'

He gave a half-shrug and smiled at Dexter as he reappeared.

'Right, Mum, I've got everything we might need.'

Scott glanced at the red backpack covering Dexter's back. 'Do you want me to carry that?'

'No, I'm fine, thanks. It's not as heavy as it looks.'

Dolly locked up the shop and joined them on their walk up to Lemon Drop Cottage to get the other bikes.

Scott was examining Dexter's bag. 'I was going to grab some water bottles from indoors. Perhaps a blanket. What have you brought?'

Dexter glanced over his shoulder as he walked beside the bike that Scott was pushing along. 'Water, snacks, a tin of sweetcorn for the ducks, antihistamine tablets, insect repellent, plasters, sun cream, painkillers, some indigestion tablets, in case Mum starts to suffer, and her cardigan for when she feels a chill coming on.'

Scott held back his laugh as Dolly frowned down at her son.

I do love this kid.

'Well, you've certainly covered a lot of areas, Dexter.'

'I was in the Scouts. I know how to be prepared. Plus, have you met my mum?'

Dolly was frowning again, and Scott couldn't hold on to the laugh that was fighting to be free. Her head sharply turned his way, causing him to quickly bite his lip. But it was no good. His whole face was smiling.

Up at Lemon Drop Cottage, Scott handed over a red bike to Dolly, grabbed some more water and a green-and-yellow picnic blanket, shoved them into his own rucksack, and led the way along Pepper Lane. 'We'll walk the bikes uphill until we get to the road past Pepper Pot Farm, then we can ride along there across to Wishing Point. There are some nice tracks down by the riverbank.'

'Are you okay, Mum? You look a bit flustered already.'

Scott turned quickly to check on her. Her cheeks were a tad pink, her lips were parted, and she had slowed in her pace. 'Oh, that's my fault. I'm walking too fast. Sorry. Let's slow down and save our energy for when we get there.'

'I'm fine,' she huffed out, clearly out of breath from stomping uphill.

Scott slowed his pace and moved to her side, grabbing the handlebars on her bike to help as Dexter passed them by.

Dolly's eyes rolled over to Scott's hand. 'I am okay, you know. I walk up and down the lane most days for a bit of exercise.'

'It's true,' said Dexter, peering over his shoulder to look back down at them. 'Mum's been looking after herself more since we moved here. She knows she'll be perimenopausal soon, so wants to try to be fitter now, in case it helps. She keeps eating oily fish too, as she worries her skin will dry out.'

Dolly stopped walking for a moment, slapped her free hand on her hip, and glared uphill at her son. 'Yes, thank you, Dexter.'

Scott slid his hand over to lightly brush against her tightly clenched fist. He waited till her eyes were on his fingers. 'We can check out that new fish restaurant down by the harbour tomorrow night for dinner if you like.'

Big chestnut eyes started to examine his face, which he tried to keep neutral.

'All three of us,' he added. 'The place has a large outdoor seating area that overlooks the boats. Dexter might like that.'

She was silent as she started to push the bike forward again. He took the fact that she hadn't moved her hand away from his as a good sign, but her lack of words was unnerving.

She glanced his way as they entered a narrow lane and climbed on their bikes.

He looked back at her face that told him she had come to a decision.

'Okay,' she said softly.

His whole being smiled as he caught up to Dexter, ready to help with any wobbles along the way.

14

Dolly

Dolly leant on the metal rail and peered down into the sea lapping against the slimy wall below. The sun was setting, the seagulls were still active, and the moored boats seemed to be peacefully resting for the evening.

Her stomach was full from one of the best meals she had ever had. Agreeing to go check out the new restaurant with Scott wasn't a bad idea. It was always nice to eat out. Plus, she liked his company.

Outside was busy but relaxed, and they had managed to get a table close to the edge. Dexter had been in his element, talking about the different species of crab and how much he adored seahorses, and then he spent twenty minutes on the subject of pirates.

They decided to grab a 99 from a nearby ice cream van for their dessert, and Dexter was currently attempting to finish his before the seagulls rudely attacked him for a share.

Scott approached and peered down at the water. His arm was pressed against hers, and she only wished it was wrapped around her instead.

Friends it is. He's got issues when we take it too far. He'll be okay. We'll be okay. It's a nice evening. I'm not going to say anything to spoil it.

She glanced his way and smiled softly.

He smiled back and gestured over his shoulder at the restaurant. 'We'll definitely have to come back here again. It was lovely, wasn't it?'

'Yes, very nice.'

'I'll have to ask Fred if he's been over to check out their menu yet.'

'We could ask him and Molly to come with us next time.'

That's okay. I can say that. We ate together before that date. Before that kiss. That wonderful, hot, sexy kiss. God, that man can kiss. I have to stop staring at his mouth.

'Yeah, I'll book a date for us all next week. Ruby can come too.'

We'll be like one big happy family. Only, we're not, are we, Scott Harper? You want me. I know you do. You just want me at arm's length when it comes to emotions. I wish you'd do something with your arms right now. And those hands. Those big, strong, man hands that knew all the right places to touch on my body. I really do have to get that night out of my head. Yeah, good luck with that, Doll.

'So, Dolly, what you got planned for tomorrow evening?'

He wants to hang out again. I can do that.

'Nothing much. Dexter is going to Daisy's for dinner, so I'll probably put a microwave cottage pie on for myself.'

His face dipped low to the side of her head. The light breeze was causing strands of her hair to lightly blow onto his cheeks, but he didn't move away.

'I'm sure we can do better than that. What about dinner at mine? We can have a BBQ for two, some wine, Arctic Roll, and then a walk along the lane to pick up Dexter.'

How does he make all of that sound so sexy?

'Sure.' A wave of embarrassment rushed over her because her voice had cracked when she spoke. Turning her head, she swallowed hard and tried again. This time with a bit more control. 'That sounds like a better plan. I'll pop up about five.'

He finally straightened, creating some space between them. Even though their arms were still touching, she missed his closeness already. She missed so much about him, especially his lips. Oh, how she loved those lips. Not a day had gone by since the kiss that she hadn't thought about his lips.

'What you thinking about?' he asked. 'You have a dreamy look about you.'

She smiled inwardly.

I'm not telling you.

'I'm just feeling really content right now.' She pointed out at the harbour. 'It's so peaceful here tonight.'

'Do you fancy a trip to the zoo on Sunday? Dexter can ask Daisy if she wants to join us. Have you visited there yet?'

'No, we haven't really had time to visit many of the attractions yet. I keep meaning to take Dexter out and about, but we've only just started to slow down recently.'

'In that case, we should make a list. There's a model village, and Dexter will love the Donkey Sanctuary. Ruby's friends with the family who run wildlife walks all over the island, and the family over at Dreamcatcher Farm let people in for strawberry picking this time of year. How would you feel about water sports? There's lots going on down the beach over here in Sandly.'

'Erm, not sure about Dexter on a jet ski, but the other stuff sounds good.'

'Okay, well, tomorrow night, we'll set up a schedule. Things to do for the next couple of weeks.'

'Why only the next couple of weeks?'

'Uhm, I don't know why I said that. We can fill up more weeks.'

'There's a Mermaid Festival coming up soon. What exactly is that about?'

Scott gestured to a bench, so she followed him to take a seat. She could see Dexter was taking pictures of the boats with his phone, so knew he'd be occupied for a while. She glanced to her side, wanting to reach over and place her hand into Scott's, but she held back, holding her fingers whilst he explained about the festival held over on Sandly Beach every July.

He squinted one eye, twisted his mouth, and put on some sort of old Cornish accent. 'Arr, it be a long time ago when a ship came to the shores of Sandly, bringing lost souls and treasure chests empty of gold.'

She giggled at his animated story-telling skills.

He smiled widely and went back to his own voice. 'The story goes, a pirate ship was here for a while, having repairs after a storm. One of the crew fell in love with a local girl, and when it was time for him to leave, he didn't want to go. His captain was having none of it. Pirates were pirates for life. They didn't get to leave, and she wasn't allowed to join them. So, the young woman went up to Wishing Point and made a wish to become a mermaid so that she could live in the sea to be close to him at all times.'

Dolly cupped her hands in front of her heart. 'Oh, that's lovely.'

Scott raised his index finger. 'Not so fast. Her wish came true, and at first all was well. But then, one day, the pirates got into a big pirate fight with another ship and the man was so badly injured the captain said he was no longer of use on the ship. He was taken to the Isle of Wight and dumped on Sandly Beach.'

'Oh, this is going to be a sad story, isn't it?'

'The man had no money, no family, and the love of his life could not step on the land. It is said, he would go to the beach every morning and find a seashell that she had left for him up by a wall that the water meets when the tide comes in. One day, all that was found on that wall was his hat, boots, and coat.'

'What happened to him?'

'Nobody knows. Some say he drowned in her arms. Others say he made his own wish and joined her. The story shifted slightly over the years, and someone started to commemorate the tale. Now, we have a festival all along the beach and surrounding area. There's music and food stalls, picnics on the beach, and all the pubs offer happy hour and free snacks. There are street performers and people walking around selling seashell jewellery and pirate hats. Some even dress up. And anyone who wants to declare their love for someone presents them with a seashell from the beach, or a bought one, and if that person wants to return the love, they go and place the shell on Mermaid's Wall. That's what that particular wall is called.'

Dolly could feel her heart swooning. She glanced up at his smiling eyes and warmed from the gentle look he was giving her. 'That's actually quite sweet. Have you ever given anyone a seashell or received one?'

He stared out at the boats, and she wasn't sure if he was thinking about anyone from his past. There was a faraway look in his eyes that said he was definitely thinking about someone.

'No, and no,' he said quietly.

I'm not sure how to feel about that. I'm happy that he hasn't had the seashell experience with someone, but then again, he has grown up here. Surely, someone would have presented him with a seashell. Look at the man. He's gorgeous. Plus, he's lovely. I'd give him a seashell. I wonder what he would do if I do that at the festival. Would he put it on the wall? Would he give me one? Oh, would you listen to me. I'm the type of daft eejit that would make a wish and turn

129

into a mermaid just to be with her man. I've got CK coming to the festival, hopefully. What if he gives me a seashell as well? Whose seashell would I place on the wall?

She glanced at Scott as he stood and made his way over to Dexter.

I wish you were my pirate, Scott Harper.

15

Scott had his phone sitting on newspaper that was spread out on the kitchen table. Its speaker was on loud, as his hands were full, painting a wooden chair that was also up on the table.

Dolly was filling him in on the latest at Wilson-Holmes Retirement Village. 'They're planning a fundraising event to help save the place, but who is going to donate money when it's just going into that owner's pocket?'

'It's to help buy him out.'

'I know, but then who owns the other half of the home? Surely, people won't give over their money under that situation. It's like they're giving her money so she can own an old people's home.'

'That's exactly what they'll be doing.'

'But she's so rich. I can't see anyone giving a rich person money. Dexter wanted to set up a crowdfunding thingy, but I've managed to hold him off, for now. I'm happy to help with a cake sale or something, but it just seems weird to donate money to someone who has loads.'

Scott homed in on a front chair leg, lightly stroking his thin-tipped brush around the curvy spindle, creating green vines. 'She's not that rich, otherwise she'd buy her brother out.'

'Well, she'll be that rich if we all give her our money to do exactly that.'

'So, what do you suggest instead?'

Dolly's sigh came through the speaker in a crackle. 'I don't know. Why can't she go and get a bank loan like normal people?'

'Maybe she's been refused.'

'Ooh, I really hate that brother of hers. Do you know what he's done now? Apparently, he's only gone and sold the fountain out the front. How do you sell a great big concrete thing like that? Can it even be shipped off to somewhere? Tessie has been asking for help for the home on the Pepper Bay group chat, but not much luck yet. Everyone's helpful, of course, but we're all a bit miffed.'

'I can ask a local solicitor if you like. My friend, Monty, is one. But I would have thought that Miss Wilson-Holmes has already been down that road.'

'My poor aunt is really stressed. And she's not the only one. She said it's making some of the residents ill.'

Scott leaned back and stared blankly at the white chair that he had been painting flowers and leaves on. 'It is sad, Dolly. Will you bring her home if she has to leave?'

Dolly's breathing hit the phone again. 'I guess so, but she was having trouble with the stairs where I live. It'll be hard for her to traipse up and down, and I don't want her to be trapped in the flat. I'm betting she won't get back all of her money from the home either, so it's not like she'll be able to afford to move somewhere else as luxurious as Wilson-Holmes.'

A text message flashed up on his phone.

Wilson-Holmes red hit one.

Scott rolled his eyes at Giles interfering.
Seriously, Giles? Red hit one? Yeah, right.

A smiley face appeared next as Dolly continued to talk about her aunt.

Scott knew Giles wasn't really suggesting they call on the best sniper in their team to take down Mr Wilson-Holmes, but it still made him grin a little.

A knock at the door took his attention away from them both. He plopped his brush in a jar of water as he stood, then headed off to the small square hallway of the cottage.

Dolly was on the other side. She lowered her phone from her ear and just stared doe-eyed at him.

He reached out and took her hand and gently pulled her into his arms for the hug he could see she needed. The freshly washed smell of her hair filled his nostrils as his head lowered to rest upon hers. Her hold on him tightened a touch, and then her fingertips started to slowly stroke his blue tee-shirt.

You need to stop doing that, Dolly. I want you so much, but I can't do this with you until after you know the truth, and I have to do it the way I planned. It will be the only way you'll forgive me for knowing all this time and not telling you. It will make it easier. Oh, please, stop. I've held off for this long. All the time we've spent together lately has been wonderful. It's just a couple more days. Come on, Scott, you can do this. Pull away. Make her a cup of tea or something. Just talk. Two more days. You've got this.

'Hey, Doll,' he whispered into her hair. 'Come and sit in the kitchen. I'll make you a cuppa.'

Her arms slid down to her sides, leaving him feeling lonely and deflated. The feeling was torture. All he wanted was to continue holding her. Kiss her. Take her up to his bedroom and stay until they had to leave for food, or water, to pay the bills, or make an appearance at Dexter's graduation.

The Mermaid Festival seemed to be taking forever to come around. He had never been so keen to attend. Writing wedding vows would have been a lot easier than the words he had gone over a hundred times in his head for the moment they planned to meet outside the spotted beach hut.

He glanced over at her sitting in a slump in one of his unpainted kitchen chairs. Even the kettle was delaying its standard boiling time. Time suddenly felt slow, endless, and frustrating.

Scott had patience. It came with his job. Not just his military job, but his artist job too. He had never been one to rush through life. He was laidback, calm, and happy to watch the clouds drift by. But new traits were developing since meeting Dolly, and he wasn't quite sure how to handle them.

At least his boss, Anna, was due back tomorrow. Then he'd have less time in the shop and more time to himself during the day. He could really get stuck into getting the cottage up to scratch, and the distraction would be a good thing, especially if it went belly-up with Dolly at the festival.

I can't think about that right now. Just drink tea and relax.

He handed over a cup and sat by her side.

She gestured at the chair on the table. 'Looks pretty.'

'Thanks. I'm going for a wild country garden look. I want to cheer up this kitchen. Make it a bit lighter in here. Everywhere, in fact. Lemon Drop is quite small. It needs light paint to open it up.'

She smiled his way. 'It's such a beautiful home. I'd love to live here.'

He noticed her blush, then turn her face away. She got up to look out the window. 'This needs a window box, don't you think, Scott?'

The idea of growing old in Lemon Drop Cottage with Dolly Lynch had no place being in his mind. Not whilst he was lying to her about who he was.

'Sure, that sounds great,' he replied. 'Any other ideas? I'm open to all suggestions.'

She sat back down and sipped her herbal tea. A gentle smile hit the hot liquid. 'I think you have it covered.'

'I'm not sure what colour to paint the main bedroom.'

'Blue,' she said quickly, then shied away her eyes.

'What kind of blue?' His voice was hushed, as though being gentle was needed.

'Sea blue. Coastal. White wood and oak flooring.' Her voice was just as gentle.

Their eyes locked, and Scott felt a whoosh of adoration fill his heart.

'Sound perfect, Dolly.'

'You would like that?'

'I would love that.'

Silence sat between them, and it was as though time had given up altogether and left the building. All that existed was an unspoken message and a strong pull of energy.

'Scott, I…'

A knock on his door interrupted her, and time resumed.

He opened the door and frowned down at the splodge of blood on his doorstep. 'Dexter, what's happened?'

Dolly was immediately by his side. 'Dexter, your leg is bleeding.'

'Yes, well spotted, Mum.' He hobbled into the kitchen.

'I'll get the first aid supplies.' Scott got on with that whilst Dolly grabbed some kitchen roll to wet and slap on Dexter's knee.

'Ow, Mum!'

'Sorry. So, what happened? Did somebody push you over, son? Tell me now. I'll…'

'No, Mum. I'm not being bullied. I fell off my bike, that's all. I was close by, which is why I came here.'

Even Scott wasn't buying that statement.

Dolly swapped the wet kitchen roll for dry. 'More like you didn't know I was here, and you thought you'd get cleaned up before I saw the blood pouring down your leg.'

'Slight exaggeration, Mother. It's just a cut. I'm thinking a sterile wipe to clean and some butterfly stitches will do the trick.'

She raised her eyebrows at him. 'Oh, is that right?'

Scott knelt to her side and took over. He could see that Dexter was right. That was all he needed. Fixing the boy's leg was a good distraction from his building feelings towards Dolly. He glanced her way for a split second and could tell she was only thinking about her son's new love for cycling. It would appear that Dexter was reading his mum's mind.

'Everyone falls off their bike from time to time, Mum. I'm not giving it back.'

Dolly huffed and clambered up onto a chair and handed him her tea.

Dexter took a sip and smiled down at Scott.

And I guess that's how they settle arguments. I should take notes. If she starts shouting at me at the festival, maybe I could just hand her my tea.

16

Dolly

The promenade was lined with small square paving stones that were engraved with names or messages from visitors over the years. The money made from selling the personalised paving went back into the local area to help with the upkeep.

Dolly stood outside the spotted beach hut, nervously circling her brown sandal over a Mr and Mrs Eley, who apparently got married two years ago.

With her stomach churning, her head feeling hot from the sunshine, and her legs weakening, she started to read the light-grey slabs to help distract herself.

I wonder if there's anyone here I know. Matloch and Kate, forever with you. I like that. Ned, Penny, and Kasey. Kasey's 1ˢᵗ beach day. Aww, that's so sweet. What else have we got here? Mackenzie, Adam, Maggie, Sam, another adventure. These are really nice. I'm going to have to find out how to get one. Perhaps I'll get one for Cianan. Cianan Lynch, now you're here too. See what Dex thinks of that. Oh, Cianan, what the hell am I doing here waiting on a man from the internet? If Dexter found out, he'd go spare, and I'd get a big fat safety lecture.

She glanced over at the sandy beach that was alive with families, deckchairs, picnics, and laughter.

Muffled music was coming from a pub over the back of the beach huts, and the smell of hotdogs was wafting her way from a nearby food van.

Her stomach was in knots, but the food was still tempting. She'd only had a banana all day, unable to eat due to worry. She still hadn't spoken to Scott about her online man, and she really wanted to let him know but hadn't found the right words.

'He's late,' she mumbled under her breath.

Most of the beach huts were opened up, with the owners sitting outside, but the one she lingered in front of was locked up, as was the rainbow stripy one next to it. At least she didn't have to worry about getting in people's way. She leant back on the door and took a sip from her bottle of water.

It was a hot day, with a clear blue sky, and refreshing water lapping at the golden sand. Dolly fancied a paddle and thought it might be a good suggestion when CK turned up. She was normally pretty good at talking to him, but now she was struggling to think up topics of conversation they could have.

Oh crikey. This is worse than waiting at the dentist. Why is he late? Maybe he's not coming.

She pushed her back off the wooden door, turned quickly, and bumped straight into a tall, broad man. Her water bottle got squashed between them, squirting the top of her pink floral dress and his pale-green shirt.

'Oh, Jesus, I'm so sorry,' she said, slapping her hand down his chest.

He stepped back to assess the damage. 'It'll dry in no time in this heat. Don't worry.' He met her eyes and frowned slightly. 'Hey, aren't you the candle lady?'

Her heart skipped way more than a beat. 'Oh God, are you CK?'

He ran his fingers through his greying hair whilst grinning. 'Wow, I haven't been called that in a while.'

She took in his features whilst feeling a little lost by that statement. He was a tad older than she'd imagined. Maybe early sixties. There was a kindness set in his green-grey eyes that settled her a touch, and the way his thick lips tilted to one side when he smiled gave off a friendly vibe. She smiled warmly, not knowing whether to shake his hand or give him a hug. Instead, she simply clutched her water with both hands. 'I've been looking forward to meeting you. Dolly, my name's Dolly.'

He tipped his head. 'Nice to meet you, Dolly.'

'What does the CK stand for?'

That tilted grin was back. 'Oh, Calvin Klein. It's an old joke. My name's Calvin.'

Now it all makes sense. Well, he seems nice and normal. But so do serial killers, I guess. No, don't think that way. He's CK. My CK, who is lovely.

'I'm so glad we're friends,' she blurted out.

His laugh was deep and husky. 'Friends, sure. But after the stuff you've been saying, I wasn't sure you would view me as a friend.'

Dolly was a little lost again. 'Of course I view you as a friend. Why wouldn't I?'

'I guess I thought you were part of the hate-campaign gang.'

'What are you talking about? You never told me about any hate campaign, or is that a joke I'm just not getting?'

He went to speak but she cut him off.

'Calvin, we've been talking online for months. I've been looking forward to this day for ages. All I want to do is hang out, have something to eat, and get to know you better. I know things can be different in person, but we connected online, right? We'll be okay. We can have fun today. What do you say?'

He appeared to be mulling it over, and she wasn't sure why.

'Calvin, do you want to go home?' she asked quietly. 'It's okay if you've changed your mind now that you've met me.'

'Erm, no. I don't really want to go home at all.'

Dolly felt her cheeks hurt, she smiled so widely. Relief filled every pore and her heart had rebooted. 'So, shall we just have ourselves a good day at this mad festival?'

He grinned, offered his arm, and said, 'Yeah, why not.'

She happily placed her arm through his and pointed down the promenade. 'Now, there's a food truck selling halloumi burgers, which have my name all over it, and then I'm thinking of grabbing a couple of beers in that pub with the live band playing on the roof terrace. How does that sound for starters?'

'Sounds brilliant. How about, I buy the food and you pay for the drinks.'

'Sounds fair enough.'

Well, he's nothing like Scott, who won't let me put my hand in my purse. I don't mind. I like paying my share. It's always such a fight with Scott. I've given up with him. Calvin seems more relaxed. I guess he's a bit nervous. That's understandable. I think that hating thing was supposed to be a joke. Not everyone's good at jokes. I'll leave that alone. This is going to be interesting. So far so good. Aye, it's definitely a good start, even though I did soak his shirt a little.

She glanced down at her damp dress, knowing it wouldn't take long to dry. Calvin was also staring at the top of her dress. Her breasts, to be precise.

No, he's just checking out where the water spilled. Although, it does look like he's checking me out.

She raised her hand to her neck, moving her elbow in the way of her boobs whilst pretending to flick back her already tied-back hair. He blinked and looked forward and that was that issue sorted.

It's good. It's okay. It's all good. Calvin is fine. I know him. He's perfectly nice and normal, and we're going to have a lovely day. I just hope I don't bump into the Walkers out with Dexter, or Scott, for that matter. Right, that's enough of that. Focus. I'm with CK. Everything will be fine. So why the hell does something feel off?

17

Scott

'I cannot believe this stupid car broke down. I said we should have jumped on the tram. It's unlikely we'll be able to park anywhere in Sandly today anyway.' Scott took a calming breath to stop himself from slamming his foot into Ruby's old vehicle.

Ruby looked out at Sandly from Sandly View, where the car had coughed, spluttered, jolted, and then died. 'I've always loved this viewing area, especially at night. Wes used to bring me up here for a snog when we were courting.'

Scott grimaced along with Freddy.

She turned to face them. 'I did say you two could go on ahead. Clive will be here soon with his tow truck to take the car to his garage.'

'We're not leaving you here on your own,' said Freddy, elbowing Scott in the ribs.

Scott checked his watch for the hundredth time. 'No, of course not.'

Freddy gestured down the road. 'You can still go, Scott.'

No, he couldn't. It was just a stupid breakdown, but whenever his family went through anything, they did it together. Well, those three did, anyway. They were going to the festival together, then Ruby was off meeting her mates, Freddy was hooking up with Molly, and he was off for the big reveal to Lady Light.

She's going to think I stood her up. She's going to be so angry. No, she won't. She'll be hurt. I've hurt her yet again.

Poxy car. Why now? It hates me, that's why. It's always hated me.

He huffed and kicked a stone over the edge of the drop by the viewing spot.

'What has got into you, Scotty?' asked Ruby, fanning her face with her straw hat.

He flapped one hand out towards Sandly, knowing full well he looked like a child having a tantrum. 'I just wanted to be there early.'

'Why, what's the rush?'

Freddy interrupted before Scott could answer. 'Mum, we seriously need to get you a car with air-con. I'm melting standing here.'

'Oh, piffle. Half the time I don't even use it. I only did today because Nora said I can park on her drive. She was only going to charge me a ball of wool.'

Scott and Freddy stared blankly at each other.

Ruby looked at the back of the car. 'It's in the boot. Nice pink colour.'

Scott rolled his eyes that way. 'There's water back there as well, Fred, if you want some.'

Freddy gave him the thumbs-up and went and opened the hot boot to pull out a bottle of water that was one more minute away from turning warm.

Scott slumped down in the passenger seat, with his long legs dangling outside. He stared down at his bare knees absorbing the heat.

'Does anyone need to do a wee?' asked Ruby.

'No,' they both sighed out together.

Ruby looked down the road. 'Ooh, heads up, lads, here he comes.'

Scott groaned, flinging his head back and bashing it on the sun visor. 'Thank God.' He clambered out the car and waited patiently for Clive to hook the car up to his truck.

The seventy-year-old man seemed to take forever. Even Freddy asked if he could help at one point, just to move things along.

Old Clive spoke to Ruby about his family first, then some gossip went back and forth about the Wilson-Holmes Retirement Village. Once the pleasantries and chit-chat were over, Clive worked at a snail's pace, and Scott was sure someone was trying to wind him up. He felt like physically lifting the old man out of the way and getting the job done himself.

Freddy had turned away, fighting back his laughter. He started texting Molly instead.

Scott had training in the area of self-control. How to calm himself, how to breathe, how to stay steady. But nothing had trained him for how to not want to throttle his aunt's old friend, who was just as hot and bothered and only trying to be helpful. Poor old Clive wasn't even charging Ruby.

Scott squatted over by the viewing area and placed his head into his hands. He closed his eyes and controlled his breathing by pretending he was working for the army again. *Game on, Harper. You know what to do. Channel that. Take it with you. Everywhere you go. It's with you.*

His racing pulse settled. The heat belting down on him cooled. And all thoughts dispersed. Scott stood, swiped back his hair, and turned to quietly watch Clive do his job. The noise around him was muffled. The dust from the road no longer an irritation, and time was of no importance. Whatever had to be done would be done. He had no control over the situation, but he did have control over himself. There was always another way.

Plan B.

Ruby was unfazed by the whole event. Freddy was so relieved Clive's truck had air-con, and Scott knew exactly what he had to do as soon as they arrived in Sandly.

The journey didn't take long, and Scott ran off as soon as Clive pulled over.

Sweat was dripping down the back of his neck and water spilled from his lips, rolling onto his chin as he attempted drinking whilst jogging. He cuffed his mouth as he hit the promenade. Slowing into a steady casual walk, as not to draw attention to himself, he flapped his white shirt to allow a breeze to enter his back. He checked his pale-blue shorts for any water spillage, saw he looked fine, hoped his face wasn't flushed and his hair wasn't looking damp, took a calming breath, and made his way to the spotted beach hut.

Where is she?

He looked both ways and down the narrow gap at the side of the rainbow-striped hut next door, even though he doubted very much she had squeezed herself down there, but he didn't want to rule anything out.

The black waterproof watch on his wrist pretty much explained why Dolly wasn't there. He was over an hour late. His eyes scanned the beach, checking every deck chair, parasol, and towel sprawled out on the golden sand. She wasn't paddling along the shoreline with Dexter and the Walkers, and there was no sign of her queuing over by the toilets.

I bet she's gone to get some lunch.

He took once last look over his shoulder before deciding to check out the food trucks along the road. As he turned, a hand shot out and touched his arm.

Scott was about to apologise for almost walking into the person, but then he saw who it was. 'Giles? What the hell are you doing here?'

'Good to see you too.'

Scott pulled him closer to the beach hut so they were out of the way of the people passing by. 'What have you done with Dolly?'

Giles grinned, then stopped when he realised Scott was being serious. 'Are you insane? Why would I do anything to your civilian online crush?'

Scott felt stupid. He knew deep down that Giles wouldn't do anything to Dolly, but he didn't have time to focus on that. 'I'm supposed to meet her here so that... Oh, why am I telling you? You already know, don't you?'

Giles bobbed his head and half-shrugged. 'Yeah, well. She's not here, because you're late. You're never late to the party, Harps. What happened?'

'Car broke down.'

Giles muffled his laugh. 'You know, it's like I'm following a soap with you two. Maybe I should watch more TV. I feel I'm missing out.'

'Giles, why are you even here?'

He tapped his own chest. 'Hey, I'm Big Bro, remember?'

'Stop telling me that you're doing your job. I'm retired.'

'Not until it says so on your file. Plus, I need to check out some things.'

Scott stopped perusing the crowds to look directly at Giles. 'What things?'

'Never mind that. Listen, you are not going to believe what happened to Dolly.'

He had Scott's full attention.

146

Giles laughed to himself, testing Scott's patience. 'I'm sorry.' He flapped one hand near his face. 'It's just so funny. You couldn't make this up.'

'Spit it out, Giles, before I wring your neck.'

'Okay, okay.' He sniffled, took Scott's water, had a sip, and was finally more composed. 'So, she arrives. Waits around. Starts to get fed up, as you do. She turns to leave, crashes into some man, spills her water on him. He's cool about the whole meet-cute thing. They get talking. Crossed wires occur. He takes full advantage. Even I held a small amount of admiration for him on that strike, but still, sleazy move. You are right to have that look in your eyes, Harps. So, moving on. She thinks he's you, and they swan off into the sunset, arm in arm. Well, obviously not the sunset, but you get the picture.'

Scott was getting more than the picture, he was getting fired up. His heart was pounding, his nostrils flared over at Giles, and his eyes set about scanning his environment again as though he were on surveillance.

'Where the hell is she, Giles?' His voice was low coming out of his clenched teeth.

'Hey, it's cool. She's safe. I have eyes on her.' He touched Scott's arm, forcing him to focus back on his face. 'Come on, Harps. I wouldn't just leave her with a lying creep. They went for a burger and beer, and they're currently making their way over to that mermaid wall place to check out seashells or something.' He glanced over Scott's shoulder. 'I really need to brush up on the local history around here.'

Scott started to make his way to Mermaid's Wall, swiftly followed by Giles. 'Who is he, do you know?'

'Calvin Wilson-Holmes. Ring any bells?'

Why does that name sound familiar? I don't know any Calvins.

147

'Slow down, Scott. Don't draw attention. You know the rules.'

Scott reduced his speed. He pushed his glasses back up his nose and checked his phone, just in case there was an SOS from Dolly, which he doubted but was worth a quick glance.

Nothing. How has she just gone off with some random man? Surely she would figure out he wasn't me. Bloody hell, Dolly. This is another level of catfish altogether. What a chancer. Wait till I get my hands on him. Hmm, how to play this.

Giles lowered his sunglasses from his head to cover his eyes. 'You know you can't kill him, right?'

'Uh-huh.'

'I suppose you could maim him a little bit. If no one's looking.'

'Uh-huh.'

'Hey, Scott, are you even concentrating?'

'Uh-huh.'

Giles took a glug of water and cuffed his lips. 'He's the guy that owns the old people's home. That's all I've got on him. For now. Oh, and he had a girlfriend. Dana Blake. You know her?'

Scott glanced his way. 'Yeah, I know her, and now I know who he is too.'

'So, what are you going to do when we get there? Are you just going to go over to her and tell her who he is and, more importantly, who you are?'

Scott swung out his arm, stopping Giles in his tracks. 'Look.' He gestured over to their left. 'There they are.'

Giles frowned down the beach at a long sea-battered wall that tilted its way down towards the water. It was around six-foot wide and appeared to have seashells around its top edges. Four other people were standing there. Two enjoying the view, and another two about to leave. Dolly and her fake friend were just stepping on to take a look at the shells that people had placed down during the day.

Scott watched Calvin's arm slip around Dolly's waist as she leaned slightly over to peer down at her foot. She started to rummage around in her sandal whilst he held her in place.

'Looks like she's got a stone in her shoe or something.' Giles pointed out the obvious.

He's touching her.

'Stay here.'

Giles went to speak, but Scott had already powerwalked away.

A hundred ways to dispose of a predator flashed through his mind as he reached the wall, but he took a breath, calmed his mind, and walked towards the end where they stood, chatting and laughing.

Within a matter of moments, Dolly turned to see him, Scott placed himself at Calvin's side, Calvin somehow slipped off the wall, and an almighty splash caused people close by on the beach to yell out that someone had fallen in the sea.

Dolly slapped her hands to her mouth. 'Oh my God.' She hit Scott in the chest as she went to pass him by. 'Did you just do that to him?'

Scott frowned. 'What? Of course not. He slipped or fell asleep or something.'

Dolly's dark eyes widened. 'Fell asleep?'

'It happens. He might have narcolepsy or…'

'Or you just did the Vulcan neck pinch on him, more like.'

Scott almost laughed. 'What? Are you nuts?'

'Oh, so I'm just imaging things now, am I? I didn't realise gaslighting was your style.'

His mouth gaped as his eyes stretched wider. 'Do you hear yourself? First of all I'm Mr Spock, and now I'm a narcissist.'

Dolly pointed below the wall where Calvin was being rescued by a group of slightly drunk young men, who happened to think Calvin's sea dive was done on purpose and was rather impressive.

'How did he end up in there, Scott Harper?' she snapped.

'I don't know, Dolly Lynch. How did you end up on this wall with him?'

Her mouth flapped open for a moment, and then it snapped shut, but Scott knew she wasn't done. She pushed him out of her way and went to storm off to save Calvin from more hardy slaps on the back and another drunken rendition of "Under the Sea".

'Dolly,' he called through gritted teeth.

She stopped, turned, then marched back. 'Look, Scott, I have been meaning to tell you about him…'

'What, Mr Wilson-Holmes?' He watched her slowly close her mouth as confusion filled her eyes. He felt the need to clarify. 'Mr Calvin Wilson-Holmes of Wilson-Holmes Retirement Village. The same man who is about to make your aunt homeless.'

She glanced down the beach for a second. 'He's… I… Calvin is… But he can't be.' She seemed to gather her bearings. 'I've been talking to him online for months, Scott. He's CK. He's an artist.'

'No, Dolly. I'm CK. I'm the artist.'

And I shouldn't have just blurted it out like that. Oh God, I feel so bad. Look at her face. I'm not sure if she's going to smack me one or cry.

He took a step towards her, but she took a step back. Her hand shot out, telling him to back off, as her other hand shakily met her mouth.

'Dolly, let me explain.' His voice was softer, but it made no difference. She had lost eye contact with him and looked as if she was about to throw up.

'You did this to me, Scott?'

A pain hit his heart at her broken voice and sad eyes. He went to speak, but she wasn't finished.

'You played games with me? All this time? I... I can't...' She glanced down once more at Calvin, who had been handed a beer and was happily glugging away. 'You're friends with him? You both thought this was funny?'

'Oh God, no, Dolly.' He attempted another step her way, desperately wanting to hold her in his arms and find a way to make all of her pain disappear. 'Please, give me a...'

Dexter called out to her from close by, interrupting anything else Scott wanted to say.

Dolly quickly turned to where he stood with the Walker family. She then glanced back at Scott, wiped her eyes, and walked away.

'Dolly, wait. Please.'

She paused for a second. 'Don't speak to me, Scott. I can't even look at you.'

He caught Giles gesturing to him to come over as Dolly marched off to be with her son. He sighed deeply, lowered his head, and reluctantly made his way back over to the promenade.

Giles smiled sympathetically as he placed his arm around Scott's shoulders. 'You had to go and push him in, didn't you?'

'He got off lightly.'

'Yep, he did. Shame about her though.'

151

Scott glared down the beach at Calvin, who was still sitting on the sand with his new mates, as though Dolly hadn't even existed. 'I'm going down there to hurt him.'

Giles tightened his grip on Scott's shoulders and pulled him the other way. 'No, you're not.' He loosened his hold and gently coaxed him across the street. 'Come on, Harps. Let's go get you some lunch.'

18

Dolly

Most people with young children had headed off home as the sun started to set and more adults hit the bars and restaurants around Sandly for the evening shift of the festival. Music drifted out of venues, and the food trucks were still going strong, even the two ice cream vans remained pitched up for the night.

Dolly had spent the rest of the day with her son and the Walker family, and she soon realised what a firecracker Tessie was, once she told her what had happened. After spilling her guts, mopping up some tears, and feeling like a prize eejit, Tessie had to be calmed down so that she didn't go off and find Scott to kick him in the shin, which was her plan.

Her friendship was commendable, and Dolly appreciated how Tessie had looked after her all day.

Poor Dexter was confused by the whole affair. He only heard snippets of info, as Dolly didn't want him knowing the full story. She was pleased that Daisy had kept him distracted. She was also pleased when Tessie offered to take him for the night, in case she felt the need to wail loudly in the bathroom, which did seem on the cards.

Molly and Freddy took her for dinner after the Walkers went home, and she felt like a lonely old soul who everyone needed to take turns caring for.

Freddy tried so hard to help sort the situation, giving it his best shot throughout the meal that Dolly only picked at. 'Dolly, you need to speak to my brother. I'm telling you, he's not some cold-hearted prankster who goes around tearing women's hearts to shreds.'

Molly nudged Freddy into silence.

Dolly appreciated Freddy's attempts to defend Scott, but she wasn't in the mood to listen.

What a day. I've been stood up, conned, made a fool of, lied to, and the day isn't over yet. What other shite can you throw at me?

She glanced up at the sky.

I've got sunburn on my shoulders, and my heart aches so much. I can't believe what has happened. All this time, CK has been Scott, and he knew. Why wouldn't he share that information? And what the hell has Wilson-Holmes got to do with any of this? Nothing makes sense, and my head hurts from thinking about it all day.

'Do you want us to take you home, Doll?' asked Molly softly, stroking her hand and smiling with full-on sympathy.

'No, ta. I'd like to spend some time by myself. You two head off.'

It took a while to get them to leave her alone, but she won in the end. She watched them make their way over to Mermaid's Wall, where they gave each other a seashell, a kiss, and a loving embrace.

Dolly sat on the small wall along the promenade, with her legs dangling down towards the sand. She smiled over at a few young couples walking along the shoreline, having an evening paddle. One lad was giving his girlfriend a piggyback, and another couple was holding hands and taking selfies.

She remembered when she used to walk along holding Cianan's hand. She loved holding his hand. It was big and strong and filled with calluses and covered her little hand fully, keeping it wrapped up safely. There wasn't one

<hr/>

moment with that man that hurt her. The only way he had achieved that was by dying.

Tears pricked her eyes.

I miss you, Cianan. Life was easier when you were around. What would you have me do now? What would you say about my stupid behaviour? I've been a fool, haven't I? Thinking I could find someone who would love me the way you did. Thinking I could trust another man enough to give him my love.

She raised her head to the darkening sky.

Oh God, Cianan. I'm so tired.

She looked back at the sea. It seemed quiet, relaxed. Her breathing moved in time with the gentle waves meeting the sand.

'I don't want to go home,' she whispered into the warm air.

'Neither do I,' said Scott.

She jumped slightly and glanced to her side as his legs swung over the wall to sit down next to her.

'Oh, Scott. I'm not in the mood to talk.' Her voice barely came out, but he heard.

'We can just sit here then.'

There wasn't an ounce of energy left inside of her to argue or even move.

A playful scream from a woman by the shore broke the silence. They both glanced her way to see the other woman she was with pretending to throw her into the sea. The happy couple laughed at each other as they made their way further along the beach.

Dolly held the faintest smile as she watched the local vet with her partner fading into the distance. She breathed out a long, slow breath and went back to staring down at her sandals.

Scott briefly glanced her way. 'I didn't know you were a fan of Star Trek.'

She would have laughed if she didn't want to cry so much. 'Dexter's a fan.'

'Oh.'

There was a stillness between them. Something bordering on a truce.

'Please let me explain a few things to you, Dolly.'

'I'm deflated, Scott. I've got no room for your... I don't even know what label to use.'

'You think I'm going to lie to you, don't you? I'm not. I want you to know all the facts. I hate seeing you like this. You're breaking my heart.'

'Well, if it's going to make you feel better, then...'

'That's not what I mean.' He shifted on the wall so that he was facing her. Just for a second, his hand reached out to her leg, but he swiped it back no sooner had his fingertips brushed her dress. 'I'm sorry. I just really want to hold you right now.' He matched her sigh. 'I always want to hold you, ever since you sat on my kitchen table with your stinging nettles rash.'

Dolly felt her lips move into the briefest of smiles.

'I've really fallen for you, Dolly. I would never hurt you. I should have come clean about who I was as soon as I found out who you were, but I got scared. I already liked you, and I was worried the whole online thing might freak you out or make things awkward between us.'

She waited for him to stop talking, needing a moment to process his words. His voice was so gentle. It held real meaning, and there wasn't a single part of her that thought he was talking rubbish. 'When did you find out?'

'When you told me about the apple-throwing incident.'

'Oh, right.'

'We've spent a lot of time together between then and now.'

She could see that his eyes looked just as sad as hers. He lowered his head to his brown flipflops, and she wasn't sure if he was going to say any more.

He swallowed so hard, she heard it. 'I wanted to be with you all the time. I was hoping you would get to know me and really like me, and either forget about *Online Me* or be pleased when you found out.'

'I'm not sure how I would have found out. Were you going to meet me here today?'

His head gave the slightest of nods. 'Yes. In the end, I thought this might be the best way to reveal myself. I was hoping for romantic.'

'But you changed your mind?'

His head shot up and his tired eyes widened. 'No. Ruby's car broke down. That's why I was late. I had it all planned out as well. I even had a speech.'

Dolly frowned with a mixture of annoyance and amusement. 'I don't understand about that other man. Why was he there?'

'Chance, would you believe. He cottoned on to the misunderstanding and took advantage.'

'So, he really didn't have anything to do with you?'

Scott scoffed loudly. 'No. Not at all. He's lucky I didn't break his jaw.' He pulled his lips in and glanced over at the gentle waves. 'I won't apologise for pushing him in the sea. He deserved way more for conning you.'

She raised her index finger close to his face. 'Ha! I knew you shoved him.'

He reached forward and gently took her wagging finger and cupped it in his hand.

Dolly felt her stomach flip as their eyes locked. She allowed her hand to be guided down to rest upon his thigh where he softly stroked her knuckles. Something suddenly felt rougher than his skin, and she glanced down to see that he had placed a beige seashell in her palm.

Every fibre of her being suddenly melted into that small ridged shell. Practically on the verge of tears, she rolled her eyes up to see his waiting. Her breath was hanging on in there at the back of her throat. 'Oh, Scott, you big eejit. I think I already love you, you know.'

He took a breath, rested his forehead upon hers, and closed his eyes for a moment. 'Even if I had a thousand wishes, I'd only wish to always be with you.'

Dolly raised her head until their lips met. Neither of them moved, allowing their mouths to simply sit against each other's for a while.

One of his fingers came up to wipe away her fallen teardrop, and she quickly clasped his hand in hers, holding it by her cheek.

'I need to go and place this on Mermaid's Wall,' she mumbled on his lips.

He pulled back a touch to look into her eyes, and once again she felt her heart melting. 'Come on then, let's walk over there together.'

She took his hand and jumped down onto the sand, and the cool golden grains immediately sprawled out inside her sandals. 'Oh, wait, I've got sand in my shoes. I'll take them off.'

'No, don't. You can't see properly at night. You might tread on something sharp. Here…'. He swooped her up into his arms and started to carry her like a bride.

Dolly giggled and rested her head against his shoulder. 'You're getting sand in your flipflops, mister.'

'I don't mind.'

She snuggled further into his hold, with not one care in the world. 'I want to hold you all night.'

They reached the wall, and he gently placed her back down to her feet. 'Yeah? Your place or mine?'

She laughed at his sexy grin that had a habit of weakening her knees. 'Lemon Drop Cottage.'

'Okay.'

'I want to go back to mine first and get a few bits, and there's just one other thing.' She paused.

How to word this.

'It's okay, Dolly. We don't have to make love tonight. We can just hold each other.'

She looked up at him through her lashes. 'Are you a mind reader now?'

He cracked a smile and lowered his eyes to her hands. 'I just want it to be right when it's our first time together. I want us both to be in a good head space. I'm going to need a lot of time to explore your body. I don't want to rush, so everything needs to be right. I want you to feel you can sleep by my side anytime you like and not feel pressured to take things further. We'll make love, just not tonight.'

'After that speech, I'm not sure I'll be able to keep my hands off you.'

He laughed and gestured to the wall. 'Put your seashell down, woman.'

The tide was in and gently slapping against the side of the walkway, so Dolly placed her small shell at the start of the wall. So many had already been washed out to sea, and she wondered if her shell had ever sat on the wall before. The thought of it holding so much love made her smile on the inside.

Scott was smiling when she turned back to him.

159

She glanced down at the sand. 'I need to find one for you, Scott.'

He stepped closer and took her hand, guiding her away. 'No, you don't. You've given me your heart. That's good enough.'

They left the wall and got a cab back to Pepper Lane, heading straight to Dolly's so that she could gather some overnight bits for her stay at Lemon Drop. The short walk uphill was taken slowly, with Scott carrying her bag in one hand and holding her hand with his other. The air was warm and muggy, and the sky was inky, revealing some stars.

They stepped inside the coolness of the dark cottage, left the lights off, locked up for the night, and made their way straight upstairs.

Dolly popped to the loo whilst Scott took her things into his bedroom.

She stopped in the doorway for a moment on her return to watch him pottering around. He opened the small square window, pulled back the pale-blue duvet, and rummaged around in a half-painted-white chest of drawers.

'I'd like to take a shower before I put on my nightie, if that's all right, Scott.'

He jumped slightly, obviously deep in thought.

She smiled his way as his eyes twinkled in the dull light of the bedside lamp. 'I feel hot and sticky from the day. And I want to put some after-sun lotion on my shoulders.'

He came over for a closer inspection of her pink skin. 'Ooh, are you sore?'

'A little bit, but I'm okay. I wouldn't mind but I smothered myself in sun lotion this morning. I guess my shoulders needed more. Unless I missed them out. Anyway, I brought some after-sun cream with me.'

His fingertip slightly stroked down her arm as his lips met her cheek. 'So, shower, cooling lotion, nightdress, then bed. Is that the plan?'

'There's something missing from that list.'

He arched an eyebrow in amusement. 'Oh?'

'You joining me for that shower. I noticed you have one installed. There seems to be a missing bath, though.'

'Ah, yes, well, that was cracked so I threw it out. But, yes, the shower cubicle is new, and I'm pretty sure there's just enough room for two.'

'So, you want to wash my back?'

He followed her out of the bedroom. 'Love to.'

The cream-tiled shower was a snug fit with them both inside, but Dolly thought its size added to the cottage's charm, and she certainly didn't mind being pressed up against Scott.

The water was turned down to lukewarm, and the bathroom window was wide open. The last thing she wanted was to feel hot and dizzy on such a muggy night whilst wrapped around such an incredible body.

Scott's lips traced her neckline as his hands explored her body. She closed her eyes and inhaled the smell of fresh sea shower gel that he was slowly stroking all over her skin.

Every inch of her was coming alive beneath his fingertips and peppered kisses.

He lowered his hands to her thighs, causing her breath to jolt and one of her legs to lift slightly up his. His hand held it in place, gently gripping her skin. She placed her arms around his neck and pressed her mouth onto his shoulder.

The water sprayed down upon their entwined bodies, cooling their building heat and hitting them in the face whenever they lost concentration of their angle.

Dolly could feel how much he wanted her, and she struggled to not take charge. His slow and steady movements were almost enchanting her, placing her into a dream-like state. Wherever he touched, kissed, or breathed on drew her further into his hold. She was ready to give herself to him completely.

He wasn't taking things any further, but Dolly wanted all of him and quietly gasped when he let out a low moan in her ear.

'Scott, I want you,' she whispered close to his mouth.

'Okay.' His words hit her lips before another heated kiss.

She joined their bodies in every way, and they both took a second to embrace the moment. Her head rested against the tiles as his mouth trailed down her neck. His breathing was heavier and his hold on her stronger. Both of his arms lifted her from the base, placing her between his body and the wall of the cubicle. Dolly held on to him, draping herself over his broad shoulders whilst listening to her name mumbled in amongst the noise of the falling water.

One of her hands reached out to the side and hit the *Off* button. The shower cut out and Scott slammed open the glass door, taking her outside, continuing on to the bedroom.

Their wet bodies hit the bedding, and he reached up to grab a pillow to tuck beneath her soaked locks that were starting to curl. He quickly took a condom from the bedside drawer, and she grabbed his shoulders, pulling him towards her. Not wanting any space between them.

Scott gazed down at her, then sat up and raised one of her legs to kiss her ankle, holding it close to his cheek. His hands stroked down her leg and back up again, caressing every inch.

Dolly followed his eyes with her own. Her heart was melting for the man. Each gentle, loving movement filled her with so much more than need and desire. He was right there in the moment with her. Studying every part of her as though he were trying to memorise and log their first time together.

The bed had absorbed their drenched bodies, leaving only their building sweat as he lowered himself over her.

She cupped his face, pressing his mouth upon hers so tightly, they could barely draw breath.

His eyes darkened and his breath caught in her mouth, and she managed to be vocal enough to tell him not to stop, to gasp out his name a few times, and let him know just how much she was falling in love with him.

Their spent bodies slumped into the mattress, still locked, as they clung on to each other as though their lives depended on it. Dolly did not want to ever let go of him. She was happy for time to freeze at that moment and never thaw.

His face was buried in between her hair and the pillow, and she could feel him steadying his breathing whilst holding his weight from crushing her. Her fingertips moved first, lightly swirling around his shoulder blade.

'Flipping heck, Scott.' Her voice was breathless and all the butterflies she had earlier had gone to her head.

He rolled his face up to look at her. 'Are you okay, Doll?' The concern in his eyes made her smile widen.

'Aye, Scott. I'm more than grand. Everything's perfect.'

He nudged her nose with his own. 'You're perfect, and I love you.'

19

Scott

Dexter was pouring himself some apple juice when Scott and Dolly burst through the kitchen doorway upstairs in her flat. Their giggling halted immediately on seeing the boy.

Dexter raised his brow. 'Oh, I see you're talking again. That's good.'

Dolly quickly brushed her hands down her green stripy dress, straightening the material from Scott's wayward hands. 'Erm, yes, about that, Dex. I want to talk to you about Scott.'

Scott wasn't sure if he should leave the room. He froze in the doorway, only moving when she nudged him inside.

Dexter held up his hand, showing his palm. 'If you're about to have a talk with me about birds, bees, and what all of this with you two means, you can save your breath. I've been hanging out with you both for weeks. It's obvious how much you like each other. I'm just glad you finally sorted things.'

'Erm…' Dolly cleared her throat and swallowed hard as she turned to Scott.

He nodded at her and smiled at Dexter. 'So, you don't mind me seeing your mum?'

'Why would I mind? She hasn't stop smiling since she met you.'

Scott loved the way that statement made Dolly's cheeks flush. She was clearly avoiding eye contact. 'Is that right?' he murmured her way.

She nudged him in the ribs. 'I'm going to make us some breakfast before we have to open the shop.'

'And I am helping you two today,' Scott told Dexter.

Dexter grinned into his tall glass. 'That's good. I can get some school work done. But who's working your shop? Surely you can't leave Stan there all day on his own.'

'Stan's fine. He's not working there now Anna's back. She's in the shop with Jake for a bit. Then they're off again. London for a week in August with the Walkers.' Scott laughed to himself. 'You've got me calling them the Walkers now. You know, Tessie and Nate aren't married yet. Their wedding is when they get back.'

Dolly pulled out a frying pan and put it on the back-right oven ring, her favourite one to use, as she had previously told him one dinnertime. 'Ooh, that'll be nice. It's like a pre-honeymoon.'

Scott shook his head as he set about helping with breakfast. 'No. It's all part of a course Tess is doing with Jake's company.'

'Oh, yeah. She told me about that. But I thought she'd completed her course.'

'I think she has to go back and forth to London at times. So, this time, the whole family is going up there with her.'

Dexter's cheery expression disappeared slightly. 'Does that mean Daisy is going away for a week?'

They both looked his way and saw the moment of sadness hit his eyes.

'Ah, it's just a week, Dex,' said Dolly. 'It'll fly by. Then you'll have the rest of the school holiday to hang out.'

Hating to be the bearer of more bad news for Dexter, Scott warily held up his index finger. 'Erm, well, actually, Tessie and Nate are going to Scotland for their honeymoon for a week after the wedding, and when they get back they're taking their girls to Disneyland Paris for a long weekend.'

Dexter lowered his head as he made his way out of the kitchen. 'She never said.' His voice was hushed and broken, and even Scott's heart went out to him.

Dolly huffed as she plonked her hands on her hips.

Scott frowned at her. 'What? Don't shoot the messenger.'

She looked over his shoulder as he stepped forward for a cuddle. 'Aw, poor Dex. I think he really likes her.'

Scott pulled her closer, kissing down her neck. 'I think I really like you.'

Laughing, she wriggled free. 'Hey, you, we've got a shop to open in a minute.'

'A lot can happen in a minute.'

He slowed down their morning by giving her a long-drawn-out kiss that had her melting in his arms. He wanted to take things further, but there was no way that was happening, not with Dexter in the other room and twenty minutes till opening. Dolly's fingers wrapping tightly in his hair wasn't helping matters.

They pulled apart for air and simply looked into each other's eyes.

Scott had never felt such a rush of emotion. All he wanted was to love her. Make love to her. Be with her always. Touching her face wasn't enough. Holding her wasn't enough. He couldn't get enough of her, and he suddenly felt vulnerable. There was a reason people in his line of work weren't encouraged to have relationships. Those emotions just broke concentration, which could be fatal.

I have to tell her about my past. No more secrets. No more lies. Just the here and now. Me and her. This life. I want this life.

Dolly lightly pressed her mouth back against his, and he could feel himself melting.

Is this what it feels like to be loved? To be wanted? Needed? She loves me.

The warmth from her tongue circling his was taking his desire up to the next level. The broom cupboard was starting to look like a good place to hide away with her.

She breathed out his name, causing his willpower to weaken. This woman, this Dolly Lynch who had taken over the haberdashery shop in Pepper Lane, this woman who he properly met via a flying apple, this woman who was digging her fingernails into his back was driving him wild with need. He could take no more.

Dolly moaned close to his ear as he lifted her up. Her legs automatically wrapped around him and her hands grabbed his face, holding his mouth on hers. His eyes were drawn to the long cupboard at the end of the kitchen that housed the ironing board, vacuum cleaner, and mop bucket amongst other household items. He was pretty sure they would fit, at a squeeze.

Her pleading voice was hushed and breathy. 'Take me somewhere, please, Scott.'

There wasn't anywhere to go without bumping into Dexter, and he sure as hell didn't want to traumatise the kid. He stopped kissing her and lowered her feet back to the floor. As frustrating as it was, he had to admit defeat.

Dolly smiled, placed one finger to her lips, held him in place with one hand firmly on his chest, leaned away, and called out to her son. 'Dexter, will you pop over to Edith's Tearoom and pick up some pastries for our elevenses?'

His muffled voice seemed to come from downstairs. 'Okay, won't be a sec.'

They waited a moment, heard the door close, and smiled at each other.

Dolly quickly grabbed his hand and pulled him to her bedroom. Slamming the door shut and locking it, she pulled him towards her and practically climbed back up onto him.

Scott didn't need a conversation about what she wanted. With her back pressed up against the door, they did as much as they could with the little time they had to join their bodies in every way.

Afterwards, they straightened themselves so they looked respectable and not so flushed. They smiled and kissed some more.

Dolly pulled him to her and told him she wanted to go again.

He steadied his breathing, not feeling as fit as he used to.

Finally, after another few minutes of not coming up for air, they were ready to open Doll's Gift House for the day.

20

Dolly

For the next two weeks, Dolly found as many ways she could to have time alone with Scott. Even though he had slept over at hers every night, she still wanted more of him, and most days she got what she wanted. They couldn't keep their hands off each other.

It was the beginning of August, and Daisy was away for the week, so Dolly and Scott agreed to focus on Dexter. They could see he looked a little lost, and as cute as she thought it was that her son was missing the girl, she didn't like him feeling so glum.

She hired Molly's younger sister Kerri to help out in the shop. Kerri was on her uni break and needed the extra cash, and Dolly was glad of the help, as the tourism in the bay had really picked up since the schools broke up for summer. Scott was busy over the road all day. Even Stan was doing more hours in The Book Gallery. It seemed like it was all hands on deck for the shops in Pepper Lane. She was glad to knock off at four every day, and nothing could encourage her to open on Sundays, not even for half a day.

The evenings and last day of the week were family time, and now she had an extra member added to the mix. Summer evenings in Pepper Bay were quickly becoming one of her favourite things. Having dinner in the quaint garden up at Lemon Drop Cottage, strolling along the beach, riding up top on the tram, or having a picnic down by Pepper River were a few things that made both herself and Dexter smile. She was so pleased she had taken the chance and moved to the Isle of Wight.

Dolly sat close to Scott in his garden, watching Dexter up by the swing, painting a gnome's hat blue. Most of the ornaments were old and in need of repair, so Scott had pulled out some of his art equipment for Dexter to get stuck in.

Scott's hand slowly stroked over Dolly's knee as the sun hid behind some fluffy white clouds, shading them for a moment. 'He looks so peaceful. Maybe I'll make an artist out of him.'

She linked her fingers through his and leant her head on his shoulder. 'I often wonder what he'll be when he's older. He's in to so much. He's already told me he's going to go to uni. I reckon he'll study something to do with science.'

'He's a clever lad.'

'How did you get on at school?'

She heard him hum and felt him kiss her head. 'Erm, average, I guess.'

'Yeah, me too.'

Dolly rolled her head up to look in his bright eyes. 'What made you join the army?'

'It just appealed to me. And after Luna died, I felt like life was too short to not get on with things you want to do.'

'Do you think about your wife a lot?'

'I don't really call her my wife inside my head. But no, I don't think about her a lot. Just from time to time she pops up. I see her sweet smile and hear her voice.' He lowered his eyes and smiled warmly at his memories. 'She was so lovely, Doll.' He took a slow, controlled breath and looked back up. 'Life's really crap sometimes, don't you think?'

Oh, don't I know it.

'Yes. I find it strange as well. I'm glad I moved us here. It feels so far away from the world, you know?'

He smiled as he nodded. 'I know.'

'I don't ever want to leave here. I wish I knew more about this place years ago, but I guess you end up where you're supposed to end up when you're supposed to be there.'

Scott breathed out a laugh. 'So that's your outlook, is it? You could put that on tee-shirts and sell them in your shop.'

'Don't you believe in destiny, Scott?'

'I believe in choices. We make them. They take us places. We don't like it there. We move on.'

'Very philosophical.'

They shared a quick kiss, then glanced back at Dexter.

'How do you think he will get on when he starts his new school next month?'

'Oh, Scott, don't remind me. He was bullied at two schools when he was younger. I started home-schooling him at one point. His last school wasn't too bad. He's always been a bit of a loner, and I worry about him out there in this big bad world without me.'

Scott pulled her closer for a tighter hug. 'Hey, come on, Dolly. He'll be all right this time. I'm sure. He's got Daisy Walker as his mate now, and have you met her sister, Robyn? She's a feisty one, like her mum. If she's on Dexter's side, no one will pick on him at school.'

'But the girls are in the year below him, so it's not like Daisy can keep him company in class.'

'I can't see Dexter wanting any distractions in class, anyway.'

She laughed, knowing that to be true. 'Oh, I'm so glad I only have the one. I get so stressed with just him, let alone having to go through that again with more. I… Oh.'

'What?'

'I've just realised. We haven't spoken about kids. I know it's early days for us, but, well, I should have told you that I can't have any more children due to getting my tubes tied. But when is it the right time to have that conversation with a new love interest?'

Scott laughed. 'Love interest? I like that.'

'Oh, you know what I mean. Did you want kids, Scott?'

'To be honest, I never wanted a family at all. My last job was time-consuming, and not many who worked in my sector had families. I chose to work in that field because I knew I wanted to be on my own. It kind of stops you looking for connections. Commitments. I guess, with my mum dying when I was so young, and my dad leaving me with my aunt, commitments and connections weren't at the top of my to-do list.'

Dolly suddenly felt nervous. A slight flutter hit her heart as her stomach churned. 'And now?'

His eyes softened as they stared into her vulnerabilities. 'I left that job. It's in my past. I've settled here. I'm doing what I love in a place I love, and then I went and met you and fell in love.'

The corners of her mouth lifted along with her heart. 'Who knew.'

His smile widened. 'Who knew.'

She reached up and stroked his hair whilst allowing herself to get lost in his eyes for a while.

'So, Dolly, what are we going to do about it?'

Her fingers were still swirling loosely in his dark hair, enjoying the softness and just being able to touch him. 'Hmm, what do you mean?'

'I mean, do you want to start thinking about you and Dexter spending more time here with me?'

'Instead of you always sleeping at mine?'

'No. I mean you two could bring some of your things over. Dexter can have his own room here, and we can start building up towards living together.'

She removed her fingers from his hair and straightened her body. 'You want us to live with you?'

'Very much, but I don't expect that to happen overnight. We can take our time. I just want you to know that's the direction I want this to go. I think this cottage is perfect for the three of us, and it always feels more like a home when you're here.'

Oh, he really does melt my heart at times. The way he speaks to me. The things he says. I wish I could be as creative with words.

He gestured towards Dexter, who appeared to have placed a gnome in the recovery position. 'Someone has to look after the gnomes.'

She laughed and kissed his cheek. 'Okay. I like your forward thinking. Do you always have to have a plan?'

He gave a slight nod. 'Never thought about it, but I guess I do like plans. They help.'

'That's your army training.'

'Probably.'

'Can I ask something about that?'

The fact that his eyes squinted a smidge and his Adam's apple bobbed made her wonder if she shouldn't ask about that time. Everyone knew soldiers had seen things that people shouldn't, but if things were going to move forward with him, she wanted to make sure Dexter was safe.

Dolly cleared her throat. 'Well, it's a bit personal, but I have to think about my son, and I know I haven't witnessed anything myself, but who is to say it's not there, and...'

'Spit it out, Dolly.'

'Do you have PTSD at all? It's just, I've seen things on the telly, and if you have any problems in that area, I would help you as much as I can, but I would want to know up front, so I'm prepared.'

'It's okay, I understand. No. I don't have that. I have seen some terrible things, but it affects people differently.'

She stroked his cheek as she quietly sighed. 'You're lucky then, Scott.'

'I know. I've seen what that life has done to some.'

'Will you talk to me about your job?'

He hesitated, making her feel she had pressed too hard.

'It's okay, Scott. I shouldn't have asked.'

'No. It's fine. I'll tell you. Just not today. Is that okay?'

She snuggled into his arms, happy to be there. 'That's okay.' Her head rolled up his top, and he lowered his head to smile her way.

'What?'

'I want to ask you to make me a promise, Scott.'

'A promise?'

'Are you ready for a promise?'

'Ah, go on then.'

They smiled at each other with affection.

'What do you want, Dolly? It's yours.'

'Promise me, you'll never return to that job.'

His smile lowered. He blinked slowly, then his nose gently nudged hers. 'I promise.'

21

Scott

'Harps, I've done something for you, so yes, I shall be expecting something in return.'

Scott shook his head at Giles through the laptop. 'You can't demand favours from me when I haven't asked you for anything.'

'Hey, I was being nice. I kind of figured you'd want to pay me back.'

'Come on, let's hear it. What have you done now?'

'You make it sound like I'm a misbehaved kid.'

'I bet you were.'

'I'll have you know I was a straight-A student, thank you very much. Remember who the brains is in our team, Clark. Speaking of which. How's it going with your kryptonite?'

Scott's eyes widened as he leaned back in his kitchen chair. 'Firstly, kryptonite? And secondly, like you wouldn't already know.'

'It's my job to know everything, but I thought it would be polite to ask. You should be happy that I make it my business to know everything, because I, my friend, have found a way to help with the old dear's home.'

'Why are you poking your nose in around there?'

Giles shrugged as he grinned. 'I don't know. When I saw *Mr All The Gear And No Idea* hitting on your girl, I thought I'd do a little digging. Hey, I was bored. I haven't got anything on till next month, so you're stuck with me. Here to help. Here to persuade you to come home. And don't say a word. We agreed you would make your decision at the end

175

of August. Well, a have a few more weeks to help you make the best choice, and we both know what that is. This life you're living now is okay for a holiday, but it's not who we are. It's not what we were trained for.'

Scott chewed on his lip, not wanting to engage himself in that conversation. He was pretty sure he had made up his mind. At least ninety-eight percent sure. He'd made Dolly a promise. It would be easy to keep. This was the life he wanted. That's why he retired. All he had to do was figure out what was going on with that two percent and if he really could ever leave his old life behind.

Stop overthinking. This is a done deal. I made up my mind before I arrived. This has nothing to do with Dolly and Dex. I want to be here anyway. It's just Giles getting under my skin, that's all. I'm settled. I'm happy. I can do this. I can adjust to any situation. This won't be any different. Think about the peace and quiet. It's going to be okay. What if I can't do this? What if she ups and leaves me one day? I can't put myself in that position. But I've told her we'll build a future together. I can't be unstable right now. Come on, Scott. Get a grip.

'Tell me your news, Giles.'

Giles rubbed his hands together dramatically, making *mwah-ha* sounds. 'This little island you come from is like a soap opera. Who needs TV?'

'What you got?'

'Juice, Harps. Juice. So, the Wilson-Holmes old lady died, leaving her fortune to get divvied up equally between the two brats, right?'

Scott simply nodded, waiting patiently for Giles to get to the point, which he knew wouldn't come anytime soon, because Giles liked to milk anything he could.

176

'He wants to sell the retirement home. She wants to keep it up and running. It's a good business. Makes sense. But word on the grapevine is *Mr Rolex* has an expensive girlfriend who would rather have a pay-out than monthly payments.'

'Dana Blake.'

'That's the one. So, the sister has to sell to give him his half. Because she can't afford to buy him out, and because of her medical history, which I won't go into for privacy reasons, the banks are reluctant to help out.'

Privacy reasons? He actually said that.

'Carry on.'

It was quite clear by the look on Giles' face that he was thoroughly impressed with himself. 'Just call me her knight in shining armour, Scotty boy, because I have the solution to her problem. I'm saving the old people from being evicted. This could well be my calling. You see, if you have power in this world, Harps, you have to use it to help people in need. I'm like an Avenger.'

'Well, okay, Captain Spy-Cam, how are you going to save the day?'

'I already did it. I sent a letter.'

The corners of Scott's mouth twitched. 'That should do it. I hope you were very firm with your wording.'

Giles rolled his eyes. 'Funny. I sent an anonymous email to their solicitor…'

'That no doubt cannot be traced.'

'Of course. So, basically, the long and short of it is, because, you know me, I like to get straight to the point.'

Scott raised his brow in amusement but stayed silent.

'Their old man had an affair many moons ago. Turns out there's another kid. I just led the lawyer down that road. Once the new daughter is involved, the fifty-fifty split won't be so much, and Miss Wilson-Holmes might be able to buy out her brother's share. She should. I've seen her finances. It's doable.'

Scott took a silent breath and tried not to shake his head at Giles' flippant manner. 'Okay, but the new sibling might just want her cut too, and then we're right back where we started.'

Giles grinned. 'I doubt that. The new sister runs a charity that helps poor communities in America. That's where she lives and works. Her organisation has its fingers in many pies all over that country. She's no money grabber. This lady is one of life's helpers, and there's no way someone like that would see a bunch of old biddies out in the cold. I think, Harps, we have ourselves a winner.'

'And nobody knows about her?'

'Nope. I guess the old man paid off her mother or something. I don't know all the details. But now the solicitor has all her details, he will have to track her down. This will slow down selling procedures for the home, and once everything is finalised, the old folk get to stay, the Wilson-Holmes siblings get a new sister, and Aunt Dolly can continue to rinse her housemates of their choccy biscuits playing dominoes.' His face zoomed out of the screen as he leaned back in his chair. 'All in a day's work, Scotty boy.'

Scott had worked with Giles for so many years, nothing surprised him about the man. 'You did good, Giles.'

'I'm the best. That's why I have this job.'

'Don't you ever want a different life, Giles?'

It was the first time he had asked him that question. A civilian life wasn't something they mulled over in their job. Their days were filled with focusing on the task at hand and little else.

Giles lost his trademark smile for a moment. 'I was in love once. It was before I met you so don't get jealous.'

Scott smiled.

'She broke my heart, as they say. I never felt the need to put myself in that position again. I've been fine ever since. Besides, I've got nowhere else to be. Not sure I'd be able to live the normal life now anyway.'

'You won't know till you try, Giles.'

'Hey, come on, Harps. Someone has to do our job. I know people out there don't even know what's going on in the world half the time, and they sure as hell don't believe that people like us exist. We're just fictional characters that only appear on shows like 24. We don't get to be part of the crowd. We're needed in the shadows.'

'Stewardson got out. He retired. And Raffa's married. He took a back seat. It can be done, like anything, if you want it enough.'

Giles sat forward, resting his chin on his hand. 'And what about Ashmount? It didn't end well for him when he left.'

'He needed help with his mental health. There are success stories out there, Giles. You know it, and so do I.'

'And you want to be one of those, do you, Harps?'

'Why not? Why can't I be one?'

'You sound like you're trying to convince yourself.'

Scott cupped his hands around the laptop and sighed quietly. 'I'm doing okay.'

'You know, the boss man doesn't like to lose good men like yourself.'

'Oh, I don't know, Giles. There will always be younger and fitter candidates coming up through the ranks.'

Giles laughed. 'Yeah, well, I've not met any smarter than me yet.'

'Well, I've met plenty fitter than me.'

A memory entered his mind of his first day in basic training. He actually assumed it would be easy. He was young, fit, and raring to go. How hard could it be? Leaving everything he knew and loved behind ended up being the easy part for him. He threw himself into army life as though he had nowhere else he could go. The people around him became his family, and his day-to-day routine was all that mattered. He pushed himself hard, and it didn't go unnoticed. But that was a long time ago, and now his body ached from time to time, and his heart found more peace back home.

'They still need your experience, Harps. They drive me insane thinking they can just sign up and do it their way. I hate breaking them in. You know I do. I hate that they're not you. We're the A Team, buddy. You know that. I need you back here.'

'No. I'm settled here now, Giles. I've hung up my hat.'

'We'll see. You've got a few more weeks to change your mind.'

I love Dolly. I'm not leaving her. I can't do that to her. Dexter has really bonded with me. I can't let him down either. No. I'm staying put. I have to.

'You think about it, Harps. Think hard.'

22

Dolly

The shop had been busy all day, and Dolly, Dexter, and Kerri had been rushed off their feet. Dolly had hoped she'd get some time during the day to go out the back and make some more candles, but no. Finally, the sign on the door was turned over to closed. Dexter slipped off to his room to do some school work, and Kerri slumped down onto a chair out the back.

Dolly glanced at the young girl, with her dyed white-blonde pixie cut, pale-blue eyes, and slim frame. She had been keeping an eye on her all day. Something was up. Kerri wasn't her usual bubbly self.

'You want to talk about it, Kerri love?'

Kerri took a deep breath. 'I'm pregnant, Dolly.'

Oh, I wasn't expecting that. She doesn't look too happy about that fact. I better tread carefully with this one.

'Do your parents know yet?'

Kerri shook her head and stared down at the table. 'They'll be okay about it. They were fine when our Harriet came home pregnant at sixteen. It's not that, Doll. I'm about to enter my third year at uni, and I have plans that don't involve being a mum.' She rolled her sad eyes up to meet Dolly's warm smile.

'You know, Kerri, it is possible to have a career and a family.'

'I know, but I wanted my career first. I planned to have children one day. When I'm in my thirties, I thought.'

'Well, life doesn't always listen to your plans.'

Not sure if Scott's learnt that lesson yet, but I sure as hell did, a long time ago.

Kerri straightened and gave Dolly a sympathetic smile. 'I'm sorry, Doll. I guess you had plans too once.'

Dolly flapped one hand. 'Oh, Cianan had lots of plans. I just went along for the ride. What his death taught me was how short life can be. How you can plan your backside off but it makes no difference. Changes happen. We don't know when or why half the time. We have little choice. We just move forward. Adapt.'

Kerri slid one of the candle moulds over to her and started to run her fingertip around one side. 'I'm going to have to adapt. I'm just not happy about it, that's all.'

'What will you do?'

She raised one shoulder to her cheek. 'See if I can finish uni. Mum will help. Shock the hell out of my boyfriend. That's another job on the list. Save as much money as I can while I'm working here and at the tea shop.'

'You're a smart girl, Kerri. I think you'll be just fine.'

'I think so too, Dolly. I'd just rather it wasn't this way.'

Dolly made her a cuppa and sat down by her side. She stroked the back of Kerri's hand and offered as many shifts as she could afford to hand out. 'Will your man help you out, do you think, love?'

Kerri glanced over her shoulder at the shopfront. 'He says he loves me. He always talks about us having a future together, but how can you ever be sure that's what they really mean? He's in uni too, and he'll be studying for way more years than me because his course is medical. This will definitely be a shock for him.'

'Not going to lie, Kerri. It's hard work raising a kid on your own. My Dex was only five when his father passed

182

away. It was a tough time for me. It's still hard doing it alone. You never stop worrying about them, you know.'

Kerri smiled over towards the stairway. 'I'd be happy to have a kid like Dex. He's got everything, hasn't he? He's so smart, he's cute, I can't even get into how good his manners are, and he's so friendly. No wonder that Daisy Walker is all over him.' She laughed, and Dolly felt her heart warm.

'And now he has put a smile on your face.'

Kerri slowly nodded. 'Yeah, I guess he has. First time I've smiled all week, I think.'

'So, who is this man of yours, anyway? Has he been in at all?'

'He came in the other day, but you were over at The Book Gallery. His name's Toby. His family run the Sunset and Sands old people's home.' Kerri snorted out a laugh. 'There's an ongoing joke that they are the rivals of the Wilson-Holmes Retirement Village, but they're not. Toby's gran has always been mates with Rebecca Wilson-Holmes. Hey, did you hear about the latest on that place?'

Oh God, what's happened now? Aunt Dolly's not said anything. Surely it can't be that bad, else I would have heard. I'm going to have to go see her.

'What's happening over there now?'

Kerri shuffled closer to the table and cupped her mug. 'Well, turns out they have another sister. She's going to be getting her share of the place now, so *Old Greedy Guts* is down a few quid, and he's so not happy.'

'Another sister? I didn't see that coming.'

'No. Neither did they.'

'Let's hope she doesn't want to sell.'

'Toby's mum reckons it's looking hopeful for the residents. This new sister is apparently quite nice. Seems like only the women in that family are nice.'

Wait till I tell Scott about this turn of events. Wait till Dexter hears. I wonder if the whispers have circulated around the home yet. Auntie will be pleased.

Kerri yawned and casually stroked over her stomach. She appeared to realise what she had done, because she stopped moving her hand and smiled to herself.

'Hey,' said Dolly quietly. 'Why don't you head off home now. Go put your feet up.'

She walked Kerri to the door and glanced across the road to see Scott heading her way.

Look at him. His shoulders are hunched and his eyes are on the ground. Why must he do the Clark Kent thing? Why can't everyone see the real confident man he actually is? What is up with him? It's like he's hiding from the world or something. Why wouldn't you want people to know who you really are? Anyone would think he was a celebrity who has to go out in disguise.

Scott pulled her back inside the shop and kissed her so hard, it took her breath away.

'I haven't stopped thinking about you all day, Dolly. Do you know how hard it is for me to keep away from you?'

She secretly smiled to herself at how good that made her feel. There wasn't time for her to answer because his lips were back on hers. They shuffled to a table, causing a pile of tea towels behind her to fall on the floor.

'Ooh, I wanted to talk to you about the tea towels, Scott.'

He opened his eyes to glance down at the crumpled pile. 'Now?'

His lips stayed with hers, so she mumbled through them.

'Customers keep asking if I have any with Pepper Bay sights printed on them. So, I was thinking, I could get some made up using your prints.'

Scott clearly wasn't interested in talking shop. One of his hands slid into her hair and the other pulled her waist closer to him. 'Sure. Whatever you need.'

Dolly giggled, and he pulled away, raising his eyebrows at her in amusement.

'You're driving me insane, woman.'

She gestured at the tea towels. 'Help me tidy up, and then I'll pop up to Lemon Drop with you for half an hour while Dexter's doing his school work, then we'll come back here for dinner, okay?'

Scott groaned and freed her of his hold. 'Can't we tidy up later?'

'The sooner we do it, the sooner we can get back to yours.'

'Fine, but let's hurry.'

Dolly laughed as she started to straighten out the chaos from the visitors of the day.

Scott was rapidly folding tea towels as though he worked on a production line and had two seconds per item before the conveyor belt carried them away. 'Hey, Doll, you want to be my plus-one for Tessie and Nate's wedding?'

'I'm not a plus-one, Scott Harper. I'm a guest. But feel free to come with me and Dex.' She felt a tea towel hit her shoulder.

Scott was smiling to himself when she looked over. 'Looks like we've got our first official family engagement then, Dolly Lynch.'

Just the thought alone warmed her whole body. They really were going to be a family. They were making a start and heading that way.

After everything I just spoke about with Kerri, can I really get excited about the future? I have to. I can't let my past hold me back. I love my Clark Kent over there. I'm going to give him everything I've got. Aye, I'll put my all and all into this. I don't know what life's going to throw at me next. Nobody does. And I don't know how long we'll get to have together, so I'm going to make every day count. I'm going to love that man. I'm going to let him into my family one hundred percent. As soon as I've checked with Dexter.

23

Scott

The wedding was beautiful, and Dolly even more so. Scott couldn't take his eyes off her from the moment she revealed herself wearing a long sky-blue dress, with tiny silver stars in her neatly pulled-back hair. He was used to seeing her wear bright colourful clothes, and she often had hairclips in that had flowers or butterflies attached. She looked so different, and if it weren't for her usual friendly smile and bubbly personality, he was sure he wouldn't recognise her at all.

The reception was held inside The Ugly Duckling, where Tessie grew up. The old pub, with its dark wood and homely vibe was full with guests. Some lined the pavement outside and others spilled over into the beer garden out the back.

Part of the grass was boarded over, creating a makeshift dancefloor, and a live band was taking turns with a DJ over the other side of the garden. Tables were lined with black-and-white buffalo check tablecloths, topped with floral arrangements made with white lilies and dusty-pink roses.

Tessie looked stunning in tall heels and a long cream dress, and her new husband's large muscles stood out beneath his white shirt and rolled sleeves.

It was a beautiful sunny day in August, and Scott was surrounded by everyone who loved him. It felt good to be home, but something was still niggling at him.

Daisy came over to the decking area where he stood with Dolly and Dexter. She smiled at everyone, then turned her attention to Dexter.

Scott could see that the boy held a touch of nerves in his small blue eyes. He gently nudged him forward.

Dexter cleared his throat as he balanced himself. 'I like your dress, Daisy. You look very pink.'

Very pink? Oh, Dex, you're killing me.

Scott pulled in his bottom lip to stop the smile that was desperate to grow on his face.

'It's a beautiful shade of pink, Daisy,' said Dolly, filling the silence. 'Right, Dex?'

Dexter nodded.

Daisy glanced down at her long bridesmaid dress, then back up at Dexter. 'Will you dance with me, Dex? I want to dance to a slow song.'

Dexter's feet were already shuffling. 'Erm, I haven't done any research on that kind of dancing yet, Daisy.'

Scott felt his hand getting squeezed by Dolly's.

Daisy frowned slightly. 'That's okay, Dex. It's quite simple. We just stand on the dancefloor and sway.' She gestured over to some adults doing exactly that.

Dexter was the one frowning now. 'Had I known you would want to participate in this kind of activity, I would have been more prepared.'

The blood was starting to leave Scott's squashed hand.

Daisy huffed at the boy. 'You don't need to be prepared for everything, Dex. I'll show you what to do. I just want to dance with you.'

Dexter didn't get a chance to respond to that, because Daisy grabbed his hand and dragged him to the dancefloor.

Scott managed to release his dead hand.

'Oh, sorry about that, Scott. I was so nervous.'

Scott laughed. 'I don't even know what to say.'

Dolly nudged him and gestured to the dancefloor. 'She's definitely a girl who knows what she wants.'

'Poor Dex. He looks lost.'

'He'll settle with her in a bit. Give the lad a chance. Watch. I know my boy. He just has to get used to things. And he's never slow-danced with a girl before. He'll be doing some calculations in his head right about now, and then...' She whacked him in the ribs with her elbow. 'Look.'

Dexter was finally holding Daisy, and Daisy took the opportunity to pull him closer to her.

Scott felt Dolly melt into his bruised side.

'Oh, Scott, they're cuddling.'

'They're dancing.'

'They're cuddle-dancing.'

He glanced down at her soppy expression. 'Do you want to cuddle-dance?'

The dreamy look in her eyes effortlessly changed to mischievous. 'I want to do a lot of things.'

A flutter hit his stomach. She knew what she was doing to him.

'I want your hands all over this dress,' she whispered close to his ear.

'Yeah? I want my hands under that dress.'

He had to cool things down, so pulled back from her light kiss on his lips. There was no way he was going to ravish her on the decking of the beer garden of The Ugly Duckling. He stared into her daring eyes.

I really could, Dolly. Don't tempt me.

Ruby approached to whisk them off to the dancefloor as the band started to belt out some lively, upbeat songs.

Scott spun his aunt around, never one to shy away from a dance. If there was one thing Ruby taught her boys, it was how to dance. She loved to jive, in particular, so both Scott and Freddy knew all the moves. Wes used to waltz her around the garden, and her own father was a foxtrot man.

189

Ruby was a force to be reckoned with once the music kicked in.

Scott had the biggest smile, dropping his guard completely, as he twisted and turned from his aunt straight over to Dolly. The sheer look of surprise on her face as he swept her off her feet made his day. She was throwing her head back and laughing whilst trying to keep up with hip movements that would score him a perfect ten on Strictly Come Dancing.

Dolly clung on to him when he pulled her close. The soft material of her dress beneath his fingers caused him to stay locked with her. He wasn't about to let go, but the music was still thumping, so he did his Dirty Dancing move on her, dipping her top half backwards, supporting her all the way.

Their mouths were inches apart as she popped back up to face him. The glow on her cheeks and her beaming smile let him know she was most definitely having the time of her life.

Molly bumped into her back. 'Sorry, Doll. Freddy keeps spinning me around. I feel a bit giddy.'

Dolly laughed. 'I know how you feel.'

They linked arms, deciding they needed a drink, and Scott was left to dance with Freddy.

Freddy spun him around and laughed when Scott tried to lift him. Ruby came over and slapped his arm.

'Pack it in, you two. You're like a couple of kids.' She marched them off the dancefloor, making room for the others left behind.

Scott rolled his eyes over Dolly, scanning her from head to toe, before he approached her at the end of the bar. He leaned over and kissed behind her ear, making her shiver. She turned to him, smiling, and then turned back to order their drinks.

Ruby tugged at his arm, pulling him over to the open fireplace. 'Hey, what's the latest with you two?'

That was her way of asking him if he was definitely sticking around. Ruby never liked him being away, and she sure as hell didn't like him working for the army. All she wanted was to see him settled, preferably in Pepper Bay.

Freddy sprung up behind them and kissed Scott on the cheek. 'Is Mum grilling you about Dolly?'

'I am not.'

They both turned to her and laughed.

Ruby rolled her eyes and crossed her arms. 'I am not.'

Scott nodded at Freddy. 'She totally is.'

Freddy swung his arm around her shoulder and drew her into him. 'Mum, he's come to a wedding with her. He spends every night up at hers, and when he's not with her, he has those dreamy eyes that say he's thinking about her.'

Scott slapped his arm. 'I don't do dreamy eyes.'

Freddy laughed. 'You so do.'

Ruby flapped her hands at them both. 'I just want to know how things are going for my boys. Is that a crime?' She shot Freddy a wide-eyed look. 'Any developments with Molly yet?'

Freddy frowned with amusement. 'What do you mean, developments?'

Ruby huffed. 'You've been with the girl for two years, son. Don't you think it's time to move things along?'

Scott grinned widely at his cousin. 'Yeah, Fred. What's the hold up?'

Ruby nudged his elbow. 'Oh hush, you.'

'Well, if you must know,' said Freddy, looking rather reluctant to speak at all, 'we're talking about moving in together. We're currently looking for somewhere to rent.'

Ruby beamed and grabbed his cheeks, pulling him down to her level for a kiss. 'I knew you'd do right by her, son.' She turned to Scott.

It was his turn. They all saw it coming.

'Well, Scotty? What have you got planned for your lady?' Now Freddy was the one grinning. 'Yeah, Scott. What's on the agenda over at Lemon Drop?'

Should he tell them he asked Dolly to move some of her things over to his? He wasn't sure. He still had concerns. He had told her one thing, but deep down, he wasn't entirely sure he was doing the right thing. Normally, when he made a decision, he stuck to it. He loved solid plans. He had made a plan last year to come home and stay. Meeting Dolly shouldn't change that. It should be a bonus. The cherry on top. The doubt at the back of his mind, pushing its way forward, was alarming, not to mention annoying.

Dolly saved the day. She came over and handed him a drink. Molly waved Freddy over to her, and Ruby was momentarily distracted by Tessie's mum, Elaine, waving her way.

Scott took the opportunity to whisk Dolly back outside. They walked over to the far end of the large beer garden and found a small bench to sit on that overlooked a narrow back road.

The sun had started to set, and the DJ had taken over from the band for a while. The air was warm, and the crowd not as loud where they sat close together.

'I was thinking, Scott, perhaps tomorrow, you could help me bring some of my things over to yours.' She frowned at his hesitation. 'Hey, what's wrong?'

I don't even know how to say this.

'I'm… thinking we could wait a little longer.'

'You don't want to do this now?'

'It's not that. It's just, I want to slow things down.'

No. No. That's not what I mean. What the hell do I mean?

'Scott, this was your idea. What's changed? Have I done something wrong? Is it about Dexter?'

'No. No. It's not you. It's me.'

I cannot believe I just said that.

Dolly shifted on her seat so that she was facing him head on. 'Scott, I need you to look at me.'

He met her eyes and couldn't make out whether they were concerned, sad, or angry. Maybe all of the above.

'Scott, I'm not a silly little girl. I'm a grown woman with a kid, a business, and my own home. I have a lot of crap in my past and a lot of hope for my future. The last thing I need is you playing games.'

He quickly grabbed her hand, afraid she might leave. 'I'm not playing games.'

She shook her head and pulled her hand back. 'I'm not feeling very stable with you right now. I told you that I love you, and I mean it. You told me that you love me...'

'And I mean it.'

'This is bigger than you and me, Scott. I have to put my son's wellbeing first. I can't afford to go back and forth with you. I have always given Dexter stability. If you can't bring that to the table, then you can't be a part of our family.'

Scott lowered his head. He needed to be clear, but it was as though the words were on the tip of his tongue but he couldn't reach them. 'Dolly, I...'

'Scott, be honest. Please.'

'It's work. I'm thinking about returning to my old job.'

Everything about her deflated instantly. Her thoughts and feelings were as clear as day. He didn't need to ask.

'You promised, Scott.' Her words were so broken, his heart took a hit.

'I know. I just don't know what to do, Dolly.'

She suddenly jumped up. 'Well, leave me alone.' Her snap was another hit to his heart. 'That's one thing you can do.'

It hurt so much, he just froze on the bench as she marched off back to the party.

What am I doing? What am I doing to myself? I was happy. I was settled. She made everything even better. Why am I messing this up? What is wrong with me? I don't even want to go back to that job, so why am I thinking about it? Bloody Giles. He planted a seed in my head, and now I can't shift it. Christ, I've just blown it with Dolly. How will she ever trust me again? She thinks I'm flaky. Unreliable. I'm not that person. What am I doing?

He stared over at the small stone wall he could see out by the road. Pressing his palm onto his forehead, he took some deep breaths.

Freddy plonked himself down by his side. 'Mate, what did you say to Dolly? She's just said goodbye and gone home with Dex.'

Scott swore under his breath and lowered his hand.

24

Dolly

Dolly sat in the garden beneath a large brown parasol at her aunt's home. She gazed across the lawn at a couple of ducks pottering around by the pond. Her aunt was next to her, sipping on cherryade and smiling through her plastic beaker. 'And what's tickled you today, Auntie?'

'I'm just happy. Can't a girl be happy without cause?' Dolly side-eyed her. 'Hmm. But you're grinning about something. Have you been gambling again?'

Aunt Dolly huffed out a laugh. 'We're allowed to play bingo in here, you know.'

'We both know that's not what I'm talking about.'

Aunt Dolly wriggled her bum, shuffling herself around a touch. 'I do have some juicy gossip, my lovely.'

Dolly figured it would be to do with the new sister on the block, but she allowed her aunt the excitement of telling the story. 'Go on.'

'Well, rumour has it, there's a deal going down. The home has been saved by a woman who runs a charity in America. Apparently, she's part-owner in this place now, or she's about to be. Mr Wilson-Holmes is getting paid off, and then he can bugger off. No one needs to see his ugly mug around here anymore.' She let out a bark of a laugh whilst waggling her pencil-drawn eyebrows.

'That's good news, Auntie.'

'Yes, and we're going to have a party once it's all settled. He won't be celebrating for too long, though. Have you heard who his girlfriend is? Dana Blake.' She peered around

195

the green. 'I can't speak too loudly, in case her mother is about. Poor Betty. Do you know, it took years for her and her old man to have a baby. They were old parents. And they spoiled her something rotten. Proper little Veruca Salt she was. Still is, by all accounts. He won't have that money five minutes with her around. She'll fleece him all right. Good job. Serves him right, greedy…'

'At least you don't have to move now, Auntie. That's the important part.'

Aunt Dolly sat back and sipped her cool drink. 'I'm glad. I'm happy here, you know, young Dolly.'

'I know, and I'm pleased that you are.'

Aunt Dolly tapped her niece's leg. 'You're a good girl. Always coming to see me.'

Dolly flashed her a grin. 'Well, somebody has to keep you on the straight and narrow.'

'That's my girl. Now, tell me, my lovely, how are things with you? Tell me some more about the lovely Superman. I've told everyone in here what a catch my niece has landed. Although, we both know, he's the lucky one.'

Great! Now the whole of this place will be talking about my breakup. Now, how to say this so that she doesn't worry about me.

'It didn't work out, Auntie. We've called it a day.'

Aunt Dolly gasped out her disapproval about that statement. 'What?' She tapped Dolly's hand on the patio table. 'Why would you let such a man go? I've seen him. I'd have a go myself if I were ten years younger. Okay, maybe more. What's wrong, my lovely? Tell me what happened. And don't skip bits. I hate it when folk skip bits. I mean, seriously, what's the point in telling a story if you're going to go and skip vital information.'

Dolly took a silent breath, relaxing the tension in her shoulders. 'I think the long and short of it is, he got cold feet.'

'Cold feet? What about? Did you start talking wedding bells?'

'No. It wasn't me at all. It was all him. He was the one who asked me to slowly move in with him, and when I went to do just that, he changed his mind.'

And I really cannot be bothered going over this again. My mind has felt nothing but frazzled since it happened. I just need to forget about him now and move on. I don't need someone messing with my emotions like that. It was such a magical day as well. The way he danced with me. His hands constantly touching me. My cheek. My lower back. Holding my hand. His tender kisses. The need in his eyes. Oh why, Scott? Why have you done this to us?

'It'll be the army,' said Aunt Dolly.

'What?'

She nodded, giving an all-knowing look. 'Does that to some of them, you know.' She gestured towards an old man wearing a baseball cap being helped along a pathway by a walking frame and male care worker. 'Take George over there. He gave forty years of his life to the navy. Tells us so many interesting stories, he does. But some are quite sad, and I'm not talking about life in the forces. I'm talking about the story he tells about his life afterwards.'

Now Dolly was intrigued. 'What do you mean?'

Aunt Dolly sniffed and pulled a white hankie from her pocket to blow her nose. She waved the material his way. 'He found it so hard to adjust to civvy street. That's what they call it. George really struggled. Maybe your Scott is too.'

Could that be why? Surely he would say. Not everyone talks about how they really feel. I did ask him about the

PTSD thing, but I never asked how he was coping not working for the army anymore. What if he has been struggling all this time and no one knows.

Aunt Dolly put away her handkerchief. 'They're different, those military types. It's all that training, and everything they get to see that's hidden from the likes of us. Makes sense when they struggle to come to terms with living on the other side. Change is hard at the best of times.'

'Do you think I should talk to him about it, Auntie?'

She gave a slight shrug. 'Wouldn't hurt.'

I feel horrible now. I just walked away without even giving him a chance to explain properly. Not that he looked like he knew what to say. This might not be the problem, but if it is, I want to at least find out.

Dolly said her goodbye when her aunt was led away for lunch. There was a bit of a kerfuffle over the cherryade, but after some gentle persuasion, heated negotiation, and a few swear words, Aunt Dolly got to take her bottle back to her room.

The hefty fountain was trickling out front of the large white building. Eros needed a scrub down, but all in all, the grey stone of the water feature was wearing well.

I wonder if the fountain will stay put now?

Dolly stepped closer to look at the pennies lining the bottom. Lots of little wishes made by visiting grandchildren. She rummaged around in her purse and pulled one out. As was custom, she flipped it into the water whilst making a wish. Hers was for her aunt to always be allowed cherryade, as the wishes had to be for residents only.

The warm smile on her face immediately turned to a scowl as soon as she saw a lying opportunist heading her way.

Calvin Wilson-Holmes.

He stopped when he saw her. A flash of horror washed across his face for all of a second.

'Come here,' she yelled at him.

He straightened his posture and boldly walked towards her, stopping just short of the tips of her toes.

Dolly poked him in the chest. 'You've got some nerve, Calvin.'

The corner of his mouth twitched up one side. 'Oh, come on. We had a laugh, didn't we?'

'You made me believe you were someone else. What kind of a person does something like that?'

He revealed his palms. 'It was just a joke.'

She placed one hand over her heart as she narrowed her eyes in annoyance. 'Aye, on me.'

He lowered his smirk, but she could still see it sitting there in his glare. 'I didn't mean anything by it, Dolly.'

'Don't say my name. You don't get to act like you know me.'

Calvin's nose almost snarled like a dog on guard duty. 'You should be a bit nicer to me. We both know I didn't slip on that wall. I could sue your little boyfriend for pushing me in the sea.'

Dolly tightened her fists and clenched her jaw. 'Yeah? Sue this.' With all her might, she pushed him backwards.

Calvin stumbled, landed on his bottom on the edge of the fountain, and then slid backwards into the water.

Dolly raised her head and marched off as proudly as she could, praying to God she didn't trip over.

25

Scott

Wes Morland's two-bed apartment overlooked Sandly Harbour. The top level flat in the old, five-story-high, red-brick building at the edge of a hilly street had a wide veranda with cream paving.

Scott sat on the balcony with an easel set up in front of him. The charcoal picture he was working on was of a moored fishing trawler. The acrylic painted art piece in front of Wes was of the horizon.

The two men had been sitting peacefully for the last hour. Scott thought he'd try something he always tried whenever he was with Wes since the divorce.

'Did Freddy tell you, we were up at Sandly View on the day of the festival? Ruby was saying how you used to take her up there.'

I'm not adding for a snog.

Wes didn't look away from his painting, but his hand did stop moving the brush. 'Leave it, Scott.' His gravelly voice rumbled as though carried into land by a storm.

He always says that.

'I just think it's nice that you have lovely memories of your time together.' He glanced sideways for a reaction. All he got was white frizzy hair, as Wes turned away.

God, this man's hard work. Sod it. I'm going straight for the jugular.

'She misses you, you know.'

A low grumbling moan came from the sixty-eight-year-old man, and beady blue eyes zoomed in on Scott.

Scott used his skills to keep his face neutral. It was a lot easier to do when he was working. Not so much when it came to his family. He continued to shade until Wes looked back at his own canvas.

'You should come over for dinner one night, Wes.'

'What, so you can set me and Ruby up? No, ta.'

Scott's shoulders slumped. 'I wasn't going to do that.'

'Sure.'

'Well, it wouldn't hurt you to sit at my table with the rest of us.'

'No. It wouldn't hurt. But I'm still not doing it, son.'

Scott hit level child-mode. 'Oh, please, Wes. Can't you do it just the once, for me?'

'Don't whine, Scott. It doesn't suit you.'

That's me told. Change tactics. Hmm?

'That Mr Hedgerow keeps popping in the tea shop to see Ruby. Think he might be keen.'

'That's nice for her.'

Scott huffed and turned. 'You hate that man.'

'None of my business what he does though, is it, Scott?'

What would Giles do? Probably cut of his income until he agreed to sit down with Ruby. Ha! No, I can't do that. Tempting, though. Oh, flipping heck, why does he have to be so stubborn?

Wes rolled his eyes over. 'Scott, stop meddling. You're too old to need your parents back together again.'

Scott scoffed, although he didn't mean to. It just came out before he had a chance to act like a grown-up. 'No one is too old for that. And while we're on the subject…'

'The subject you brought up.'

Scott cleared his throat and swallowed. 'Yes. Well, can't you at least be friends with her?'

'We are friends.'

'You barely speak to her.'

'Works better that way.'

Scott started to clean his hands on a piece of grey cloth that sat upon his lap. 'She still loves you, Wes.'

'And I'll always love her, but that doesn't change the fact she cheated on me.'

'It was before Freddy was born. And you weren't even married then, or dating properly.'

Wes widened his eyes and lowered his paintbrush. 'I only found out a few years back, and besides, does it matter when it was? It happened. And as far as I was concerned, she was my girl back then. I knew I was going to marry her, and she treated me the same way. Your dad had just left, Scott. I stepped up. I took you away on that fishing trip to help you and her. And what was she doing while we're away? Shacking up with some holidaymaker who had only come down for a couple of weeks.'

'She said sorry.' Scott made sure he kept his tone hushed. The last thing he wanted was to make Wes think that it wasn't a big deal or that he was on Ruby's side.

'She's sorry she hurt me, but it doesn't take away the pain, son. So, let's not go on, eh?'

It was heartbreaking all round, and Scott hated that they were divorced. Freddy was mortified and almost gave up on love altogether. Even when he started dating Molly, he couldn't bring himself to commit to her.

Scott stared out at the harbour. Seagulls were flying overhead, and a few people were walking around down below. Some taking pictures of the boats. One couple was leaning against the rail, holding hands and staring out to sea.

I wish that was me with Dolly. I miss her. I wonder what she's doing now.

As if reading his mind, Wes asked, 'Why did you break up with young Dolly?'

How does he know about that? Freddy, I bet. I wonder who else knows. Dexter hasn't spoken to me. Dolly must have told him. He probably wanted to know why I wasn't around. Please don't hate me, Dex.

'Well?'

Scott was being given a taste of his own medicine. He knew that Wes knew that he didn't want to talk about his love life, or rather, lack of one. 'Well, I'm thinking about returning to my old job, so it wouldn't be fair on her.'

Wes slammed his brush down and spun on his chair to look directly at Scott. 'Oh, is that right?'

Scott was suddenly reduced to a child again. Only Ruby and Wes had the ability to make him feel that way. He wasn't having any of it. Wes was about to be told. 'I can do what I want,' he snapped.

Wes had a much louder, deeper snap. 'Oh, really?'

Scott's attempt to be the alpha failed miserably.

Wes hadn't finished. 'You listen to me, son. You've done your time in that job. You're settled here now, and here you're staying. If you think that Ruby can take any more of your gallivanting, you're wrong. You, lad, are staying put.' He paused, glancing over at Scott's picture. 'Is it money? Do you need money?'

'No. I don't need money.' Scott's tone was as deflated as his broken heart.

Wes homed in on him. 'You told me that you were happy here. What's changed?'

'I really don't know.'

'How can you not know?'

Scott gave a half-shrug. 'I was happy, but then I met...' He stopped talking.

'Oh, I get it.'

'Get what?'

'You're scared.'

'I'm not scared.'

Wes nodded and sighed. He turned back to his painting and picked up his brush.

Scott huffed. 'I'm not scared of anything.'

Wes hummed to himself for a moment. 'Hmm, that's what you thought. Then you went and finally opened up.'

'What's that supposed to mean?'

Wes was thoroughly engrossed in the horizon. 'You never cry, Scott. You didn't even cry when Luna died. Have you noticed that about yourself, son? You just won't cry.'

Yes. Of course I know that about myself. What's that got to do with anything?

Wes went back to humming, and then he laughed to himself.

'I'm not scared,' snapped Scott.

'You're in love, Scott. Of course you're scared. It's one of the scariest things in the world. It makes you vulnerable, and that's the one thing you hate.' He glanced over at him. 'Ever since your mum died and your dad left, you won't stand for vulnerable. You won't stand for a lot of things. That's why you ran away with the circus.'

Scott rolled his eyes.

Wes smiled and went back to his picture. 'Have you not figured that out about yourself yet? You got too close to young Dolly, and it scared the crap out of you. Your only answer to that problem is to run away.'

I'm not running away. Am I? I love her, and I want to be with her. I made a plan for us. It was a good plan. I liked it. She liked it. I was happy. We were happy. Everything was perfect. Then what did I do? I pushed her back a step.

Thought about going off with Giles. Bloody hell! He's right. I do want to run away just to save myself from any pain that might happen down the road.

Wes sniffed in the warm, salty air. 'You can't control life, Scott. If she leaves you one day, so be it. If she dies on you, it's tough. You can't do a thing about it. You just have to enjoy the good times as best as you can while you have them. The last thing you do is throw them out with the rubbish. You're lucky you got to find such love in the first place.'

I am lucky. She's lovely. She's everything.

'So, what are you going to do about it, son?'

Scott lowered his head. His breakthrough moment was tarnished by the fact that he had messed things up so spectacularly with Dolly. 'She doesn't trust me any longer. So, there's little I can do now.'

The last time he had cried was when his mum died. This was the closest he had come to feeling the prick of tears hit his eyes. He tugged on his fingers, sniffed, and looked over at his uncle, who was simply watching him.

'Tell her the truth, Scott. She'll understand.'

Will she? It's only just started to make sense to me.

Wes pursed his full lips and nodded. 'I'll make you a deal. If you open up to the girl, I'll come to dinner one night.'

Scott held back his building smile. 'With Ruby there too?'

Wes went back to his painting whilst grumbling. 'Yeah, with Ruby there too.'

'And you won't stay silent like you normally do when everyone is around?'

'That's rich, coming from you.'

Scott frowned.

Wes pointed a finger over at him without looking. 'Are you going to stop acting like someone else and start showing the world the real you?'

I think I might have already started doing that since hanging out with Dolly. It's quite possible that Clark Kent has finally lost his glasses. Obviously, I can't lose mine. I won't be able to see. I could just wear my contacts, but I like my glasses. Yes, my Clark Kent disguise is no longer needed. I don't have to hide out in the open anymore. Not now I'm retired. Not now I'm making a new life for myself. Dolly sees the real me anyway. And when I catch up with her, she's going to know everything about me. It's time. It's my time. No more running. No more hiding. No more worrying that someone else might leave me.

'I'm ready for my life here, Wes.'

'Good. About time. Now, stop talking and let me get back to my painting.'

Scott smiled to himself. Everything felt lighter, and he, too, could now concentrate on his artwork.

After a moment of silence, he side-eyed Wes. 'You could bring Ruby some flowers,' he mumbled.

Scott flinched as a splat of blue paint hit his cheek.

26

Dolly

'Dex, my battery is low. It might run out in a minute. I'll be home as soon as I can. Stupid car just stopped. If you can call Ruby for me when you get this message, tell her I'm running late because her car broke down, but I'll get something sorted... Oh, flipping heck.' Dolly glared at her mobile phone as it died right there in her hand. 'Great!'

She tossed the phone back into her bag and then flung that over to the back seat.

When Ruby had offered her use of the car for all the running around Dolly had to do that day, the last thing she thought would happen was her being left stranded somewhere between Sandly and Pepper Bay.

She glanced out through the front windscreen. It was still light out, but it was almost eight o'clock at night.

With no phone, no working car, and only a vague idea how to walk home from her current position, she stayed put for a while.

Oh, what a day! Aunt Dolly's cherryade fight, stupid Calvin will probably try to sue me for pushing him in the fountain, and the supermarket had run out of Jaffa Cakes. What kind of a supermarket runs out of Jaffa Cakes? I could really go for one now. At least I got all my orders shipped off today, so there's a plus. Dexter's eaten already, so I don't have to worry about him. I've had a sandwich, but I know I'll feel hungry soon.

She flung her head back onto the headrest. 'Argh!'

A heavy sigh later, all thoughts went elsewhere.

I really miss Scott. Those large hands of his all over me. Touching me. Kissing me. Making me feel wanted, needed, loved. I love that earthy smell he sometimes has, and the way he smiles for real. No hiding. No pretend shyness. Just him. And those glasses. Does he even know how sexy he looks wearing those things? God, that man is sex on legs. And he was mine, for a while anyway. Now he's gone.

She turned to see a face staring at her through the window on the passenger side of the car. The scream that left her lungs made them both jump.

It was Scott. And he was frowning at her with confused amusement. The back of his knuckle tapped the window.

Not sure I want to open it. Not sure I want to talk to you, Scott Harper, even if you do have sexy knuckles that I want to kiss right now. Why doesn't he lower his hand?

He twisted his mouth to one side, revealing his frustrated look. The tap came again. This time harder.

She could see out of her peripheral vision that he was sitting on his bike.

'Dolly, open the window.'

You're not the boss of me.

She folded her hands in her lap and turned up her nose. There was a dark patch of something resembling smudged mascara rubbed into the sun visor above her that caught her eye. She decided to focus on that and ignore antsy pants outside.

Another thump hit the window.

'Dolly. Don't ignore me.'

Thought you were leaving. Going back to your old job. Off you go then. Goodnight.

She was sure she heard him sigh.

'Dolly, will you please talk to me? Just open the window. I want to know what you're doing sitting along here on your own in my aunt's car.'

The softness mixed with desperation in his voice reached in and tweaked her stubborn heart, immediately turning off the cool air swirling there.

Ruby's car was quite old and didn't have any fancy gadgets such as electric windows. One stretch later, and the window on his side was rolled down.

'Dolly, what are you doing out here?'

'The car just stopped.' She said it whilst still staring at the dirty mark.

'How long have you been sitting here?'

'About twenty minutes. Not sure.'

'Is Clive coming to get the car?'

She finally moved her head to look over at him. She wished she hadn't. Bright blue eyes were twinkling back and his kissable mouth held the slightest of warm smiles. Her eyes rolled to his chin. Just underneath was where she loved to kiss. It was as though it was calling her name, beckoning her forward.

'Dolly?' He was pressing for some sort of response.

She floated out of her daydream of kissing him under his chin, along his neck, all down his chest.

'Dolly?'

'Erm… who is Clive?'

Scott rolled his eyes. He got off his bike and leant it against the front of the car. Then he came back to the window, reached in, and pulled the door open.

She tried not to frown at his uninvited invasion into her personal space. Partly because he wasn't close enough. She swallowed hard as his long legs struggled to fit in the front.

He pulled the chair back, making more room, and then shuffled around to face her. 'Have you called Ruby?'

'No. I only had a small amount of charge left on my battery, so I called Dexter instead. I left him a message. Well, part of a message. My phone died.'

'This car breaks down a lot. Clive is my aunt's friend. He has a tow truck, and he normally takes the car back to his garage.'

She watched him whip out his phone and make a couple of calls. One to Clive, and one to Ruby. Each conversation lasted all of two minutes. When he was finished, his chest lifted and fell in annoyance.

'Clive won't be able to get here for another hour.'

Dolly shrugged. 'That's okay. I can wait.' She waggled a finger at the windscreen. 'You can go.'

'I'm not going.'

'I'm fine. You don't need to wait with me.'

'I'm not going.'

There wasn't much around for a good game of I Spy, so Dolly went back to staring at the black mark. She did glance at his hands, but the thought of them gripping her thighs only made life harder.

'Dolly, I want to talk to you about us.'

Her heart flipped, and the salmon in the sandwich she had eaten an hour ago had come back to life to flap around in her stomach.

'There is no *us* anymore, Scott.'

Even lightning wasn't as powerful as the jolt she felt hit her when his hand shot over and grabbed hers.

'Dolly, I'm sorry. Please hear me out. I love you so much. You're killing me here.'

Good to know I'm not the only one suffering.

'If you love me as much as you say, then you wouldn't walk away from me.'

'That's what I want to talk to you about. I made a mistake. I froze. That's not me. I'm a plan man. I know what I'm doing and when I'm supposed to be doing it. I set up plans for us. But I froze, Dolly. I panicked.'

She turned to look directly into his eyes. They were worried. That much was obvious. 'I can't do fickleness, Scott. I have a kid to think about. I don't want to bring someone into his home who doesn't know if they're coming or going. I want stability for my son, and myself.'

'I understand. Please, give me another chance. I'll do better. I'll show you I'm not fickle.'

'How can you show me, when you aren't even sure?'

'But I am now. I didn't know what was happening to me. But I spent the day with Wes, and he got me thinking about a few things. He pointed out that all I do is run away. Not to hurt people. To protect myself. Isolate myself.'

Their fingers were entwined and she could feel his hold tighten.

'Christ, Dolly, I've never loved anyone the way I love you. I'm not leaving. I'm not going anywhere. Please don't leave me.'

The twang of pain in his words reached every fibre of her being. It was too much. That angry wall she had built up was falling down, brick by brick. It was so hard to hold back, but how could she trust him again? What if he changed his mind once more?

He let go of her hand and reached up to place his fingers into the back of her hair. 'I promise you. I'm not going anywhere,' he whispered.

The lump in her throat hurt to swallow, but she got there. 'You promised last time.'

'Technically, I didn't break it. I didn't actually leave, after all.'

She rolled back the tears pricking her eyes so that she could glare at him.

Scott recoiled. He looked submissive. Clark Kent was back.

There was something so vulnerable about Clark that made it hard to hate on him. Maybe that was the ploy. Scott Harper was a lot smarter than he had people think. He seemed to like fooling everyone. Was he fooling her? Was he putting on an act to get what he wanted? Could she really trust this man who says he loves her, wants to live with her, but then does U-turns at the last minute? What was missing? Something was missing?

He leaned closer and placed his mouth gently on the side of her neck, and Dolly no longer cared about what was bugging her.

The light brush of his lips upon her skin caused shivers that came rolling in like waves created by the appearance of Poseidon himself. His hot breath carried down to her collarbone along with a guttural moan.

'Dolly…. Dolly…. Dolly.'

She closed her eyes for a moment, embracing every peppered kiss.

'God, I want you,' he whispered down into her top. 'I really want you.'

Every inch of her was coming undone. He had her. Right there, with his simple sentence, he had her. The control he had over her emotions was annoying, satisfying, and overwhelming. How could he just render her useless like that?

What am I going to do about it? How can I control this? We need to talk some more. I have things I want to say.

His other hand reached over to nestle on the inside of her thigh. She twisted his way, giving him more access to her body. The hand in her hair tightened, and the lips on her skin edged up towards her parted mouth.

Things need sorting properly. A conversation is needed here. God, his hands. I love his hands. Oh, he's moving his mouth to mine. He's going to kiss the life out of me any second now. I have to speak. I have to...

'Scott. Lift my skirt higher.'

His mouth was on hers before she could add any more words. Deep, hard kisses jolted her head backwards. He caught it, holding her in place. Keeping her with him.

Dolly's body was doing its own thing. She started to slide over to his lap. The gearstick was in her way and then the dashboard. The roof felt too low, and the seats too small. Hands were frantically clawing at clothes as their bodies tried to wriggle around the compact car.

'Do something, Scott,' she breathed out, panting in his ear.

He attempted to lift her, but there wasn't enough room. Her skirt was hitched up around her waist, allowing his hands access to her knickers, and she so wished she had put on her best pair that morning.

The back seat was drawing nearer as he wriggled them both that way. One of his long legs was stuck between the front seats, and she heard him swear under his breath. Her head tilted against the side window and something pinged in her back, but she didn't care. His mouth not leaving hers was all that mattered. They both knew that.

Scott raised himself over her, but there wasn't room for their bodies to entwine the way they wanted. He went to move away, but she cupped his face and pulled him back,

213

kissing him with so much intensity, she could feel him melting into her.

She scrambled her hands down to his trousers, but she couldn't quite get to where she wanted to be. He tried to lift himself to give her access but banged his head on the roof.

'Dolly, I...' His broken words were breathless.

She gripped his hair, trying to pull him closer. 'Get me, Scott.'

'I'm trying.'

They wriggled some more, feeling around for space, trying to hold on to each other whilst looking for leg room, any room.

Scott jolted up, swearing about the car. He caught his breath and gazed back down at her squashed body.

Dolly smiled up at him, needing him, wanting him so badly.

He bit his bottom lip and gave her the smile she knew to be real. The one that caused her internal satnav to direct him straight to the bedroom.

His eyes darkened. A beat. No movement. And then. 'I really need to get you home.'

Dolly's breath caught in her throat. She rolled her head slightly towards his arm and lightly brushed over his bare skin with her lips. 'I really need you right now.'

Without removing his eyes from hers, he slowly lowered one hand to her thigh, and Dolly was lost in him.

27

Scott

Cramp in his left leg and the fact that Dolly had been partially satisfied caused Scott to straighten himself and climb back into the passenger seat. He turned to look back at her straightening her skirt and tidying her hair. That messy bed hair that he had twirled and curled, gripped and held. *Christ, I need to finish the job. Look at her, she wants more from me. I want to give her more. I need some more space. We need to get home. She's killing me here.*

He jumped up as best he could and leaned towards her for another kiss. She helped out by shuffling forward. Her hands were back in his hair. He was back to trying to move the seats.

'Scott, you know what I want.'

Her breathy voice hit him in all the right places.

'Yep.'

He felt the smile on her lips as she said, 'Well, what are you going to do about it?'

He breathed out a laugh and pulled her bottom lip into his mouth. 'Oh, I'm going to do a lot about it, as soon as I get some room.'

She laughed and pushed him backwards, placing one hand on his heart. He took it and pulled it to his mouth, kissing her knuckles. One sweet kiss at a time. She leaned forward again and smooched his right cheekbone.

'Come on, help me into the front.'

He flinched as her knee hit him in the head, then he made an *oof* sound as her hand slipped and caught him in the groin.

'Ooh, sorry.' Dolly stumbled back into the driver's seat with a huff.

They took a moment to regain some composure, and Scott let out a long sigh. Within seconds, they were back to looking at each other. She grabbed him by the scruff of his neck and thrusted her mouth straight onto his. Scott climbed to his knees, towering over her, swamping her into the small seat.

'Scott, I…' Her words faded onto his tongue.

All he thought about was how much he needed her. He would do anything for her. Anything she asked.

'You're so beautiful,' he whispered to her neck.

Her finger slowly traced over his jaw and slipped inside his mouth. He closed around it whilst keeping eye contact.

'I don't need room. I need hours. Hours with you, Scott.'

He pulled her finger from his mouth and kissed the tip. 'You can have a lifetime.'

'Take me home.'

He went back to his seat and glanced outside. It was getting late but still light. 'We'll walk back, drop the keys to Ruby, Clive can pick them up from her, and then we'll head to mine for a bit before spending the night at yours.'

Her eyes rolled to his mouth. 'I like your plan.'

'I was hoping you would.'

She arched her eyebrows and grinned. 'What else is in your plan?'

His eyes were on her legs. If he could move objects with his mind, that skirt of hers would be back around her waistline. He showed her the desire burning in his eyes and then smirked, knowing the spot he had just hit when he saw her cheeks flush. He liked that look. All of her looks were perfect, but the one where she showed she wanted him was his favourite. Her lips would part, her eyes would glaze over, she'd lean a touch closer to him, her cheeks would glow warmly, and that's when he knew she was ready to be kissed. Yeah, that was definitely his favourite look.

He stared at his favourite look, and it gave him goosebumps and hungry eyes. But the poxy car that hated him so much was getting the last laugh, as usual. He really needed to get home. There was so much exploring to do. And there was still more talking to be done, but that was something that could wait its turn. The priority was to get naked with Dolly and make love all over his house.

She stroked his leg and gestured at the door. 'Come on, before it gets any later.'

He agreed, so they got out and locked the car. He handed his phone to her so she could send Dexter a quick text to update him whilst he removed his bike from the bumper. An idea sprung to mind, making him smile to himself. He just hoped she was up for it.

'Hey, baby, you wanna ride?' He waggled his eyebrows and flashed the smile he knew weakened her.

She rolled her eyes and approached the bike. 'Is that your best line?'

He laughed and gestured at the handlebars.

Her eyes widened with amusement. 'You're kidding, right?'

There was something else in amongst her reluctance. There was mischief, wonder, and a hint of excitement. He knew she was going to sit there.

'Wait. There's a blanket in the boot. I'll fold it up and place it on the handlebars. You'll be more comfortable that way.' He got busy with that, watching her as much as possible as he set the wheels in motion for their trip home.

Straddling the bike, he held it securely as Dolly placed the green blanket down and clambered on top. He leaned towards her back and kissed her head.

'I love you, lady.' He sensed her smile.

Dolly yelped out a playful scream as they took off down the road.

The bike wobbled a bit at first, causing Dolly to curse and Scott to laugh.

'I've got you,' he told her.

It didn't help when she raised her legs and tried to lean back into him.

The summer night was warm, light, and quiet, and Scott had never felt so alive with happiness before. He kept his eyes on the road, over her shoulder, with the occasional glance at her mousey hair and side of her neck. He had to concentrate, for both their sakes. There was a good chance he would ditch the bike, take her and the blanket into the trees and make love till the sun came up.

Dolly yelled out to the country lane. 'I blooming love this, Scott Harper.'

He grinned like the cat who got the cream and all the milk too.

This was the last thing he expected on his ride home from his uncle's place. To see his aunt's car parked alongside the road and then see Dolly inside felt like a sign, and he didn't believe in signs. But if there was someone trying to tell him something and it led him to being able to be back in the arms of the woman he loved, then he was taking it, full on.

Her fingertips moved over slightly to briefly touch his hand, sending even more sparks of love into him. He started to pedal a bit quicker.

Dolly was still laughing and making it known to him every so often that she was having the time of her life up front.

He pressed forward so that his shoulder touched her back and she slipped herself down onto the bar below and rested on him, telling him she loved him. With his eyes on the road, he kissed the side of her hair and then nibbled on her ear, making her giggle.

As soon as the door to Lemon Drop Cottage closed them inside, they stripped each other of all clothing within record time, and Scott carried her upstairs to his bed.

She leaned up on her elbows and traced over his chest with her eyes. 'So, what are you going to do with all this room?'

He did a couple of star jumps, just to make her laugh. It did the trick. She curled up, clutching her stomach with laughter.

'You big eejit.'

He climbed on the bed, pulling her legs down, and she immediately wrapped them around him. He untangled himself from her hold. 'Don't you trap me. I need some space here. That car has taught me a valuable lesson.'

'Oh yeah, what's that?'

'Not to take your body for granted.'

He liked her laugh. The way her face came alive and her eyes sparkled.

He lowered his head to her stomach and kissed her belly button. 'I'm going to kiss every inch of you before we leave here, and then when we get back to yours, I'm going to go over the map I made with my mouth all over again.' He lifted his head to smile at her. 'And I might even take the same route first thing in the morning.'

'Is that right?'

'Shh!' He raised her arm and kissed her elbow. 'Excuse me, I have a body to explore. You just close your eyes and mind your own business.'

Dolly laughed and quickly sat up. 'Can't I come along on your journey?'

He playfully arched an eyebrow. 'Not sure what you mean.'

She licked his cheek and matched his building grin. 'I want to explore too.'

He held back his laugh. 'Did you just lick my face?'

'It was calling me.'

'And what did I taste like?'

'Not going to lie. You don't hold as much flavour as a Jaffa Cake, but, hey, I'm not going to complain.' She licked his cheekbone again and winked.

Ha! What am I going to do with this woman? Well, I can think of a few things. Let's start with the bit behind her ear. See who wins that round.

He nuzzled his nose into her hairline and lightly brushed his lips over her skin. His smile widened on her ear as soon as he heard a raspy moan and felt the change in her breathing.

One of the things he loved was when he knew he had her. How she melted before him. But it was a two-way street. And when it was her turn to own him, he crumbled. He had never begged anyone before for anything, but with her, he had no shame. He pleaded for her touch just as much as she did for his. It felt good. She felt amazing. Everything about being up close and personal with her heightened all emotions. Just like that, she could bring him to his knees, and God, did he love that feeling.

28

Dolly

Dolly sat in her kitchen going over the talk in her mind that she wanted to have with Dexter about Scott. There were plans and steps to move forward, but none of that could take place without her son's approval. She knew he liked Scott, that much was obvious, but joining them all as a family was something else altogether.

Dexter hadn't known life with a father figure. Dolly was his everything, and they got along just fine that way. Now she had two men in her life that she loved dearly. She just hoped she could make it work.

Scott seemed so determined. They had such a long chat about their relationship. He liked plans, and she liked stability, so together they created some sort of unwritten, foolproof agreement about how they wanted life to be for them. It was almost as if they had invented their own board game. A roadmap. A spreadsheet. A way forward that kept them both calm.

She was putting her trust in this man. Giving him so much more than the benefit of the doubt. She had given him her heart and soul, and now it was time to share her child's space and safe zone. The safe zone that she had created for him the day his father had died. There was no way she was going to allow anyone or thing to enter that precious place. That was Dexter's. He got to say who came in. She wasn't about taking that choice away from him.

Dexter mooched into the kitchen, heading straight for the fridge for some apple juice. 'Do you want some, Mum?'

She eyed the bottle being wiggled her way and gave a slight nod. 'Aye, go on then. And then will you sit here with me a moment, son? I want to talk to you about something important.'

He glanced over his shoulder and then went about sorting the drinks. 'What is it?' He sat opposite her, with eyes wide and his worried face switched on to high alert.

'Don't worry, baby boy, there's nothing wrong.' She used words she knew would soothe him.

He settled back into his chair and sipped his juice. 'Thought you had bad news.'

'No. No. Nothing like that. This is about me and Scott.'

'I'm just glad you made up.'

She studied his nonchalant expression. 'He wants us to grow as a couple, Dex. As a family. The three of us. He's asked if we would consider moving a few of our things over to his, and how you could set up one of the bedrooms as your own.'

Dexter frowned with confusion. 'So, I'd have my own room at Lemon Drop?'

'Yes. Eventually, he'd like us to all live there together, but he thought it would be for the best if we do that slowly, over time.'

'What do you think about his proposal?'

'I like the idea. I like him a lot, Dex, and he likes me and you very much, but, well, you know, this isn't something we've done before. He hasn't lived with anyone either, so it'll be new for all of us.'

Dexter seemed to be nodding to himself. 'I think it's very responsible of you both to take it slowly. After all, we haven't known him long. But, I do like him, Mum, and I can see how much you like each other, and that makes me happy.' He slipped his hand over the table to hold hers. 'I want you to be happy. You deserve it, Mum.'

Dolly controlled her breathing and emotions in front of him. She didn't want to cry. 'It's not about what I deserve, Dex. It's about what's right for you.'

Dexter sat back, appearing to mull over his next sentence. 'Mum, you can't not live your life because of me.'

'You are my life, Dexter Christopher Lynch. Don't ever forget that. I would never do anything that you wouldn't like. Your opinion is what matters most. I won't make you live with a man just because I'm in love with him. You have to feel comfortable. You need to be happy.'

He gave the slightest of shrugs. 'I've always been happy, Mum. You've given me a great life. I always count my blessings for having you as my mum.'

Hold it together, Doll. You've got this conversation. You know what a sweetie he is, but get down to the nitty-gritty. He can't just agree for my sake. I need to make sure he's okay with Scott.

'I'm the one who's blessed, Dexter. You're a good kid, and I know I have been lucky. What I want to talk about is your feelings towards Scott, I guess. You've never had a father around, and he's not going to be that, of course, but he will be a male role model in your life, and stuff like that can rub off in many ways.'

'I know. He's pretty decent. I can't see him being a bad influence, if that's what you might be worrying about.'

She shook her head and leaned forward, clasping his glass in her hands to stop him from taking another sip.

'Dex, I think we both know that Scott's one of the good ones, but this isn't really about that side of things. It's about your whole life changing because of the moves I make in my life.'

'So far, you've made good, sensible decisions for us as a family. I don't have any reason not to trust your judgement, Mum.'

It wasn't something she wanted to smile about, but it was hard to hold back after that statement.

'I've tried my best, Dex. Lord knows I've tried.'

He wrestled his glass from her grip so he could take a gulp of apple juice. 'I know you're not the best cook, and you're the clumsiest person I know, but I'd still pick you if we had to choose our own mums.'

Dolly breathed out a laugh through her nose. 'Oh, that's really kind of you to say, but let's just go back to the clumsiest person you know. Surely, that can't be right.'

Dexter raised his brow as his blue eyes twinkled her way. 'You remember that time I'd hurt my foot and you carried me inside and banged my head on the doorframe? What about when you tripped entering the living room and your glass of water went all over me. And that time you accidentally set fire to my bookcase, while I was in the room. Do you remember custard-gate? All over my lap.'

She had no choice but to laugh out loud. 'My goodness, is it any wonder you're still alive with me around.'

Dexter laughed with her. 'Well, you certainly keep me entertained. Now, Scott can take the brunt of it all. You've already knocked him off a ladder. I don't think he knows what he's letting himself in for.'

She shook her head as she placed one hand over her heart. 'Oh, that was shocking, wasn't it? I could've killed him. I elbowed his lip the other day by accident. I think he's taken to ignoring all the bumps and bruises he's received since meeting me.'

Dexter finished his drink and placed it down slowly, twiddling the glass around in circles. His eyes rolled over to meet hers and his mouth pulled in his bottom lip.

'What, Dex? What do you want to say?'

'I'm glad you found a partner again, Mum.'

'Are you sure about that?'

He nodded. 'Yes. I've heard all the stories about Dad. I know how much you loved him. Sometimes I've thought about how sad you must be being on your own.'

'Hey, I've never been on my own. I've had you, and that was enough. I've never felt like I needed anything else. Honestly, Dex.'

'But you tried dating that time back in Hastings, and we ended up with the cheater coming over a few times for dinner.'

She shook her head at the memory she rather she didn't have. 'I was trying to introduce him to you bit by bit, but it wasn't right, was it, Dex? You remember how quiet dinnertime was when he came over? We didn't laugh or chat like we do.'

'I never liked him, Mum. I just didn't know how to tell you that.'

'Which is exactly why I need you to be one hundred percent honest about Scott. I can't live my life with someone and then later on you rock up with a sentence along the lines of, *I never liked living with that man.*'

He nodded. He understood completely. Dexter was the easiest person on the planet for Dolly to have a conversation with. They had always simply got each other.

'I would have told you about the cheater, Mum. I just didn't have to in the end because it ended. Had you asked me back then if I wanted to live with him, I would have said no straight away.'

'Well, that's good to know.'

Dexter stopped playing with his glass and leant over the table, drawing her towards him. 'You made a good decision with that one, Mum. As soon as you found out about him, you walked away. I know I can rely on you to do the right thing by us.'

Dolly smiled warmly at her beautiful child. 'You always have to tell me everything though. I'll always be on your side. Always. And I'll always do whatever is best for you. You come first. Always have. Always will. I need that ingrained into every part of your being.'

'I kind of think you gave that away by being a helicopter mum.'

'I am not a helicopter mum.'

Dexter snorted out a laugh. 'You so are.'

Dolly huffed and slumped back in her chair. 'Oh God, Dex, what am I going to be like when you start school next week?'

His button nose scrunched as his lips curled. 'I dread to think.'

She tapped the table. 'Come on. We need to discuss Scott.'

'I thought we had.'

'You did? You're finished?'

Dexter nodded his reply.

'You don't have questions, son?'

He thought about it for a moment. 'Well, I think it's going to be okay with Scott. He seems to blend in quite nicely with us. Plus, we're not moving in overnight. We're going to do it gradually and get used to each other some more.' He smiled widely, soothing her worries. 'I like it, Mum. I like him, and I love Lemon Drop Cottage. Will I be able to decorate my own room over there the way I want?'

'Of course. Scott said you can do what you want. He told me to tell you that outdoors is for impression and indoors is for expression. So, feel free to express yourself.'

Dexter's smile widened even further. 'I think we should buy him a new gnome. It will be our way of adding our touch to the place.'

'I like that idea. I've already given him a candle. Can you believe he didn't have any? Well, except for that power cut emergency supply.'

Dexter stood. 'I'm going to get ready for Robyn's birthday party, and tomorrow I'll look online for the perfect gnome.'

'Good plan. And I'll tell Scott we've made our final decision, and perhaps we can take some of our bits and pieces over there after dinner tomorrow night.'

He walked over to her and hugged around her shoulders, giving her a peck on the cheek. 'I love that we moved here. Thanks, Mum.'

29

Scott

Scott and his boss, Anna, were walking up Pepper Lane, heading towards The Post Office Shop. They stopped at the turn off to Walk Walk Road, as Anna had grabbed her back and puffed out some air.

'Are you okay, Anna?' Scott rested one hand on her shoulder whilst looking down at her large baby bump.

Anna straightened, brushed back her dark bob, and smiled weakly. 'I'm okay, Scott. Just walking slower and slower these days.' Her ice-blue eyes twinkled his way as she let go of her back and nudged his arm. 'Come on, let's get up to the shop. You get those parcels sent off, and I can finally get my hands on Tilly's rosemary bread. I've got such a craving for the stuff, and it only seems to go down well when it's Tilly's homemade one.'

Scott smiled as they stepped onto the dry muddy track that made the road that led all the way up to Dreamcatcher Farm. 'Tilly always makes the best bread. You'll be lucky if there's any left at this time of day, though. She's known for selling out first thing in the morning.'

Anna nodded as she waddled on, avoiding small ditches made by the worn-in tractor tyre marks on the ground. 'Stan normally gets there first thing when he goes for his early morning walk. I called Tilly yesterday and asked if she could make me another one for tonight.'

Scott laughed. 'Have you already eaten all of this morning's loaf?'

Anna bit her lip and lowered her head from the sun. 'I sound so greedy, but it's not me. The baby loves the stuff.'

'That's it, blame it on the baby.'

She groaned, stopped walking, and rubbed her lower back again. 'Ooh, I've had lower back ache since last night.'

Scott offered his arm for her to cling on to. 'You should start thinking about putting your feet up now.'

Anna scoffed. 'Please. You sound just like Jake. If he had his way, I wouldn't be allowed to walk at all. I've always been a big walker. My body is used to it.'

'That may well be, but you're heavily pregnant now. There's a lot more weight pressing down on your legs.'

Anna groaned. 'More like my bladder.'

Scott gestured up the road as he guided them both around a dip. 'Look, Joseph's truck is outside the shop. I'll get him to drop you back up to Starlight Cottage when you're done.'

'Oh, Scott, don't you start bothering people for me. I'm fine. It's just a bit of backache, that's all.'

'Do as you're told for once, else I'll call your husband and tell on you.'

Anna burst out laughing. 'If you call Jake and tell him I've got backache and need a lift home, there'll be a helicopter landing in front of us in about five seconds flat. And it'll have a doctor inside.'

Scott smiled warmly down at her. 'Yes, he can be a bit dramatic, can't he?'

She nudged his side. 'Now you're being polite.'

Scott held the old wooden door to the shop open for Anna to step inside. From the outside The Post Office Shop looked like a country cottage, but inside was a big area that stretched quite away back and was filled with all the bare essentials the locals might need.

A woman with dark wavy hair and big chocolate eyes was standing behind the counter, writing in a notebook. She gazed up to see her customers. 'Scott, you got parcels? I was about to shut-up shop. You're just in time. Here, hand them over.'

Anna leaned back against him as soon as he placed the parcels down. 'This shop always smells lovely, Tilly. Fresh bread is one of my favourite smells.'

Tilly smiled, then frowned. 'You okay, Anna? You look a bit pale today.'

'Just hot and puffy with backache.'

Tilly looked at Scott. 'Go out back to the kitchen and get Anna a drink, will you, Scott.'

Scott did as he was asked whilst Anna sat on the chair that Tilly pulled out from behind the counter. He could hear them talking whilst he got on with his task.

Anna was grateful for the water that Scott handed over, taking what looked like a much-needed gulp.

He gestured at the small square window that was next to the door. 'Your dad about, Tilly? I saw the truck and was going to ask him to drop Anna up the lane.'

'Oh, no. I was using it at lunchtime. I haven't taken it back up to the house yet. Here…' She reached over the counter and handed him the keys. 'You can drive Anna up, Scott, and then drop it off on your way back.'

He pocketed the keys. 'Cheers, Tills.'

Tilly flashed him a smile as she went back to sorting his parcels. 'So, how's it going with you and Dolly? You know you two are the latest hit around here.'

Anna laughed into her glass of water.

Scott frowned playfully whilst nodding. 'Yes, I know. Can't keep anything to yourself around here.'

Anna lowered the glass to her lap and glanced up at him. 'I remember when I first came here. I couldn't believe how close everyone was in Pepper Bay. I was the one who was the talk of the town then. I like how friendly you lot are. It didn't take long for this place to feel like home, and that wasn't just because of Jake. It was because of everyone here.'

'Aww, Anna,' said Tilly, smiling over at Scott. 'We are a lovely bunch.' She laughed as he grinned.

'Well, I love it here. Jake took me to so many different places for our honeymoon, and as wonderful as that was, this is still my favourite place.'

I guess I've always thought that too.

'Where is Jake?' asked Tilly.

'He's at a meeting in Sandly. Work thing. He should be home soon.' She yawned and then winced.

'Come on,' said Scott, taking her arm. 'That's exactly where you need to be.'

Anna slumped back onto his arm as Tilly went off to fetch the loaf of rosemary bread that she had stashed out the back. Scott was just concentrating on Anna.

She doesn't look right to me. Probably just that back pain. Let's hurry and get her settled.

He pulled the truck keys out of his pocket as Tilly handed over the bread. 'I'll see you in a bit, Tills.'

They went back outside into the warm evening and Scott helped Anna into the dusty red pickup truck. She groaned and held her stomach as he drove slowly over the many bumps in Walk Walk Road. He tried to slow down as much as possible, not wanting her to feel even more uncomfortable than she was obviously feeling.

'Anna, when's the baby due?'

'Not till early October. Well, that's what I was told. Why? You think all these aches and pains I've had since last night is labour?'

He turned left on to Pepper Lane. 'Is it getting worse?'

She winced as she shifted on her chair. 'Yes.'

'How about we drive up to the hospital, just to check things out?'

'Okay, but let's not call Jake until we know for sure. He'll only freak out and panic.'

Scott breathed out a laugh and adjusted the air-con on the dash. 'Okay.'

'Do you think Tilly will mind us taking the truck for this long?'

'No. She'll be fine. I'll call her and explain when we get to the hospital.'

'It's probably a false alarm. The baby can't come this early. It's too small right now, isn't it? Unless the dates are wrong.' She stopped talking, and Scott guessed she was silently doing some calculations.

'Did you find out if you're having a boy or girl?'

'No, we decided to have the surprise.'

He wanted to help keep her mind off things, so carried on chatting about anything he could think of. 'Got any names picked out yet?'

'Well, Jake wanted to name the baby after his grandparents, but his brother, Josh, you know Josh, right?'

'Of course.'

'Well, Josh had the same idea, so they did this thing where they put Edith and John's names in a hat and each picked one. Which, to me, doesn't make any sense.'

'What do you mean?'

'Well, wouldn't it make more sense if whoever has a boy first calls it John, and Edith if it's a girl? But they said what if they both have boys. So, anyway, I just let them get on with it, and Joey didn't care either, although I do suspect that she would rather have herself a little Edith, because she runs Edith's Tearoom. I'm happy for her to have the name. It seems more fitting for her.'

'What name did you get?'

'We got John, so if it's a girl, we're a little stuck at the moment. Jake wanted to name her after me, but I said no to that. I think it might be a boy, but who knows. At least if it is, he'll have a name straight away.' She laughed and then grabbed her side.

'Anna?'

'Ooh, Scott. It really bloody hurts.'

'Okay, I'm not going to drive like a maniac, but I am going to just speed up a bit.'

'Oh God!'

'What? What's happened?'

'My waters have just broken.'

'What! Erm, it's okay. Just hold on, Anna. We'll be there soon.'

'I'm not sure this baby is going to wait, Scott. I feel the need to push.'

'No. Don't you push.'

'Oh God.' She started to scramble with her dress, pulling it up to her thighs and grabbing at her knickers. 'Scott, I swear I can feel something.'

He quickly pulled over. 'Okay, Anna, listen to me. I once delivered a baby when I was in the army. There was gunfire and chaos and all sorts going on, but I was all she had, and we got on with it, so I have that level of experience.'

She grabbed his hand and squeezed the life out of it. 'That's good enough. Do something, Scott.'

'I'm going to have to take a look, okay?'

233

'I really don't care, just get on with it.'

The yell that shot out of her clenched teeth jolted right through him. Her hand was gripping his left shoulder, holding on for dear life as he lowered his head to awkwardly remove her underwear.

Oh bloody hell, I can see the head. Stay calm. Breathe. Focus. You've got this.

He straightened and grabbed his phone and called an ambulance. The lady on the other end of the line was calm, caring, and reassured them that the paramedics were close.

Anna wasn't listening. She was almost zoned out with pain, and Scott was concentrating as though he were defusing a bomb, which was something he only ever had to do once in his job. And once was enough.

'We need to get you in the back, Anna.'

'I'm not bloody moving.'

He ignored her screams, because there was no way he could deliver her baby whilst they were both crushed up in the front of the truck. 'Anna, we need more room.'

Whilst she gritted her teeth, puffed, and gripped her fingernails into his arms, he managed to lift her into the back of the pickup. He pulled his shirt off, placing it beneath her, ready for the baby.

Anna was growling rather than screaming, puffing and clenching her teeth, and muttering some swear words in between loud breathing and Scott's calm and direct instructions.

The woman on the phone was talking all the way through the birth, and sirens were loud and clear just as a little girl came into the world.

Scott quickly wrapped the baby in his shirt and lifted the tiny girl to his face, checking she was breathing. Car doors and footsteps were all he heard, then the faintest of cries, which brought a smile to his face and a new beat to his heart. Anna had tears rolling down her pale cheeks as Scott showed her the baby's little face just before a male paramedic clambered up into the truck to check on Anna. A female medic appeared and took over from Scott, asking him questions whilst wrapping a blanket around the infant.

He waited till she went back to the ambulance, then dropped back to his heels, taking a breath whilst looking to the sky.

Focus, Harper. Mission incomplete. Finish the job.

He turned his attention back to the scene in the truck. The paramedic told him that he was going to transfer Anna to the ambulance, and then he went off to get the gurney. Scott took her up into his arms, ready to lift her down. Her body felt weak, and her face matched. She slumped into his hold, breathing steadily whilst closing her eyes.

'It's okay, Anna. I've got you.'

The ride to the hospital didn't seem to take long, especially with Scott asking all the questions he knew Anna would want asking. There wasn't much coming back to them. They were told the baby was going to be taken straight to the premature baby unit and not to worry, as she seemed fine. Tiny, but so far so good.

Scott checked his shorts for his phone so that he could call Jake. 'Anna, I've left my phone in the truck. I'll call Jake as soon as we arrive.'

'Mine's in my bag.'

He glanced around his feet. 'Yeah, I think that's in the truck as well.'

The female paramedic told them they were two minutes away, and that seemed to relax Anna, whilst Scott was still in working mode.

There's no room for panic in a crisis. Those are the words Giles would often say. Where the hell are you now, Giles?

He was so used to having him in his ear, guiding him, instructing, telling him the next move, that he felt a little lost without his voice. There was no one. Just himself and his training in keeping calm and getting the job done. No matter what.

Anna reached over for his hand, and he held on, smiling her way, showing her positivity in his expression. Another technique he had learned. Keep them reassured at all times. It wasn't just him who wasn't allowed to panic.

They arrived at the hospital and were taken straight to a ward, where he waited patiently by her side whilst she was checked over. They listened to a doctor explain about the baby unit next door and were told the baby was doing well.

'Anna, I need to find a phone so I can call Jake.'

'Please don't leave, Scott. I want you to sit with my daughter. I don't like her being all alone.'

A nurse reassured Anna that there was a very nice team of people who worked in that unit who loved babies and would take good care of her little girl.

Anna didn't seem to listen. She tried to get out of bed in a hurry, blacked out, and was settled back down by Scott, who had caught her mid-fall.

Scott was told by the nurse that Anna was probably in need of iron tablets and would see to it that she started a course immediately. Meanwhile, Anna was given a cup of tea and some biscuits to help up her strength a little, which Scott had to practically force her to take, as she was still busy trying to find ways to leave her bed.

'Anna,' he scorned, using his firm tone. 'Stay still and drink the tea. I need to find a phone so I can call Jake.'

A midwife handed Scott her mobile and told him to make his call. He thanked her and quickly got on with his next task. Jake wasn't answering, so he called Ruby. After the initial shock, Ruby assured Scott she would track down Jake and get him to the hospital.

Anna still wasn't settling, so Scott told her that he would go check on her baby, but the nurse stopped him before he had even made it out the door.

Only parents were allowed in the baby unit, but Anna kicked up such a fuss, they finally allowed Scott to sit with the baby until Anna was a bit stronger to get out of bed. He offered to push her in the wheelchair, but the doctor was back in the room and wanted Anna to stay put for a few more minutes. Anna really wanted Scott by her baby's side, so she pushed him away, telling him exactly where he was needed.

He went to the baby unit and was told to scrub up at a large trough-like sink and was then given a blue gown to wear, which he was thankful for, having surrendered his shirt to the newborn. He had no idea where it had ended up.

The tiniest baby Scott had ever seen had been well and truly cared for by the staff in the unit. He looked down at her beautiful face and smiled. She was sleeping as though there wasn't a huge amount of fuss just made over her entrance to the world.

'Hey, little one. What a fighter you are, eh? Born in the back of a pickup truck. You'll definitely have to buy one when you're old enough. Your mummy will be here in a minute. Meanwhile, you're stuck with me. I'm Scott. I'm the one who will teach you self-defence when you're older. Trust me, no one's going to mess with you. Not on my watch. But for now, you just rest. Build your strength. There's a saying where I used to work… Strength is all in the mind, and the mind is only strong when rested.'

He rolled his eyes over to the doorway to see Anna being wheeled in. He helped place her wheelchair in a good spot and stood back, giving her space with her baby.

Not sure if I should just leave now or what. Oh, hell, I was supposed to meet Dolly at mine. She's moving some stuff in with Dexter. She's going to think I've changed my mind again when I don't open the door. Christ, please don't tell me she's thought that and gone home. Ruby would ring her. Wouldn't she? Why would she? She was only instructed to find Jake. Great! Just great.

He stared back down at Anna as her hand found his. Her blue eyes were smiling wearily up at him.

'Thanks, Scott. So much.'

'Hey, you did all the work, and you were brilliant.' He glanced back at the doorway, as his eye caught Jake looking nervously around the room. 'Anna, look.' He squeezed her hand and gestured over at her frazzled husband.

Jake spotted them and quickly headed straight for Anna. Scott got out of the way and watched with the slightest of smiles as Jake bent to his knees and clutched his wife into his chest as though she was the air he needed in order to breathe.

Scott saw tears pricking azure-blue eyes when Jake rolled his head up to speak softly with Anna. He took another step back, trying to give them their privacy.

I need to get back to Dolly. Explain what happened. She'll be okay once she hears about this. I just hope she's not hurting right now.

Jake glanced up at him, and Scott couldn't quite read his expression. He looked like a man with one hundred thoughts rushing through his mind at once, but there was definitely relief amongst the emotions. That much, Scott could make out.

Jake turned to the baby, staring silently for a moment at his sleeping daughter. He then stood and approached Scott, wrapping him in a bear hug. 'Thank you so much, Scott. I'll owe you forever for looking after my girls.'

Scott was relieved when he was finally free. He took a much-needed breath and smiled. 'Hey, congratulations, mate.'

Anna tugged Jake's wrist, pulling him down to her level so she could whisper in his ear. He smiled, nodded, and turned back to Scott.

And why are they both grinning at me like that?

'What?'

'You ask him, Jake.'

Jake kept his voice low and his smile in place. The tears were still sitting in his eyelids, and his hand was not letting go of Anna's. 'We were wondering, if it's all right with you, we'd like to call our daughter Harper.'

There was a warmth that hit Scott that he had never felt before. There was no holding back the smile breaking through as he breathed out a laugh through his nose whilst nodding his approval. 'That's... I'd love... Of course. I'm honoured.'

'Thanks, Scott, once again, for everything.' Jake shook his hand and gently squeezed his arm.

'You're welcome. Look, I'm going to head off home now if I'm not needed here any longer. I need to get Joseph Sheridan's truck back to him.'

Anna smiled up at him before turning her attention back to her daughter. 'Okay, Scott. And thank you once again. You really are a super man.'

Scott lowered his head, feeling a touch bashful for real for the first time.

Jake quickly reached into his pocket for his wallet. 'Let me pay for your cab back to the truck, Scott. It's the least I can do.'

Scott pushed his hand away. 'Thank you, but it's fine.' He leaned over Anna and gently kissed her cheek, then got another hefty hug from Jake before finally managing to leave.

He tucked the front part of the blue gown into his shorts as he quickly made his way through the hospital to grab the first cab he saw waiting outside. He ordered the driver to his destination as though the young lad was a private in the army chauffeuring his superiors. It earned Scott an eye roll and a huff that he ignored.

The sight of the truck did little to bring Scott out of work mode. He tidied up as best he could, jumped in the front, and headed straight for Dreamcatcher Farm.

Tilly was amazed by the story of Harper's birth, and so relieved everyone was doing okay. She immediately updated the Pepper Bay WhatsApp group with the news, and Scott made his way back home to see if Dolly was outside, by any chance. He guessed she wouldn't be. The fact that there wasn't one message on his phone from her told him she hadn't heard the baby news yet.

30

Dolly

'Mum, Scott's banging down the back door now. You're going to have to speak to him at one point. Why not now? He's shouting something about a baby, the last I heard.'

Dolly curled her legs up on the cream sofa in her living room.

Dexter sat down at the other end. 'We can't ignore him forever.'

She snorted out a huff. 'Oh, we can.'

'At least hear him out.'

'No. I'm done with his excuses, Dexter. We were supposed to be moving in some bits, but was he there? No, he blooming well wasn't. No doubt changed his mind. Again.'

'Again?'

'Well, that's all I'm going to take from the likes of him. He can get stuffed, so he can. I'm not dealing with his back and forward.'

Dexter turned to her phone on the pine coffee table. 'He's ringing again.'

She snatched it up and switched it off.

'I don't think he's going to go away, Mum. He's banged down the front door, now he's around the back. The phone hasn't stopped ringing, and his muffled shouting is still going on. One way or another, the man is determined to be heard.'

Well, I'm not listening to him. I know exactly what he will say. Oh, Dolly, I got scared again. Oh, Dolly, please don't leave me. Oh, Dolly, I'm joining the army again. He better not. I'll smash him in the face. See how he likes that. Of all the cheek. He shows up here, hours late, thinks we've all got to hear what he has to say. Well, hear this, Scott Harper, bugger off.

She shot her head towards the kitchen. 'I'm going to go open the window in a minute and throw a bucket of water over his head if he doesn't shut up.'

'No, Mum. You're not doing that.'

'Oh, why doesn't he just take the hint and go away and leave us alone, Dexter?'

'He probably wants to apologise. Mum, I have to say, you are being a tad harsh.'

Her eyes widened as far as they could go. 'A tad harsh? I gave that man a second chance, and what does he do with it? Sod all, that's what. Leaves us standing on his doorstep with our luggage. And does he call? No, he doesn't.'

'You could have called him.'

'No, I flipping well couldn't have. I'm not chasing after the likes of him, son. I am so over that.' She shuffled to the edge of her seat and sat up straight, wagging an index finger his way. 'You and me, we've always had stability. If you think for one moment that I'm going to let him come along and make waves in our calm harbour, then you've got another thing coming.'

Dexter slumped his shoulders.

You don't know what he said to me last time, Dex. All his lack of commitment. He's just running away again. Well, he can run the bloody marathon for all I care.

Dexter smiled weakly, obviously wanting to tread carefully with his words. 'Maybe I should go to the window and just tell him to go away.'

'Yeah, and then throw something at him.'

'No, Mum.' He got up and made his way into the kitchen, swiftly followed by Dolly. He glanced over his shoulder at her to see her eyeing up the eggs. 'No, Mum.'

I'm fuming. I cannot believe I fell for him all over again. I believed him. I actually believed him. Oh, we'll move in together. We can be a family. We'll do it properly, over time. Allow everyone to adjust to the changes. And I went and had that chat with Dexter about him. What a complete mug I've been.

'I'm just glad we found out exactly how fickle he is before we moved in. How selfish is that? He was happy for us to uproot out lives, knowing full well he wasn't sure.'

'Erm, Mum. You should come look at this.'

Dolly glanced over to see Dexter peering out the closed window. 'I'm not interested.'

'Well, you might be if you looked.'

'Has he brought a ladder round? He'd better not think about climbing up here.'

'No. He doesn't have a ladder.'

Curiosity got the better of her. 'What's he doing now? He's gone quiet.'

'He's currently staring at his feet.'

Oh, what should I do. I bet he's got his stupid Clark Kent face on. He'll want me to see him looking submissive. Make me feel sorry for him. Nope. I'm not falling for that. I'm not looking.

'Come away, Dex, before he spots you.'

Dexter turned to reveal the confused amusement washed over his face.

'What's that look for, son?'

He gestured towards the window. 'It's what he's wearing, Mum.'

'Oh Christ! Is he in his army uniform? Has he come to show us he's going back? He's really leaving.'

'No. It's not that. Come, look.'

She shook her head and folded her arms in a huff. 'You just tell me.'

Dexter sighed. 'I can't be entirely sure, but I'm pretty sure…'

'Oh, Dex, spit it out.'

'It would appear he has hospital scrubs tucked into his shorts.'

'What?'

'You know, like a surgical gown.'

'I know what you mean. I want to know why he is wearing that?'

Dexter gasped. 'Oh, Mum, what if he's just escaped from the hospital.'

'What are you talking about? People don't escape from hospital.'

'They might.'

'Why would he escape from hospital?' She slapped one hand over her mouth. 'What was he doing in the hospital?'

Dexter's phone bleeped. He pulled it out of his pocket to check the screen.

'If that's him, ignore it. I'll…'

'It's not. It's Daisy. She's… Oh… Aww, that's so sweet.'

'What is?'

Dexter glanced up from his phone. His blue eyes were smiling. 'It's Anna and Jake. They've had a baby girl.'

'Oh, that's lovely.'

Dexter went back to the screen. 'She's in the premature baby ward.'

'Sweet Jesus! Is she all right?'

He looked up with eyes wide. 'She's tiny, but will be fine, Mum.'

Dolly clasped her hand over her heart, gripping her tee-shirt tightly. 'Oh, bless her tiny heart.' She waved at his phone. 'Does Daisy say anything else? How is Anna doing?'

'Wait a minute, Mum. Daisy's written an essay here.'

She waited patiently for him to speed-read his way through Daisy's text message, waving her hand at him every so often.

Dexter's eyes widened and his mouth gaped. He let out a hushed gasp and stared over at the window before looking back at her.

'What? What is it, Dex?' Dolly could feel her heart pounding in her chest. She prayed Anna was all right.

'It's Scott, Mum. He delivered Anna's baby in the back of Joseph Sheridan's pickup truck on the way to the hospital.'

They took a moment to simply stare at each other before slowing turning their heads towards the kitchen window.

Within a beat, Dolly rushed over and slung it open so fast, the frame rattled. To her dismay, Scott was nowhere to be seen. She turned sharply to Dexter. 'He's gone.'

Dexter ran to the living room to check the front. 'Mum,' he called. 'Mum, he's walking back up the lane.'

Dolly sprinted down the stairs, through the shop, and out into the dying light of the summer night. 'Scott,' she cried out. 'Scott.'

He stopped walking and quickly turned.

She ran towards him whilst telling him to wait. Before he could speak, she propelled herself into his body. His arms shot out in reflex, catching her, holding her, drawing her closer to him.

Dolly started to kiss all over his face. 'I'm so sorry,' she mumbled on his skin. 'I'm sorry, Scott.' She peppered his forehead and cheeks, his lips and his nose. 'I thought you'd left me again.' Her voice was breathy and muffled.

Scott slowed her down. He pulled her away from his face and smiled happily down at her. 'I'm never leaving you. Wild horses couldn't drag me away.'

'Oh, Scott.' She pressed her mouth onto his and pulled him close again.

'I love you, lady,' he whispered on her lips.

She came up for air and stroked one hand over his cheek. 'Oh, Scott, what a nightmare. And I mean all of it. Me thinking you'd changed your mind again. Anna going into early labour. You playing out your very own scene from Call the Midwife.' She slowed her breathing. 'How are you?'

He breathed out a laugh and nodded. 'In need of a top and a cup of tea.'

'I can see to that, and then how about something to eat and a cuddle on the sofa?'

He rested his head down onto hers and gazed into her eyes. 'That sounds perfect.'

Dexter shouted out from the living room window. 'They called the baby Harper.'

Dolly turned back to Scott to see his wide grin and a wash of proudness fill his gorgeous blue eyes. 'So, Pepper Bay has got its very own little Supergirl.'

'Yes, I guess so.'

'Come on, handsome. Let's get you settled for the night. At least you have some bits moved into ours.'

'Seems we've already made a start.'

She wrapped her arm around his waist, took another glance at his hospital gown, shook her head at herself, and led him back to her home.

'Got any Jaffa Cakes, Doll?'

She nudged his side, trying not to laugh. 'I'll give you flipping Jaffa Cakes, mister.'

31

'I'm going to miss you, Harps.' Giles sniffed and then revealed his big cheesy grin.

Scott smiled back. 'Hey, I haven't given you my decision yet.'

'It's the last day of August. I think we both know you're not coming home.'

'I am home, Giles.'

Giles leaned back in his chair, zooming out from the screen on Scott's laptop. 'Yeah, that much I gathered. I've been with you all summer, and I can see that even if you wanted to return, you wouldn't be of any use to us now.'

Scott huffed out a laugh. 'Thanks!'

'We both know what I mean. Having a family distracts your mind. You would be playing it safe all over the place, worrying about Dolly and Dexter if anything happened to you.'

'I think they would be fine. They've done all right up to now.'

'Yeah, I know, but still, you know how it goes in our line of work. We need people without emotions.'

There were many days where Scott felt like a robot in his job. He always kept Ruby, Wes, and Freddy at bay in his mind. Giles was right, loving people too hard interfered with dangerous tasks. Not many of their colleagues had a home life. He never thought he'd have one at all.

'I'm happy here, Giles. I feel settled.'

'Are you going to tell her the truth about your past?'

'You know I'm not allowed to tell her.'

'I know, but you're allowed to tell her what you did, just not exactly what you did.'

Scott nodded as he sighed. 'I plan on telling her that much. I don't want to hide away anymore. Has my file been cleaned?'

'On it as soon we say goodbye.'

A wave of emotion filled Scott's heart. He had spent so many years with Giles. It was going to be strange not having him around.

Giles winked. 'Go on. You can say it. You're going to miss me.'

The corners of Scott's mouth curled, even though he tried to hold it back. 'I'm going to miss you, Giles.'

'Good. I should hope so. Maybe I'll check in on you from time to time. Don't worry, I won't interfere with your humdrum life. You won't even know I'm there.'

Scott glanced at the ceiling out in the hallway of Lemon Drop Cottage. 'Stay out of my smoke detector.'

'See you on the other side, Harps.'

A lump stuck in Scott's throat as Giles signed off for the last time. He held his fist to his lips, staring at the blank screen.

I really will miss you, Giles. Be lucky, mate.

A knock on the door disturbed his thoughts. He closed the laptop and slowly made his way to see who was knocking.

The delivery man handed him a plant, tipped his head, smiled, and walked away.

Scott looked down at the tiny blue flowers in his hands. He picked out the card that told him they were forget-me-nots. A laugh left his parted lips as he closed the door and turned in the hallway. He raised the plant up and looked at the smoke detector, not really sure if Giles was watching.

'As if I would ever forget you, Giles.'

He took the plant into the kitchen and was about to look up care instructions for it but stopped when Dolly opened the front door.

'Hey, my lovely, what you got there?'

He kissed her head as she snuggled under his arm.

This is the perfect time to tell her about my past. Get it over and done with once and for all. Then we can just enjoy our new life with no secrets.

'Forget-me-nots from my old work colleague, Giles. It's his retirement present for me.'

'Oh. That's nice. So, erm, you definitely retired then. You told them. There's no chance at all you can return now.'

He turned so their eyes could meet. 'Hey, it's over. It's done. I've finally said goodbye to that life. This is the life I want now.'

Dolly flung herself into him, kissing him hard.

Scott smiled on her mouth. 'I love you too.' He pulled back and encouraged her to take a seat. 'Let me explain my old job to you, Doll. It's time you knew the truth. I want to tell you. I don't want it hanging over us.'

She nodded, looking apprehensive. Clasping her hands together tightly on her lap, she gave him her full attention, ready for whatever he was about to hit her with.

Scott swallowed down some dryness and sat by her side. 'Okay, well, I was in the army for a good few years when I was offered a different role in another sector. It was still military, just more back seat.'

'You mean a desk job?'

'No. I mean a shadow job.' He could see from her confused expression that she had no idea what he meant. 'Think James Bond.'

It took a second, but then her mouth gaped and her eyes widened. 'You were a spy?'

He waggled one hand in front of his chest. 'Sort of.'

'Sort of?'

'We use the term, field agent.'

'So, you did secret work for the government?'

'Well, we like to think of it more along the lines of doing secret work for our country.'

'Were you ever in any danger?'

Be honest, Scott.

'Most of the time.'

Dolly's hands were turning white, she had them clenched that tightly. He leaned closer and took them in his, soothing her nerves by stroking over her fingers.

She started to focus on his movement. 'You kind of hear about those jobs, but you only really think about them in films or in books.'

'Yeah, I know.'

Her eyes shot up, meeting his. 'Are you allowed to tell me this?'

'Only this much. You know, some people I worked with are married, have kids. We're not all loners, but it helps. They prefer that. I started to know I wanted out a couple of years ago, but it wasn't until last year that I put the plan into action.'

Dolly was still looking slightly nervous. 'Are you safe, Scott? Are we safe?'

He raised her hand and kissed her knuckles. 'Dolly, I swear to you, you are perfectly safe, and so am I. I had a different identity there. Here, I'm me. I'm nobody. I'm forgotten. Right now, as we speak, Giles is wiping me from the system. I no longer exist there. It's over.'

She pressed his hand to her mouth. 'Oh, Scott, of all the jobs in the world, you had to go and pick that one.'

A laugh left his mouth as he smiled. 'Someone has to do it, believe it or not.'

'I'm just glad it's not you anymore.'

'So am I.'

A moment of silence sat in the air. Dolly lowered his hand from her mouth and sighed. The slightest of smiles hit her lips, causing Scott to wonder what was going through her mind.

'Come on, spit it out, Doll. What are you thinking?'

Her eyes rolled to the floor. 'I was just wondering if Lemon Drop was this sweet little cottage that doubles as an assassin's lair.'

Scott couldn't help but laugh. 'Assassin's lair? Really?'

'I'm picturing a stash of guns under the floorboards, secret panels that open up to reveal knives and tear gas. A bunker in the garden that holds fake IDs, an assortment of money, grenades, and a clean shirt. I can see you being prepared like that.'

'You know, you watch too many movies.'

The fact that her eyes hadn't left his, told him she was examining him for evidence.

Her eyes rolled up to the ceiling. 'Does the thatch open up into a helipad?'

'No, but there's an idea.'

Dolly stopped smiling. 'Scott, are you really safe?'

'Yes, Dolly. I'm just Scott Harper from Pepper Bay, who works in a book and art shop, paints pictures, and spends all his spare time with his beloved family. It's as simple as that.'

She grabbed his face for a quick kiss. 'So, definitely no guns in the house?'

'There's nothing here that can hurt Dexter.' He glanced at the doorway. 'Although, those gnomes outside are a bit shifty. I'd keep my eye on them if I were you.'

She laughed, making him relax. He needed her to believe they were safe. With Giles on his side, there was no way anyone would ever get to him or his family. That man could cover tracks more than a snowstorm. He studied her eyes.

She seems calm. Probably thinking about spy films now. That's okay. It's better for her if she leans towards the fantasy side. Just see all the martinis and tuxedos, Dolly. Action men swimming underwater in wetsuits. Cracking computer codes and dancing the night away with beautiful women wearing long gowns. Okay, maybe not that part. And I'm definitely not telling her about the emergency box beneath the garden shed. What does Giles call it? Every field agent's lucky charm. Yeah, right. No one has ever had to use theirs, so maybe that's the lucky part.

He leaned forward and kissed Dolly's cheek, taking longer than a peck would take.

You're my lucky charm, lady.

'I don't think we need to tell Dexter about your old job, Scott.'

'Agreed.'

'Does your family know?'

'Nope.'

'Do you want to keep it that way?'

'Yep.'

She giggled close to his ear. 'Just you and me then.'

He cupped her face and nudged her nose with his own. 'Just you, me, and the gnomes.'

'So, what's the plan now, Jack Bauer?'

'Well, first of all, no more secret agent jokes. And secondly, we move forward with our plan.'

253

Dolly wriggled out of his hold. 'Oh, you and your plans. At least now I know why you're so fixated with having them.'

He glanced at the tiny blue flowers on his table. 'How about we go and plant this in the garden?'

'Good plan.' She tugged him back towards her as he grabbed the plant and went to walk away. 'Hey, Scott. Thanks for telling me the truth about your life.'

'You're my partner, Dolly. You deserve to know about me.'

She smiled and followed him into the garden. The sun was strong and the sky baby-blue. A sweet smell wafted their way from the pink salvia bush that Scott knocked when he reached down to hold her hand as he walked along the pathway, one step ahead.

'So, Scott,' she said quietly. 'I was wondering... You know how James Bond has a different woman every...'

'Didn't happen.'

She went to speak again, but he turned quickly, swiped her off her feet, and dropped to his knees on the grass, gently placing her down and leaning over her whilst stroking her hair away from her face. Their lips met and just for a moment the garden and his past no longer existed.

'Scott?' she mumbled on his mouth.

'Hmm?'

'You came back to Pepper Bay to settle down by yourself, so why did you decide to add me into your life?'

His blue eyes smiled her way, hinting at mischief. 'Ooh, I don't know. I guess I've always had a thing for apples.'

* * *

If you enjoyed this story, why not come back for another
visit to Pepper Bay with Rory and Tilly.

The Post Office Shop

Tilly Sheridan is fifty, perimenopausal, single, and pretty
much lives in dungarees. Her daily life consists of running
her family's small shop on Dreamcatcher Farm, where not
much goes on. The last thing she expects to happen in her
life is to fall in love with an ex-criminal.

Rory Murphy has just finished a fifteen-year sentence for
robbery, but he is not the same man who first walked into
that prison. With the help of a mentor, he changed his life
whilst still behind bars, and now he has been given the
opportunity of working on a farm to help him integrate back
into society. He's expecting early starts, long days,
backbreaking work, and lonely nights, but he finds
friendship, family, and love in Pepper Bay. Is it possible for
him to finally have a good life? Not if his past has anything
to do with it.

Lightning Source UK Ltd.
Milton Keynes UK
UKHW012025021222
413123UK00006B/263